BLACK WINGS, GRAY SKIES

HAILEY EDWARDS

Copyright © 2022 Black Dog Books, LLC

All rights reserved.

No part of this book may be reproduced in any form or by any electronic or mechanical means, including information storage and retrieval systems, without written permission from the author, except for the use of brief quotations in a book review.

This is a work of fiction. Names, characters, businesses, places, events and incidents are either the products of the author's imagination or used in a fictitious manner. Any resemblance to actual persons, living or dead, or actual events is purely coincidental.

Edited by Sasha Knight
Copy Edited by Kimberly Cannon
Proofread by Lillie's Literary Services
Cover by Damonza
Illustration by NextJenCo

BLACK WINGS, GRAY SKIES

Black Hat Bureau, Book 4

Monsters with a taste for children are nothing new, but fairy tales never mentioned this nightmarish predator. Rue has her hands full tracking the creature hunting the streets of Charleston, but a call from home divides her attention—and her loyalties.

A stranger has come to Hollis Apothecary, asking questions that prickle the hairs on her nape, but she can't abandon the victims based only on a bad feeling. The pit in her stomach only grows when the stranger takes a hostage and makes his demands. He wants to talk to Rue, face to face. Or else. What he has to say will change her life, and her perception of her past, forever.

1

Forearms braced on the chill metal railing, I gazed out at Charleston Harbor from the Battery. From here, I had a clear view of Fort Sumter, Castle Pinckney, Fort Moultrie, and Sullivan's Island Lighthouse. Behind me sat a trim row of historic, and historically important, antebellum mansions with price tags in the tens of millions. White Point Garden wasn't far. And, being a peninsula, the Atlantic Ocean swirled around us.

Charleston might be a small city, but it was plenty big enough for our missing kids to get lost in.

A breeze ripe with hints of green apples and smoky cherry tobacco teased my nose, and I filled my lungs. I bargained with Asa to wear his long hair loose today, and the wind thanked me for it, teasing the velvet black strands. The way the ends whipped into his serious peridot eyes must have driven him nuts, but he let me enjoy myself.

Probably because his inner daemon was counting down the hours until I brushed out the tangles.

The bar through his septum glinted, titanium bright, and his rough-cut druzy earrings sparkled in the sun as he approached me.

"We have another victim." Asa mimicked my pose, his hands tight on the metal. "A seven-year-old boy." His fingers flexed. "Andreas Farmer."

"Human?"

"Yes."

The most peculiar aspect of this case was the choice of prey: human children.

A classic, yes, hence the storybooks, but few predators dared hunt them openly in the era of cellphones, hobby drones, and traffic cameras mounted at every intersection. Shadows were no longer dark enough for monsters to hide in. Not with humans wielding night vision goggles and brandishing thermal imaging.

Modern technology was its own kind of magic, and paranormals were rapidly losing ground to science.

The parents had no idea what had happened to their children. Neither did we. They assumed the boys had been kidnapped, because we couldn't afford to let them think anything else. Even with what we knew, we were no better informed, really. We assumed, given paranormals' tendency toward predation of humans, that we were hunting a killer and not a serial kidnapper, but we simply didn't know yet.

Ding. Ding. Ding.

What a way to ring in the new year.

Early-morning sunlight glittered on the water, but a chill had settled in my bones. "Are we sure...?"

"There was no body," he allowed, "but the child lost too much blood to have survived."

The same as the others.

"Where was he taken?"

"Fort Sumter." Asa reached over, twining his fingers with mine. "His parents both work full-time, so they enrolled him in an educational day program at his school. The program offers students adult supervision during holiday breaks when parents are unable to watch their kids for extended periods. The curriculum is heavy on field trips, and that's how his group came to tour the island. They were scheduled to leave at noon, but he didn't get back on the boat. His teacher worried he might have climbed where he shouldn't have and fell in the water, but the park rangers didn't find anything. Neither did Marine Patrol or the Coast Guard."

Civil War-era cannons, hulking cast iron beasts, made popular jungle gyms at Fort Sumter, and kids never thanked adults who warned them away from dangerously good fun.

"A large blood smear," he continued, "was discovered by a young girl this morning. The body volume of blood was nearby in the grass." His fingers twitched in mine. "The girl and her little brothers are visiting their grandparents in Charleston over the holidays. It's family tradition to visit a historic landmark a day to keep the children occupied during their long break."

The layout of the fort was hazy in my mind, jumbled with other maps I had skimmed. "Where did she find the blood?"

"In an alcove where restoration work is being done on a cannon."

"Those poor kids." I blew out a breath. "I'll file the paperwork to have a witch sent to them."

The director—well, one of his underlings—would lie about what agency offered the children help adjusting to their trauma. Say anything, do anything, promise anything. Whatever it took to get a Black Hat special agent through the door. From there, the family would receive the same treatment I had administered to Camber and Arden. Except in a much higher dose. With no follow-up appointments.

Should they recall any damning specifics later, they might rate a second consult.

Their final.

With anyone.

Ever again.

That fear lived in me every day when it came to the girls, but they had me, and now they had Aedan too. The director himself couldn't touch a hair on their heads without bringing my wrath down upon his.

After checking my phone for the millionth time, I forced my thoughts away from home. "Where's Clay?"

Asa jerked his chin behind me, and I twisted around to find Clay bristling with armloads of bags.

Dressed in his Black Hat finest, he cut a trim figure. The formal suit made the purple beehive hairstyle he rocked that much more ridiculous. No. I take that back. What pushed it over the top was the glittery grape eyeshadow. He drew wide-eyed stares and more than a few smiles, but no one dared to laugh outright.

When you were seven feet tall and four hundred pounds, no one questioned your fashion choices.

Except me.

"Tell me who did this to you." I pounded a fist over my heart. "I solemnly vow to exact vengeance."

"It was me," Colby chimed from within the wig. "Isn't he pretty?"

"In that case," I backpedaled so fast I was in danger of falling into the ocean, "he's never looked better."

Lash extensions fluttering, Clay laughed at me with his eyes, happy to sparkle if it gave Colby joy.

For a guy without organs, he had the biggest heart of any person I had ever met.

"You visited the city market." Asa eyed the paper bags. "I thought you were scouting for a new hotel."

The one we hit last night crawled with agents like ants on a mound, which made me twitchy.

Our trio didn't blend in with the other teams. Part of it was fear of my reputation. Part of it was curiosity over my disappearance. And part of it, I suspected, was the peculiar magic thrumming through me these days, drawing unwanted attention to my power signature as the familiar bond bound Colby and me tighter to one another.

Sooner or later, they would figure out I no longer practiced black magic.

Until then, the fewer Black Hats who knew about Colby, the better.

"We had more important business to attend." Clay breezed past us. "The business of breakfast."

The smells hit me a heartbeat later, and my stomach rumbled when it identified the sources.

"Biscuits?" I pushed off the railing. "Cajun boiled peanuts?"

"Also teeny-tiny sweet potato donuts dusted with sugar, coffee for Ace, and Arnold Palmers for us."

"That sounds amazing," I confessed, "but the hotel—"

"The guy at the hotel gave me a coupon for Bridge's Biscuits when I turned in our keycards. He wanted us to get fifteen percent off an amazing breakfast to start our day off right. Who am I to deny his final wishes?"

"That makes it sound like he bequeathed you the coupon on his deathbed…"

"Shh." Clay pressed the black coffee into my hand. "Just eat, drink, and be grateful."

The sip of scalding hot coffee puckered my lips with its bitterness, but Asa watched with rapt attention that made it hard for me to swallow. I slid my eyes to his, our gazes locked, and heat swept through me.

"Enough of that." Clay plucked the cup from my hand and passed it to Asa. "Here's your tea, Dollface."

"Sweet tea?" I cracked the lid and sniffed. "Heavy on the lemon."

"That's an Arnold Palmer for you." He doled out a paper straw. "Half tea, half lemonade."

"Ah." I offered it to Asa, who tasted it with a considering hum, before I drank. "I like it."

"Next time, you go first." Clay scoffed at my easy approval. "Then give me your unbiased opinion."

Beside me, Asa focused on his coffee, his expression bland if you didn't know his tells.

"Don't look so smug." I elbowed him in the ribs. "Your spit has ruined food for me."

Finger tapping the lid on his drink, he eyed my straw. "It's not the saliva so much as it's—"

"No one cares about the specifics," Clay cut in. "You two take your bag and swap spit muffins over there. Way over there. Colby and I, the normal people, will eat our breakfast on the steps."

A golem and a moth girl were as far from normal as a witch and a dae, but I was too hungry to argue.

"Then Asa and I will eat our breakfast on the seawall."

"Hey, Hairnado." He flicked an elastic at Asa. "Pull that mop out of your face."

"Hairnado." Colby snorted. "Good one, Clay."

Though my eyes couldn't detect the gleaming pedestal under Clay's feet, I suspected Colby had set him high up on one.

Several yards away, Clay plonked down with his back to us. With much enthusiasm, he launched into the tale of how General P. G. T. Beauregard watched the bombardment of Fort Sumter from the piazza of what Clay called the Edmondston-Alston House, which signaled the start of the Civil War.

His choice of location, across the street from the historic home, and his topic, Fort Sumter, told me there had been time between card swipes on his shopping spree for him to catch up on our latest victim. In his way, he was preparing Colby for what lay ahead. Namely, a small island in the distance.

A brush of my fingers down the leg of my pants comforted me that my wand and kit were within reach.

The familiar bond with Colby was my greatest weapon, but I preferred not to lean on her too hard. More than any other case that came before, this one would establish our work routine, and I wanted firm lines drawn to create a healthy work and play balance that allowed her to contribute while still being a kid.

Once they settled in, Asa sat on the concrete with his back against a post, giving him a view of the street. I joined him, hanging my legs over the wall, letting them dangle above the water, and dug into the bag.

"Let's see what we've got." I extracted two small clamshell boxes. "Which do you want?"

A slash of marker indicated biscuits. One sausage, egg, and pimento cheese and one sausage with gravy. Two sides of grits rested in the bottom, along with plastic utensils and various condiment packets.

"I don't enjoy pimento cheese."

"Are you sure?" I lifted the biscuit, brought it to my mouth, and bit down. "Mmm. Pimento-y."

Equal parts suspicion and hunger warring on his face, he watched me chew. "That's not fair."

"All's fair in love and biscuits." I laughed at his torn expression. "It's actually not that bad."

The mixture of cheese, mayonnaise, pimentos, and spices wasn't my favorite, but it was edible.

"I have an idea." He wet his lips. "On how to improve its flavor."

After I swallowed, I waited to see which of his hungers would win. "Oh?"

Asa leaned in, sank his teeth into one pimentoless corner, and gulped with a pained noise.

"Who would have guessed that pimento cheese was dae kryptonite?" I surrendered the second box, still piping hot, to him. "Here." I divvied up the grits next then explored the condiments. "Sugar or cheese?"

"You don't have to eat that abomination." He grabbed for the biscuit in my hand. "I don't mind, really."

Ignoring the obvious lie, I nudged him with my knee. "Sugar or cheese?"

"I don't understand." He eyed the contents of the bag. "What about sugar or cheese?"

"In your grits." I resisted moaning around the next mouthful of pimento, aware the only reason its taste had turned addictive was the dae sitting beside me and our shared fascination. "Which do you prefer?"

"Pepper and ketchup."

Sausage went down the wrong pipe, and I coughed biscuit crumbs into his face. "Eww."

The only way to dress up grits was to mix in sugar, as the goddess surely intended.

"You asked." He picked at the lid on his grits. "I learned it from Clay."

"Clay is a culinary heathen who changes how he eats grits as often as he switches up his hairdo." I noticed Asa hadn't begun his meal. "Can you eat if I don't christen your meal first?"

The weird factor lessened for me if I teased him, like our shared ancestry was a private joke.

"Yes," he said slowly, toying with his fork, still in its wrapper, "but your proximity dictates my hunger."

The cure, according to Clay, was to mate Asa. Or mate *with* Asa? A fine line separated the two, but I had yet to ask for clarification. Willful ignorance? Yes, please.

As much as I wanted my palate back, I couldn't let taste buds make life choices for me.

"Give me that." I stole his food, took a dutiful bite of each item, then passed them back. "Dig in."

The food interested him after that display, but he stole my fork before I could snatch it.

While he shoveled in his meal, I picked at my grits, gave up on them, then checked my phone.

Again.

"The girls are fine." He held out *our* fork, laden with sweet creamy grits dense enough to hold their own on the tines. "Aedan would have called if there were any problems."

"It's hard leaving them with a relative stranger." I forced myself to pocket the cell. "A strange relative?"

Aedan, my *almost* cousin, had little experience blending with humans, let alone under scrutiny from two girls with no filters. As the newest addition to the Hollis Apothecary staff, the better to protect Camber and Arden when I traveled for work, he was clocking eight-hour shifts. Without me there to ensure he wasn't overwhelmed by stimuli, or his nosy coworkers, his probationary period had escalated into a trial by fire.

Far from ideal conditions for an aquatic daemon.

"Aedan wants this to work." Asa fed me another bite. "You're all the family he's got left."

"He has siblings." I pondered whether the grits had been prepared with cream cheese. "But fosterage…"

To keep them safe from discovery by their eldest and uber homicidal sibling, Delma, he had placed his younger brothers and sisters in ironclad fosterages that guaranteed anonymity. Even from him. I had since killed her in a challenge she issued, but what was done was done. Aedan had no recourse. He was alone.

Except for me.

"He can't take them back." Asa read my mind. "He won't see them again until they're of legal age."

"Do you think he'll live in my backyard until then?" I was joking. Mostly. "He seems happy out there."

Camp Aedan, as Colby and I called it, had been a stopgap measure to help him get his feet under him. He had nothing when he came to us but had since inherited the wealth Delma had spent decades amassing. In his mind, it was blood money, earned with his siblings' lives, and you couldn't pay him to spend it.

There was no rush to kick him out of his tent by the creek. It wasn't like I kept preapproved daemon renters on file, eager to take his place. He wasn't paying anyway. It wasn't truly a gift if it came with a price tag.

Aedan felt safe there, sharing land with his new and *slightly* less murderous relative.

Behind those wards, he was snug as a bug in a rug, and it gave me a rush knowing he trusted me to protect him. Blame it on my white witch roots, the ones that craved a coven, a community. Or blame it on the whisper of conscience growing stronger in my mind every day.

Refuse to allow past missteps to dictate the path of your future.

You don't owe anyone a smile when life is kicking you in the teeth.

Every day is a new chance, a new choice, a new challenge.

Honestly, it was like a fortune cookie factory of positivity up there these days.

A high-pitched squeal snapped me out of my head as a laughing father swung his pink-cheeked daughter in the air and caught her against his chest. Giggling and squirming, she wriggled until he put her down.

Part of me wondered if my dad had ever played with me like that.

Hard not to think of him, after Colby gifted me a rare photo of my parents for Christmas.

Ahead of her father, the girl ran to the railing, gripped a pole, then popped her head through the bars.

After her joyous squeals, her frantic screams didn't register until the man rushed to her, peered over the edge to the sandbar below, and gulped hard. He jerked his daughter to him, hefted her onto his hip, and then scanned the Battery for help.

Two Black Hat agents on a case stuck out like sore thumbs anytime. With me in civilian clothes, I imagine the scene could be interpreted as a high-value target, a socialite or politician's daughter, out for a picnic. With her bodyguards.

"Call the police," the man yelled. "There's a..." He cradled his daughter's head, forcing her to rest against his shoulder. "Just do it." He bounced her lightly on his hip, as if she were a much smaller child. "Please."

That was all the civic duty the man had in him before he swept his daughter down the nearest steps into a gray sedan parked snug against the Battery. He wedged into the traffic faster than Asa and I could rise.

We crossed to where the girl had stood and leaned over for a better look.

As we did, a foul stench hit my nose, one I recognized as if it were a perfume I had been born wearing.

Black magic.

Sneakers dotted with cartoon characters acted as a flotation device for a skinny leg bone bobbing in the surf.

"Call the director." I gritted my teeth. "Looks like we have our first body."

2

The Charleston Police Department had two wargs who worked in patrol, and I requested they meet us at the crime scene. The male was short, thin, and Scandinavian in coloring. The female was a head taller, in faded civvies with the CPD logo, and could have been cast as a shield maiden in a Viking documentary.

She was also deep in conversation on her phone, a growl present in her voice, her eyes gone amber.

"Agent Hollis," the male greeted me. "We appreciate the call."

A faint accent flavored his words, but not one I could place. New York maybe. Or New Orleans. There was a surprising amount of overlap between the two if you listened close.

"I regret the circumstances, but it's nice to meet you both. I hope together we can solve this case before more innocents are hurt." I indicated Clay, who gave no hint his personal style made this awkward. "This is Agent Kerr." I nodded at Asa. "This is Agent Montenegro."

Hidden within Clay's wig, Colby kept still and quiet so as not to tip them off to her presence.

"I'm Officer Vandenburgh." He hooked his thumb at his partner. "That is also Officer Vandenburgh."

"Great delivery." Clay acknowledged the man's dry humor. "You ever consider standup comedy?"

"We have five kids under six." He huffed a laugh. "I only tell knock-knock jokes, and the audience prefers I repeat the same ones over and over." He scratched his cheek. "They like to shout out the punchlines."

With a terse final word, Mrs. Officer Vandenburgh pocketed her cell. "Sorry about that."

"Sitter issues?" Her husband sighed at her confirmation. "What did the terrors do this time?"

"Our triplets are teething, and our twin girls are over their little brothers chasing them and biting them." She included us in her explanation. "Not even our mothers will watch them until they grow out of this."

Aside from Colby, I had no experience with kids. I could sympathize with the Vandenburghs' mothers for not wanting to be responsible for entertaining five kids who could turn into wolves and gnaw on them.

"Enough about us," Mr. Officer Vandenburgh, noticing my awkward silence, broke in. "Where is she?"

She was a stretch. There wasn't enough to confirm gender without testing, though the sneaker might give us a hint.

"The remains are this way." I hooked a thumb over my shoulder. "We didn't disturb the scene."

Aside from shooing off seagulls eager for an easy meal, we had no reason to venture down to the beach. The leg had washed ashore, securing our evidence and leaving us to wait on the police. Normal protocol it was not, but so many missing human children were a ticking time bomb. We had been authorized to use all available resources to put an end to this as fast and discreetly as possible.

And if that meant asking for an assist from officers with the keenest noses in the business, then so be it.

"God," Mrs. Officer Vandenburgh breathed. "That poor child."

"Might be a boating accident," her husband murmured. "A three-blade propeller can inflict one hundred and sixty impacts in one second. Amputations aren't that rare, even in adults. What makes you think this is one of yours?"

"The smell," I answered for us. "You didn't notice?"

"Yeah." Mr. Officer Vandenburgh flushed to the tips of his ears. "We just figured it was…"

"Me."

"Sorry about that." His wife palmed the metal railing. "We don't see many black witches up this way."

Now that was interesting, and it was news to me. "You don't say."

Mrs. Officer—much easier to think of her that way—leapt the railing and stuck an impressive landing.

"I figured it was a peninsula thing." He gripped the rail next. "I hear that magic and water don't mix."

For now, I had no reason to believe, aside from the smell, that a black witch might be involved. The truth was, you didn't have to be a witch to dabble in the dark arts, and I couldn't afford to get fixated on the idea this was yet another case with a Black Hat rogue agenda.

That was how mistakes got made. How killers walked free. Neither of which was an option here.

Once Mr. Officer's boots hit the sand, he and his wife began a preliminary examination.

The tender way the officers handled the remains, the care with which they treated the scene, spoke of heartache that throbbed so deep only another parent could grasp the breadth of that loss.

To give them privacy, Asa and I blocked the Battery path ahead while Clay did the same behind us.

The fewer humans who saw what had attracted our attention, the better.

A small eternity later, Mrs. Officer called up to us. "You can come down now."

Clay leapt the rail, sank up to his ankles in sand, then lifted his arms toward me.

"Come on in, Dollface." He made grabby motions. "The water's fine."

Even the most ambitious waves lapped the shore yards away from him, so I doubted his authority on the matter. Had this not been a crime scene, I suspected he would have caught me, walked me into the surf, then dunked me into icy water. With the Vandenburghs looking on, I figured the odds skewed fifty/fifty.

Professionalism and golems did not always go hand in hand when an opportunity for mischief arose.

"Are you serious?" I measured the distance. "You expect me to jump?"

Impact with Clay was the next best thing to a head-on automobile collision with a concrete pylon.

Chivalry was not dead, as Asa showed by swinging over the railing to land nimbly on the hard-packed sand beside the smirking golem. Pivoting toward me, Asa opened his arms in a clear challenge to Clay's offer.

As a witch, I was the least agile person on our team, but sheesh. It wasn't like I was human.

Determined to prove a point, I sat on the seawall, gripped the railing at my chest, and slid beneath it.

The mushy patch where I landed sucked me down to my ankles. I windmilled my arms to recover my balance, almost face planted, overcorrected, then fell backward onto my butt with a grunt-squeak.

Black witches don't grunt-squeak, and they don't earn reputations as klutzes.

Because they kill the witnesses.

Both guys stared at me, and the faintest snickers drifted from Clay's hair.

Why had I quit eating hearts again?

There must be a good reason, but it was eluding me just now.

The warg couple exchanged nostalgic glances that made me

curious if they had pegged our team dynamic yet. Maybe Asa and I reminded them of the early days of their partnership. Or they thought I was an idiot for making a fool of myself rather than accepting help when it was offered. Hard to tell.

No one said a word about my damp butt as I picked my way to the wargs, the guys falling in behind me.

The only secrets to be revealed were in the remains themselves, which gave us more freedom to explore without fear of contaminating the scene. Location, currents, and tide might tip us off to the general area where the leg entered the water, but I wasn't holding my breath.

"Apologies," Mr. Officer greeted me, his nostrils wide. "This smells nothing like you."

The remains or the magic lingering on it, I wasn't sure, but I decided he meant well either way.

Asa stood behind me and to my right, but he didn't shrink into himself to put the couple at ease. As much as I wanted to believe it was a sign of him embracing his power, I decided it was a bureaucratic pissing match happening on an animalistic wavelength I wasn't picking up on.

"There's enough tissue to run DNA." Clay squatted for a better look. "That will take twenty-four hours."

Magic, in an effort to remain relevant and not simply a wonder, had spawned forensic fields with special skills that allowed results to be in the hands of any agency willing to pay the fee within hours rather than days or weeks. The director sponsored several branches relevant to the Bureau's interests. In exchange for a discount on bulk services, of course.

With a snap, I put on latex gloves. "Do you mind?"

The couple exchanged a weighty glance then Mr. Officer pulled out his phone. "Do you?"

"Record away." I knelt to stabilize myself then set to work on untying the sneaker. I tugged slack in the laces, stretched the tongue up and the sides out, then freed the shoe from the swollen foot. I glanced at the logo on the inner sole. "Girls, size seven."

"That isn't conclusive of gender," Mrs. Officer warned me. "Kids wear hand-me-downs all the time."

We had detailed descriptions of what the victims had been wearing, so it was easy enough to check.

"True." I held the shoe while Mr. Officer snapped pictures. "Can you forward us the photos and video?"

"Sure thing." Mr. Officer requested my email address. "I'll ask you to do the same, going forward."

After helping them bag the shoe, I removed my gloves, tucked them in my pocket, then rose.

"Of course." I shook his hand and then hers. "You have our full cooperation."

"Who is *our*?" Mrs. Officer swept her gaze up me. "You're not FBI."

Mysterious disappearances and kidnappings involving children fell within FBI jurisdiction.

Good guess, wrong Bureau.

"FBI isn't that diverse," her husband agreed. "Black witch, golem, and..." he flared his nostrils, "...daemon with a hint of fae."

"Your lives will be much happier and longer if you take us at face value." I winced at how it sounded. "I'm not threatening you." No one with a lick of sense went after a warg. They ran in packs for a reason. "I'm telling you our boss doesn't like when people ask questions."

If they didn't know, then they didn't need to know.

That was the company line.

Look at me, toeing it.

Oh, how times had changed.

"All right." Mrs. Officer spread her hands. "I've heard about shadow organizations. Enough to know I don't want to find myself on the wrong side of one." A thread of steel laced her voice. "As long as you're here in good faith, we have no problem." She flexed her fingers, and pelt sprouted across her hand. "Fair warning." Her nails sharpened into claws, and she pointed one at me. "Harm an innocent in our city, and I will give you a tour of the bottom of the ocean and a free pair of cement shoes."

The reasoning behind Asa's uncharacteristic boldness crystalized in an instant.

Our city.

"You're the Charleston alphas," I realized. "I didn't see that in your files."

"I can neither confirm nor deny that." Mr. Officer twitched his lips, enjoying how the tables had turned on us. "But I would be afraid of my wife, if I were you. I have days where I wake beside her in a cold sweat, and that's after thirty-five years of marriage."

"Ignore him," Mrs. Officer told us then cocked an eyebrow at her mate. "You're worse than I am."

"Not even close."

"Remember our first year on the force as mates *and* partners? Oh. That's right. You weren't there." Mrs. Officer snorted. "Every time you saw me in danger, you sprouted fur and got sent home."

"That's not true." He tugged the ends of her hair. "Sometimes, I sprouted claws instead."

"Count your blessings." She swatted him. "Warg males will literally mark their territory."

A sudden itch reminded me of the bracelet on my wrist. The one woven from Asa's hair.

Used to the weight of its purpose, the comforting scratch against my skin, I rarely thought of it anymore.

"Daemons will too." I crimped my lips. "They're just sneakier about it."

"I'll call the cleaners," Mrs. Officer offered. "File the paperwork via your agency, and you'll be granted a temporary login so you can access information as it's uploaded to our regional database."

Cleaners specialized in erasing signs of paranormal activity. They swore oaths of impartiality and vowed to seek justice for all supernatural factions. They worked for themselves, but organizations could buy in. The membership fees funded investigations as well as industry advancements, and it provided cutting-edge services smaller towns couldn't have afforded on their miniscule budgets otherwise.

However, the director all but owned the cleaners. As in the entire organization. Their database was a curated version of the one the Kellies maintained for Black Hat. Their oaths of neutrality might as well have been made on bended knee before him.

"Thanks." I appreciated the inclusion. "I'll do that."

Now I had no choice but to file, since they would expect me to track the case through their connections.

Better to let them see I was signed in and active on their network than wonder why I didn't need to be.

Lucky for me, Colby excelled at cyber drudgery that made my head throb.

Our team left the officers to wait on the cleaners and returned to the top of the Battery to gather our things. I was out of bravado at that point and allowed Asa to boost me high enough for me to reach the railing and haul myself over it again.

Except for a curious bird, a plump royal tern, no one had bothered our abandoned breakfast.

I was tempted to finish eating to avoid wasting the food, but I didn't like how the idea made my stomach clench. As much as I hated to admit it, the scene hadn't cost me my appetite. But maybe it should have?

A lifetime of inflicting horrors on others for purpose or pleasure had numbed me to most terrible things. Only now there was a whispery acknowledgment from my fledgling conscience when I should feel sad or angry for what was done to a victim. I wasn't sure carnage would ever bother me again, but that nascent tug of conscience whispered it was okay if it did. That no lacquered cane waited, eager to whack my knuckles for showing emotion, for empathizing. But I couldn't shake a lifetime of conditioning so easily.

"You okay?" Clay bumped my shoulder as I set out for the SUV. "You've got that look on your face."

Blinking away the fear I might not live up to my own expectations, I asked, "What look?"

"The look that tells me you need a second breakfast to recover the calories you burned climbing."

Accidentally on purpose, I stuck out my foot and tripped Clay, who toppled into the bushes.

Without hesitation, Asa dove in after him, ripping the poufy wig off his head and holding it high.

Clay yelped at the sting and stumbled out the other side, patting his shiny bald head in horror.

"What the f—" Clay bit down hard, "—*fudge* did you do that for?"

"Oleander." Asa exited the bushes. "Every part of the plant is toxic."

"Goddess bless." I spun on my heel, hit the nearby stairs, and rushed onto the sidewalk. "Colby?"

"I'm fine," she called out, laughing. "I'm upside down, but I'm good."

Clay escaped unblemished, but Asa had splotchy hands. The fall must have snapped limbs and exposed him to sap.

"I should have recognized it." I took the wig from him, and my fingers tingled. "I wasn't thinking—"

"Let's get Shorty to the SUV." Clay stole the wig. "Then we'll revisit what the hell city planners were thinking when they planted murder bushes along one of the city's biggest tourist magnets."

Not waiting for us, Clay booked it toward the SUV, leaving Asa and me to play catch-up.

"No one got hurt." Asa tucked his hands into his pockets. "Except the wig."

Now that he mentioned it, I wasn't sure if Clay was in triage mode for Colby or his hairdo.

"Everyone knows about oleander." I flung my hand toward the neat row of bushes. "What kind of witch misses that?"

"One whose thoughts were on the case and not on the hat tip to confederate tea."

Tour guides loved to talk about how Southern women brewed oleander tea for Union soldiers. We'd had a close encounter with a ghost tour last night and overheard the tale. Had it been here, at the Battery, I might have put two and two together. As it was, I figured the plants had been grown in secret.

Apparently not.

"You have a lot on your mind." His voice softened. "Your grandfather, your grandmother, your cousins."

"Who am I that I have family drama?" I noticed more blisters forming on his hands and slowed to a halt. "Technically, I've always had family drama, but that was only the director and me. Now I have a psycho granny blowing bubbles in a marsh, a dead cousin's ashes in my safe, and her brother living in my yard."

"You're also trusting Aedan with two of the most precious things in your life."

"The girls," I agreed. "Part of me wonders if they're better off if I don't come back."

Factor in the online sales, and the store did well enough to support them both. Without me.

"They love you." He stopped beside me. "They would always choose to have you in their lives."

"We can't know that." I took his hand in mine. "They might never forgive me."

For what I had done. For what I had let happen to them. For lying to them.

"They love you," he repeated. "They would understand, in time."

"Let's hope we never find out which of us is right."

"You shouldn't touch me." He stiffened when I tightened my grip. "You don't want a rash or worse."

"I like touching you." I sandwiched his hand between my palms. "Hold still."

Allowing my eyes to drift shut, I pushed healing magic pulled directly from my bond with Colby into Asa. A warmth built between us, soaking into his skin, but daylight nulled the usual light show.

"There." I took his other hand. "Let's give you a matched set."

A soft curve to his mouth, he held still while I tended him, watching me the whole time.

"You're staring." I had my eyes shut, but I felt his intensity. "Take in the historic sights, why don't you?"

"I prefer the view from here." His breath coasted along my throat. "I never tire of looking at you."

"Oh, you will eat those words." I opened my eyes to find our noses almost brushing. "Now you have to see me every single day. You don't get a vacation when a case ends or get to jet off when one begins. You're stuck with me twenty-four-seven."

"I know." His smile turned wolfish. "It's my new favorite part of the job."

"Mmm-hmm." I brushed my lips over his, tasting salt. "We'll see."

Ahead of us, Clay stood with his hands on his hips, one foot tapping. "Done yet?"

"Almost."

I fisted my hand in Asa's hair and hauled him back to my mouth, savoring every corner.

The growl that pumped through his chest was cut short when Clay bulled between us with a grunt.

"You're worse than teenagers." He opened the front passenger door. "Get in, Dollface."

Once he had me shut in, he marched Asa to the driver side door and shoved him behind the wheel.

Twisting in my seat, I checked on Colby. "You okay back there?"

"The wig protected me." She scrunched up her face. "I'm not sure it would have hurt me either way."

As a creature forged from the soul of a fae girl? Or as an otherworldly moth with a pollen addiction?

"We can go to our new digs, shower, and regroup." Clay rocked the SUV as he settled. "We need to get out of these clothes." He pointed to the built-in GPS. "I've already put in the address."

A hint of *something* lingered in his voice, probably having to do with the *new digs* he hadn't mentioned securing earlier, but I didn't stop to analyze it.

Clearly, he wanted to surprise us, and we were at his mercy.

Ten minutes later, Asa was pulling into a parking deck off Hasell Street. The area was pocked with restaurants, but I didn't spot a hotel on the way in. Clay didn't enlighten us either. Just smiled and loaded his arms with wig boxes then waited for us to take the hint and catch up to him.

The parking deck lacked an elevator on our end, so we took the stairs. As soon as Clay hit the sidewalk, he made a tight right turn and stopped before a set of double doors that led, I thought, into a barbeque joint. Except, upon closer inspection, the restaurant was gutted top to bottom. Closed for good then.

Clay punched in a code he read off his phone that unlocked the doors, then he called for the elevator.

"I'm getting horror movie vibes here." I peered around him. "Where are we going?"

"You're questioning Charleston's quirky charm." Clay nudged me back. "Just give it a minute."

We gave it a minute and a half before the elevator arrived, and its doors slowly peeled aside.

Asa stuck to my side, his expression distant, his attention somewhere else. By some miracle, we all fit in the car together. And yes, I did the math to ensure our weight fell below the guidelines. *Well* below.

The ride up lasted another eternity, which gave me plenty of time to skim a printed note that informed passengers the ride was ninety seconds up and ninety seconds down. It advised us to enjoy the ride.

A geriatric ding announced our arrival on the top floor, and the doors opened onto a short hall.

We clogged the exit in a rush of sharp elbows and angled shoulders in our mutual eagerness to escape.

"This is unexpectedly nice for lodgings above a sketchy vacant rib shack."

One thing was for certain. No one was going to stumble over us here by accident.

"Please sign the guestbook like that." Clay chortled. "I'm sure the owner would *love* it."

Another hint of that *something* had me asking, "Who's the owner?"

"Frank Tally." He wiggled his phone at me. "He's the father of a cashier from Bridge's Biscuits."

I committed the name to memory—the restaurant, not the father—in case I needed another grits fix.

"A random cashier gave you a tip on where to stay?"

Granted, Charleston was a major tourist destination, and plenty of locals had their own side hustles to cash in on. Real estate was a big one. Lots of old buildings got chopped up and remodeled into vacation rentals.

"What can I say?" He grew wistful. "We bonded over a shared love of pimento."

"She could tell he was a tourist from his accent." Colby rolled her eyes at his dramatics, which she not so secretly loved. "She asked where he was from, what brought him to the Holy City, where he was staying. The usual chitchat. He said he hadn't decided yet and asked if she had any recommendations as a local."

Pretty standard, especially if she had a reason to angle the conversation in that direction.

"Her dad renovated the upper floor," Clay cut in. "She texted me the address and told me to check it out on the VacayNStay app. She promised I wouldn't find a better deal for easy downtown access, and I took her word for it. Her freckles made her seem trustworthy, and who am I to doubt a lady's beauty marks?"

"You just wanted her number."

"True." He held up a finger. "*But*, as fate would have it, this is also a prime location."

At this rate, he was going to sprain an elbow patting himself on the back.

"For once, your flirting paid off." I noticed bronze plaques beside each doorway. "Which ones are we?"

"The Sweet Caroline and the Charleston Shuffle, but I rented all four to give us the entire floor."

"Cute names." I had to admire clever marketing. "How big are these suites?"

"Kitchen, breakfast nook, bathroom, bedroom, and living room. Our two have fireplaces. For ambiance."

"Mmm-hmm." I took Colby from him, purple beehive updo and all. "Meet back in thirty?"

"Sure."

Asa, still in his head, didn't say a word as he entered their suite then closed the door behind them.

"Any idea what that's about?" I aimed for the table to set down the wig and begin extraction. "He was quiet the whole way here."

"I dunno." She climbed out and shook off her wings. "Where's my laptop?"

Unsure what to do with the wig, I used a small trash bag from the kitchen to secure it for Clay.

"Hold your horses." I carried her to the sink. "You're taking a bath first."

"*Ugh.*"

A bath for her involved a very gentle, very careful, very short sprinkle of water across her body while she was in her biggest form to give her wings the most stability.

To distract her, I asked, "Can you file the paperwork for me with the cleaners?"

"Sure." She snorted. "It's a waste of time, but protocol is protocol."

Why the director didn't bring Black Hat mainstream boggled my mind, given he held controlling interests in so many other organizations and collected patents on magi-tech advancements in the criminal justice field the way some folks collect trading cards.

We couldn't remain a shadow organization forever. Not with modern technology making it near impossible to bluff your credentials. Used to be, you could flash a police badge or an FBI badge, and no one thought to question you. These days, you could buy either online, and no one believed you were who you said you were without first calling headquarters and having your badge number verified.

But he was the boss, and Colby didn't mind the legwork. She had plenty of them, after all.

"Okay, smarty fuzz butt, not everyone has access to our resources. We have to play it cool."

"Speaking of playing…" she flicked water in my face, "…I need to check in with my guild."

The suite was decorated in soft blues and whites with a beachy vibe. The front wall must have been store windows at some point in the building's history. It was easy for me to drag the small table into a thick ray of sunlight and plunk Colby down on a towel to air-dry while she chatted with her friends.

Soon fierce roars clashed with battle cries as orcs met their regularly scheduled doom.

With that familiar soundtrack in my ears, I began warding our floor to keep out uninvited guests.

3

We booked a sightseeing tour to Fort Sumter the next morning with the same company and on the same boat as our latest victim, Andreas Farmer, to give us a chance to nose around without arousing suspicion.

So far, the most peculiar thing we had encountered was the absolute lack of anything peculiar.

No gawking, no gossip, no speculation, no rehashing of the sordid details.

The total lack of interest, as if nothing untoward had happened yesterday, left me wary.

Without holiday fluff pieces to fill airtime, the local news had sensationalized the kidnappings before the Bureau reached in and pulled the plug on coverage. Even the retroactive media ban they slapped on the most damning aspects of the case couldn't erase damage done by linking the victims in the public's mind.

Cleaners worked fast, but they tended to cover up paranormal involvement rather than erase the crime. Phones made documentation simple, and social media shared breaking news as it happened.

It was easier to spin a story than squash it when multiple human witnesses guaranteed the spread by word of mouth.

Yet there hadn't been so much as a whisper about Andreas, or the other missing kids, in the ticket line.

"Ace and I will clear the top deck," Clay said as we stepped on board. "You clear the bottom."

Patronizing? A little. We were on a small boat, so Clay felt comfortable letting me hare off on my own.

The overall aesthetic of the *Bo-na-na Fanna* was steamboat, but its majestic paddlewheel was a decal on the side, a homage to its ancestry. The upper deck accommodated a bar selling snacks and sodas, as well as a couple dozen plastic lawn chairs for tourists to sit in during the crossing. But that wasn't my domain.

No.

I had been relegated to the dining area, easy to examine through the glass, and the bathrooms.

"It's always locked," a woman said from behind me as I peered in. "Only the crew goes in there."

"Looks fancy." I turned with a smile for her. "Do they do those nighttime dinner cruises too?"

"What don't they do?" She rolled her eyes. "Anything for a buck."

"You sound like you've been on this boat before." I kept the ball rolling. "Are you from here?"

"I'm Tracy Amerson. I teach at one of the local schools." She angled her face, daring me to recognize her profile. "My student was..." She pinched her lips. "He was the boy in the news."

There was no stopping a brief mention of a missing child discovered by a vacationing family in a popular tourist spot, but the disappearance had been reduced to a thirty-second sound bite on the local stations.

"Oh no." I clutched my nonexistent pearls. "I skimmed the news on my phone, but it didn't register."

No one onboard had so much as said *hello* to us, yet here stood his teacher, eager for a chat.

Maybe I ought to take solo bathroom detail more often.

"I was supposed to watch him, protect him, but he disappeared." She bowed her head. "I just thought…"

Performing my role to the hilt, I gentled my expression. "You need closure."

"I must've been to Fort Sumter a hundred times." She hunched her shoulders. "I've gone each year since I took up a teaching position. The kids are my responsibility, and I failed in the worst possible way. That I brought them here for the day program makes it that much worse." Tears slid down her cheek. "They're supposed to be safe with me while their parents are at work. Now the whole program is under review."

Sympathetic noises on my end kept her talking while I puzzled over why she chose me to approach.

Had she been wandering the boat, the better to castigate herself, only to discover a type of solitary madness that might push her to speak to total strangers until recognition dawned on just one face?

There was something very wrong with this boat, and, I suspected, with her.

"Rue?" Clay ambled down the stairs. "Everything okay down here?"

Jumping at his voice, Tracy offered me a fleeting smile that didn't reach her eyes.

"It was nice meeting you." She edged past me into the bathroom. "Enjoy your tour."

Once the door shut behind her, I joined Clay. "That was Andreas Farmer's teacher."

She hadn't used his name, but that tracked if it hadn't been released to the public yet.

"Really?" He raked today's wavy blond hair out of his eyes. "That's interesting."

Together we climbed the stairs to the upper deck and found Asa holding us seats.

For the safety of our fellow passengers, his hair was braided tight to prevent any hand-chopper-offing.

When he saw me, he smiled, and the thick bar piercing his septum caught the light. Bone-white ceramic with gold veins mirrored in his hoop earrings. They looked good on him. But then again, as the man fanning his cheeks across the aisle would attest, everything was improved by Asa wearing it.

Plunking down beside him, I filled him in on my brush with Tracy Amerson.

"Killers often return to the scene of the crime," Asa mused. "Do you think she's involved?"

"Hard to say." I replayed our conversation. "She approached me and waited to see if I would identify her before she brought up the boy. I can't tell if she was that desperate for connection, or if she was that freaked out no one seemed to notice or care if Andreas was missing. It also makes me wonder if she's para. She's kept her head, and so have we, but everyone else on board is la-de-da."

"We'll keep an eye on her." Asa put his arm around my shoulders to pull me close. "See what she does."

"The island is small." Clay, still standing, watched the boat's wake. "It shouldn't be hard to track her."

"Are those..." Colby gasped, "...*dolphins?*"

Eyes bright in the shadow of his jacket, Colby peered around his lapel out at the water.

"Sure are, Shorty." He moved to the rail to give her a better, and safer, view. "How many do you count?"

With the two of them occupied during our trip, I turned my attention to Asa. "Hi."

"Hello." The edges of his mouth twitched. "Come here often?"

A snort burst out of me. "I can't believe you went there."

"I've gone many new places since I met you."

"Yes, well, I did steal your first kiss."

"I didn't mean it in the literal sense."

Flames erupted in my cheeks, and I cleared my throat. "I knew that."

Soft chuckles shook his shoulders while he watched me burn.

Grumbling under my breath, I fussed, "How did I end up the pervert in this relationship?"

"I like it." Asa leaned over and captured my ear between his teeth. "You have such interesting ideas."

A groan clawed up my throat, part pleasure and part embarrassment, and his answering growl made me shiver.

"Keep your teeth to yourself, mister." I shoved him back. "There are kids present."

"Can I ask you a question?"

"Depends." I squinted at him. "Is it pervy?"

"No."

"Oh, well." I sighed dramatically. "There's always next time." I nudged him. "Ask."

"Does the water call to you?" He gazed out at the ocean. "I wondered if it did, if it ever has."

"No." I joined him in watching the bustling harbor, filled with yachts and…a floating tiki hut? "I don't have an affinity for it, as far as I can tell. I was surprised to learn I came from aquatic daemons. I thought I would feel *something*, but I don't." I rested my chin on his shoulder. "Can I ask you a question?"

"Of course."

"Do you have an affinity for fire or some other element?"

Until Delma used her power to allow us to view Calixta through a column of water, I hadn't known it was a talent some daemon possessed, and I had no thoughts either way on my lack of talent in aquatic areas.

I was a witch. I had magic. Magic could do pretty much anything. I saw no reason to be greedy or bitter.

"No," he said softly. "My father's legacy is pain."

"Orion Pollux Stavros," I murmured. "Master of Agonae." I thought about it. "As in agony?"

"Yes." He angled his head toward me. "I didn't inherit the gift, if that's what you want to call it."

"So, there are more than elemental daemons?" I really ought to knuckle down on researching daemons, and fae, rather than showcasing my ignorance to Asa. "There are types that control or affect emotions?"

"There are all manner of daemons. Dae are even more diverse in our talents."

Uncertain how to ask, I tiptoed around my intentions. "Are there many with your unique skill set?"

"You're asking about the daemon. How separate we are from each other." He watched a gull soar past. "I'm not the only dae with issues that manifest in a split personality." He dipped his gaze. "It's common. Not the level of autonomy that my other half has, but some degree of independent thought or action."

As far as I could tell, he and his daemon were two wholly separate identities who shared a body. But not the same form. I wasn't sure what bound them. Their soul? And, if he grew to accept that part of himself as an equal and integral part of the whole, would the daemon meld with Asa until they were one being?

All good intentions aside, his mother had encouraged his extreme body dysmorphia until he reached this point. I didn't want Asa to be at odds with any parts of himself, but I also hoped the daemon was here to stay. Which meant I would keep my lips zipped on my personal preference. Mine didn't matter. Only his.

If a day came when he had to make that choice, he had to do it himself, for himself. Himselves?

"You're not the only special snowflake," I teased to get us out of our funk. "I'm evil incarnate, so there."

"Yes." He brushed his lips across my forehead. "I could tell when you were willing to put your life between Colby and anyone who crossed her. I thought to myself—that woman is a vile stain on witchdom."

"You kind of did think that," I reminded him. "You hated me on sight."

"I wanted to bite you on sight," he countered. "It wasn't until I saw Colby that I misjudged you."

"Bite me?" I jerked back. "Are you serious?"

"Just a nibble." His smile bared straight white teeth. "I was fascinated from the moment I met you."

Fascinated with a capital F? Or intrigued? I was too chicken to even tease him about that.

"I wanted to punch your face in." I smiled through a wince. "I don't react well to people threatening Colby, or me, or threatening to take Colby from me." I held up a finger. "It was a very pretty face, though, and I would have been sad about ruining it."

"I somehow doubt that."

Static crackled as the intercom woke, and the captain began reciting safety instructions for our excursion.

Reminded we were on a job, I sat upright, tucking away thoughts of Asa biting me to savor later.

Before we were allowed off the boat, a wiry park ranger climbed aboard to bark a second set of rules for exploring the island. The entire speech was safety conscious, but it didn't mean much to young kids who had been cooped up for thirty minutes and who wanted to run wild as soon as their feet hit the ground.

To avoid the stampede, we hung back and let everyone else disembark first.

Everyone except Tracy, who had holed up in the ladies' bathroom for the duration.

Based on the sniffles I overheard from a locked stall, I suspected she had lost her nerve and elected not to go ashore, and that worked for me. Here, she was contained. That freed us up to examine the crime scene without dividing our focus. Plus, the quiet time ought to soothe her enough for a quick interview.

The wiry ranger eyed us with suspicion as we crossed the gangway and waved us off to one side.

That he zeroed in on Clay's slightly bulging suit pocket left my fingers tingling for my wand, paranoia screaming he had noticed Colby, but he was likely just worried Clay was wearing a concealed weapon.

"Can I help you folks?" His gaze slid between Clay and Asa. "You're mighty dressed up for tourists."

"We're bodyguards." Clay jerked his head toward me. "The boss's daughter wanted to see the fort, so here we are." He stepped closer. "You got a problem with that?"

"No," the ranger said at last, cracking his neck. "Just antsy, I guess, after yesterday."

Aside from Tracy, I had yet to encounter a soul who acknowledged Andreas Farmer's tragedy.

This made two people unaffected by the other passengers' mysterious localized amnesia.

Interesting.

"We heard about the boy in the news." I tried for politician's daughter over socialite. I wasn't a people person by nature, so it was a safer bet. "I'm sorry you're having to deal with looky-loos on top of your regular duties."

"All part of the job, ma'am." He tipped his hat, buying the act. "I apologize if I offended."

"I appreciate that you take your job, and the security of your visitors, so seriously."

A proud smile cracked his weathered cheeks, and he pointed toward the flagpole.

"The program is about to start, if you want to climb up Battery Huger. Otherwise, feel free to wander."

"We'll do that." I infused warmth into my tone. "Thanks again."

We took his advice and located the stairs. Good thing too. From there, we could see the entire island, all two hundred and thirty-five acres, including an offset sandbar locals were using as a private beach to sun and picnic on.

My initial takeaway was that everyone in Charleston must own a yacht or boat or kayak. People here lived on the water. Boats were crammed full of laughing families and friends, music poured from Bluetooth speakers, and no one appeared to notice it was the last gasp of December before the new year took its first breath.

Then again, maybe that explained why everyone was partying. Kids were out of school, the ball drop was coming in fast, and people loved to get a head start on the hard liquor holidays.

Beside me, Clay made an appreciative noise when a silver-haired woman dressed in a navy-blue string bikini began dancing in the surf. Two other women joined her, and he watched them laugh and splash with undisguised appreciation for their curves. To the point I had to pinch his side to yank his attention away from their frolicking.

Even from this vantage, I could read disappointment in their postures when he turned his back on them.

With Clay's height and build, he was easy to spot, and the silver fox still had her eye on him.

Cheeks puffing on an exhale, he forced himself to focus. "How did they take a kid in broad daylight?"

"Between the rangers, the teachers, and the other kids," I agreed, "we ought to have witnesses."

Our suspect took him during the tour, hid him until everyone left, drained his blood…and then what?

"Andreas should have been screaming for help." Asa scanned the horizon. "How did no one hear him?"

"We've got black magic traces on the leg." Clay zeroed in on me. "Can you sense any magic on the island that could tie it to this disappearance?"

Sometimes I hated being the authority on all things gruesome.

We didn't all get to grow up to be sugar and spice and everything nice.

I was sugar and spice—in the kitchen—and everything occult.

"Depends on how well the cleaners did their jobs." I exhaled. "So far, I've got nothing."

Maybe we would get lucky when we looped around to examine the alcove where the blood was found.

A buzz in my pocket had me stepping away to answer my cell. "Hollis."

"You sound so official," Camber teased. "Are you wearing a suit right now?"

"I'm allergic to good tailoring." I relaxed into her voice. "I wear a bag over my head to hide my shame."

Arden chimed in, alerting me I was on speaker. "Then shouldn't you be wearing a bag over your outfit?"

"It's a symbolic gesture." I fell into our familiar banter. "To what do I owe the pleasure of your mocking?"

"A man came in about ten minutes ago," Camber explained. "He asked to speak to you."

Had he been a local, they would have said so. His being a stranger made me anxious. "Did he say why?"

"Only that he wanted to speak to you." She made a thoughtful sound. "He was…odd."

"He wore a black suit," Arden contributed, taking over for Camber. "It was old-fashioned."

"The way he spoke was kind of British but not?" Camber snapped her fingers. "I got it. It's like that made-up accent they used in Hollywood in the forties. What was it called?"

"Mid-Atlantic," Arden supplied. "A mix of American and British English someone invented for funsies."

"I know you didn't go with us to the midnight showing of *It's a Wonderful Life*," Camber rattled on, "but it's that accent. Listen to Donna Reed's lines, and you'll get it."

That showing had been an attempt to socialize Aedan that had resulted in him making two friends aside from the girls. I hadn't gone, because I hadn't been invited. Selective memory was a marvelous thing.

Perhaps I ought to invoke it to forget I was too old and uncool to rate a ticket. "Anything else?"

"No." Camber paused to confer with Arden. "I don't think so."

"We thought you should know," Arden finished for her. "Just in case."

"Thanks for the update." I forced myself to play it cool. "How's everything else?"

"Business as usual," she assured me. "Actually, we should go. A customer just walked in."

"Let me know if Mid-Atlantic Man comes by again." I backed away from the railing. "Talk to you later."

The phone rang again almost as soon as the previous conversation ended.

"He was a black witch." Aedan kept his voice low. "The way he dressed? It was Black Hat, but vintage."

"Vintage?" I mulled that over. "Do you think he's old, or is it an affectation?"

"Between the accent and the outfit, he could have walked out of a black-and-white movie."

Life on the road would be so much easier if I owned a satellite in orbit above Samford.

Now that we knew Mayor Tate's dirty little secret, that the security cameras mounted throughout downtown were dummies, I had to think Clay was on to something when he jokingly suggested we begin methodically wiring in real ones.

There might come a time, and soon, when I required the ability to watch over the town when I left it.

On a less extravagant budget than, say, outer space.

"Keep an eye on the girls." I squinted against the sun. "Make sure they get home before dark."

"Okay." He muffled the receiver. "Hey, Arden. Sorry for taking a personal call on store time."

"You're fine." An edge of curiosity seeped into her tone. "I thought you were laying low?"

Much like me, he was trapped in the narrative we spun to explain his presence. We couldn't very well tell the town he was okay now because I murdered his sister in a duel. Or that he was insta rich and, oh yeah, daemon royalty adjacent. No. He would have to remain a victim in the eyes of the town until they saw him heal and grow, and they determined he had come out the other side victorious.

The process was familiar, since I had gone through it myself. Samford had embraced me, shown me how to find happiness in simple things, and given me space and time to mend the damage done to me over a lifetime of choosing the darker path each and every time it presented itself to me.

"I am," he rushed to assure her, "but there's a feral hog nosing around town."

"Wildlife relocation, right?" Her interest sounded genuine. "I forgot you did that."

Yet another lie spun to protect him, and to cover for him helping us hunt supernatural creatures.

"Only in special cases these days."

A laugh from Arden caused Aedan to catch his breath, and it made me want to pop an ibuprofen.

"Isn't your client still on the phone?"

"I gotta go," he told me quickly. "I'll touch base if I catch that hog near town again."

The call ended, and I smiled to know my sort of cousin was on the job.

But who was this *feral hog*, and what did it mean that he had come looking for me?

And why was I suddenly craving bacon?

The gourmet donuts Clay provided for breakfast had been amazing.

A dozen stuffed with cranberry jam, coated in a goat cheese glaze, topped with candied rosemary. And a dozen made from corn lemon shortbread, filled with sweet corn custard, topped with a blueberry glaze.

Basically, bacon or no bacon, my stomach had no right to complain.

The ranger's presentation was wrapping up as I made my way back to the guys. I listened to the tail end of it then updated them on the feral hog situation. Until we knew more, I was willing to stay in Charleston. But the second piggy raised a red flag, I was flying home, case be damned. I owed Camber and Arden that much.

"Let's meander toward the back stairs." Clay led the way. "The cannon alcoves are down there."

A few of our fellow passengers decided to sprawl on the small patch of lawn and stare out at the ocean. They looked content with their lives, happy for the sun and an excuse to spend the day outdoors. What they didn't look was wary the same thing that happened to Andreas could happen again.

"The calm is eerie." Asa watched the tourists. "No one is concerned about their children."

Twenty-four hours after a boy disappeared, they should have been afraid for them.

Honestly?

They should have stayed home.

Plenty of folks avoided the news for the sake of their mental health, me among them when I wasn't on a case, but you would expect someone to have said something to parents about the disappearance before they walked up to the ticket window.

"This cover-up is bigger than the cleaners." I checked with my gut. "A spell was cast over this island."

Too bad the moisture in the air would have begun eroding the spell as soon as it was cast, so any signature the practitioner left behind would be smudged beyond recognition.

"A spell?" Clay cocked his head. "Wouldn't we have felt it?"

"Any magic would have to overcome the volume of tourists and the salt water, which is running water." I figured they both knew the issues inherent with that, but thinking out loud helped me. "The best they could have done was anchor a spell to a foundational object on this island. Say, Battery Huger."

"That means the spell has a limited scope, right?"

"Anyone who comes chasing a whisper of a news story will forget why they were here after they set foot on magicked ground." I smoothed my palm over the Battery, searching for any lingering power. "As time goes on, this type of effect fades on its own. With an island? I estimate it'll be gone in a matter of days."

"But you don't think cleaners did this."

"No." I couldn't shake the feeling. "I don't."

We reached the alcove flagged in the report. There sat a chained-off cannon, mid-restoration, but the earth beneath it held no signs of the bloody mess that had sent the vacationing family into a tizzy.

After identifying the exact spot using crime scene photos, I crouched to place my hand on the bare earth.

"This much the cleaners did do." I dug my fingers into the soil. "The area has been magically bleached."

There were no clues left to discover, no magic trail to follow, no evidence to link the leg to this place.

"The spell on the island's not strong enough to influence paranormals," Asa ventured. "We're a diverse sampling, and we're unaffected."

"No one on board acted right either." Clay swept out a hand. "For them, this was just another day."

Meaning whatever influenced them had taken root prior to boarding and lasted the length of the trip.

"The boat wouldn't hold a spell long enough for it to be worth the effort." Objects in motion tended to shuck enchantments. A floating object? Total waste of effort. "Patriots Point makes more sense."

The check-in area kept people queued while waiting for their boat to arrive. It was an ideal setup to hold everyone steady while subtle magic wiggled into their minds that would be reinforced at the fort.

"The ranger on the dock initiated a confrontation," I reminded them. "Where does he fit?"

"Good question." Clay mulled it over. "The teacher wasn't *as* confrontational, but still."

"She also hasn't left the boat," Asa pointed out. "We should head back early, check on her again."

"She must be para to be unaffected." I tried not to leap to my next conclusion, but I already had a spring in my step. "That doesn't mean she's our dark arts practitioner. She might simply be a para who works in a human field. Same for the ranger." I explored the alcove for any hidey-holes. "She might have confided in me because she sensed my otherness. It must have freaked her out, no one talking about Andreas. So, she tested me."

Done with my inspection, I dusted off my pants as I stood and headed toward the dock.

"Or—" Asa resumed his earlier speculation, "—she's a killer returning to the scene of the crime who got spooked when she bumped into you because you passed her test. You knew about Andreas."

"Kidnapping human children is begging to get noticed." Clay kept pace with me. "If that's what the perp wants, they won't be happy their crimes are being swept under the rug. They'll escalate until they get the recognition they crave."

Frantic shouts drew my attention to the waiting boat where a man leaned over the edge to vomit.

"She's dead," he called to another deckhand on shore. "She's...*really* dead."

He emptied his stomach over the side again then slumped into a chair.

Human ears wouldn't have picked up their conversation, but if I heard it, then Asa and Clay had too.

We wove through the other passengers to reach the dock but

found a ranger blocking the gangway with his broad shoulders. His posture struck me as military, and his expression dared us all to try his patience.

Unease crawled through me when I noticed he wasn't the man who pulled us aside for a chat. Several of the rangers were on duty, but I would have expected them to all come running after the scream. Unless, maybe, he ducked into the Battery and missed the commotion.

Around us, the crowd gathered, everyone concerned or curious, most having no idea what was wrong.

"Ladies and gentlemen," the ranger announced, his voice low and rough. "We must ask you for your patience. The boat has experienced a mechanical issue and will be unable to bring you back to shore." His white-knuckled grip cinched around the railing. "That gives you thirty bonus minutes to tour the fort."

The guy was a pro, I would give him that. He kept his composure, and the people listened to him, but his competence left us with the thorny issue of how to get on the boat before the human police arrived and muddied the investigative waters.

Time to get ahead of this story before it gained legs.

First things first, I texted my old pal Marty and told him to rouse the other agents sitting on their thumbs at the hotel we ditched. They needed to work with the Kellies to get between this incident and the human press. He was, as always, super helpful and a joy to converse with. Not at all a jaded has-been too lazy to do his job without me threatening to shove my sneaker so far up his butt that he choked on my shoelaces.

Then I sent a plea for assistance to the Officers Vandenburgh.

"I can check things out."

Whirling toward Clay, I pegged the tiny voice emanating from his pocket with a glare. "No."

"I can fly in, fly out, and no one will see me."

"You're not going alone." I slashed a hand through the air. "The killer could still be in there."

The kidnapper targeted kids. Not fae kids, as she had been, but I wasn't taking any chances.

Until we knew if this killer and our kidnapper were one and the same, I was clipping her wings.

Huffing her annoyance, she put on her headset then slouched into Clay's pocket to pout.

"You're the aquatic daemon." Clay mimed the dog paddle. "Show us how it's done."

Had the cannons been functional, I might have aimed one at his head then lit the fuse.

Arms falling to his side, he read murder on my face and fought not to laugh. "Too soon?"

"I'll go." Asa shed his jacket and passed it to me. "I'll need cover."

"What kind of..." I watched his nimble fingers work his shirt buttons, "...cover?"

"The kind that will conceal a full moon on the rise." Clay snickered at my unhinged jaw. "Can you arrange for a lunar eclipse?"

Concealment spells were tricky bits of magic that required flexibility to warp a person until they blended in with their surroundings, but I knew Asa. The shape of him. The feel of him. The fine details I cataloged when he wasn't looking. I could manage cover to and from the water, with Colby's help.

"Yes." I shut my eyes against temptation. "Give me five."

A slow exhale gave me the focus to reach through the familiar bond. Palming my wand, I gestured Asa to come to me. A tap on his shoulder wrapped a thick blanket of misdirection around him that would shield him from prying eyes but allow me to watch.

Us.

I meant us.

For his protection.

Totally a safety precaution.

His shirt hit me in the face, startling my eyes open, and I worried I might have to use it as a napkin as saliva pooled in my mouth.

"Are we sure this is a good idea?"

As he held my stare, he smoothed a thumb over the button of his pants. "Do you have a better one?"

About to tell him that, yes, I had several, I squawked when Clay slapped a hand over my mouth.

"Do *not* answer that, Dollface." Clay puffed out his cheeks. "Or I'll be the next one to barf."

A hard glower convinced Clay to remove his hand before I removed it for him, which he would *not* enjoy.

"You're strangling my shirt." Asa tugged down his zipper. "What did it ever do to you?"

"The shirt was hogging the view," I said in a breathy voice like a lovesick fool. "You are so beautiful."

That last part slipped out before my brain caught up to my mouth, but it was true.

A disbelieving sort of wonder stole over his features. "You think I'm beautiful."

The idea I might be the first person to accept him, daemon and all, threatened to break my black heart.

Resting my hand on his cheek, I confirmed it. "Inside and out."

"Hallmark..." Clay tipped back his head and implored the sky, "... I've got a movie idea for you."

A moth-sized snicker escaped from his pocket. "They don't do Halloween specials."

We really had to work on her eavesdropping on adult conversations.

Hmm.

A soundproof pocket spelled into Clay's wardrobe would do the trick.

"Rude." I glowered at the pair of them. "I might be a witch, but I'm also a woman."

Asa turned his lips into my palm. "My witchy woman."

The oxygen evaporated from my lungs as if they were soda cans crushed flat with a stomp.

"You two are mushier than oatmeal." Clay curled his lip. "The bland kind that comes in packets."

Air rushed in, allowing me to think clearly, and I stepped back from Asa. "That's just plain mean, Clay."

Clothes piled in my arms, I turned away while Asa shucked his pants, which he draped over my shoulder.

On my best behavior, for Clay's sake, I counted back from one hundred under my breath.

When I turned around, Asa was gone, and Clay was cleaning off a spot for the clothes he took from me.

"Ace will be back soon." Clay slung an arm around me. "He's got this."

"I know." I leaned my head against him. "I just worry."

"He's got a daemon under his skin and his mother's cleverness to boot." Clay smiled. "He'll be fine."

Everyone always said that, and everything was always fine.

Until it wasn't.

4

The dented bullet in my pocket kept me oddly centered as I rolled it between my fingers, considering it had been lodged in Asa once upon a time. It was both talisman and reminder that he wasn't invulnerable. Even his daemon had weaknesses.

Ten minutes after Asa left, I began to have trouble breathing.

Fifteen minutes in, and I was a fish gasping for air in a dry tank.

Twenty minutes in, I spelled myself the same as I had him then stripped to my underwear.

Hidden from sight, I was ready to dive in after him...

...when he rose from the surf looking like he ought to have been the Haelian Sea royalty instead of me.

The swim had caused one braid to come undone. The other held on, but it was matting from the salty water. His eyes were brilliant in the sun, glittering like gems, and when they raked down my body, I flushed from head to toe.

"Rue?"

Reading me with terrifying ease, he opened his arms. I slammed into him before I realized I had made the choice to go to him. To *run* to him. He lost his balance, probably something to do with how my legs had snaked around his hips. We toppled backward, landing in a puff of loose sand.

"It's okay." He spoke the words against my throat. "I'm fine."

"I'm the one who's fine." I held on tighter. "Why are you soothing me?"

"You're shaking." He ran his hands up my back. "You were worried."

"Don't flatter yourself," I grumbled. "I'm half naked. I'm just cold."

Beneath me, Asa's soft laughter shook my entire body, but he didn't call me out.

"There are laws about indecency," Clay said from nearby. "Why are you two always breaking them?"

The urge to pepper Asa's face with kisses and cling to him like a barnacle surfaced within me, this fragile want that scared me spitless.

"Why can't you let us break laws in peace?" I heaved a sigh, grateful for the excuse to extricate myself with grace. I stood, feet to either side of his hips. "Just once, you could wait and see what happens."

"I know what would happen." He tossed pants at Asa's face. "That's why I don't want a front row seat."

"Fascination is gross," Colby said from Clay's pocket. "I'm never dating. Boys are too much trouble."

Oh, yes.

A spelled pocket was happening as soon as I had a minute to work out how to safely craft it.

"I'm glad one of the Hollis girls has sense." Clay exhaled. "We can't be too hard on Rue. Fascination makes her brain sizzle like bacon on a griddle. All that delicious fat is cooking out, leaving her crunchy."

"Huh?" Colby wiggled in his pocket. "What does that mean?"

"My thoughts exactly." I chose to miss the point on purpose. "Are you trying to tell me you're hungry?"

"Shorty, plug in, okay?" Clay helped her settle. "Dollface, do you know me at all?"

"So, that's a yes."

"I wouldn't cry if we hit an all-day breakfast spot after this."

Much like me, Clay wasn't as affected by gore and tragedy as most people would be.

We weren't normal. By any metric. We had to grow thick skins to survive the Bureau.

"The donuts were phenomenal," he continued, "but not very filling."

"You only ate, like, eighteen of them."

"It's not my fault you and Ace are lightweights. Who only eats three donuts?"

"That's all we had time for before the Hoover in the backseat sucked down the rest."

"You knew the risks, and yet you let me hold the boxes."

"What did you find?" I offered Asa a hand up, and he took it. "Does it tie into our case?"

"Tracy is dead." He shucked his soggy underwear. "I've never seen anything like it."

Neither had I.

Goddess bless, Asa was not just a little naked, but all the way naked, and I was staring.

Clay dug his fingertips into my shoulders and spun me in the opposite direction faster than I could blink.

"Put that away," he scolded Asa. "Can't you tell this trembling virgin is terrified of the one-eyed snake?"

"Really?" I cranked my head toward him, only to get smacked in the face with my discarded clothes. "That's what you went with?"

He had done me a favor, really. I didn't want Asa to feel like I viewed him with the same raw hunger as a fresh heart, warm and dribbling juices, because drool flecked my parted lips. Even if it might be true.

"The connectors in your brain shook loose." He massaged my scalp while I dressed, mostly to control the direction of my head. "I had to act fast to preserve as many cells as possible."

"And you thought pulling out the one-eyed snake would do the job?"

"No." He tugged the end of my hair. "Pulling it out caused the problem in the first place."

The peep show was over by the time Clay finished teasing me, for which I was grateful.

There was a time and a place for lascivious thoughts, and right now was neither.

Dang it.

With a flick of my wand, I dissolved the spell concealing us before our absence made us suspect.

"There was no body, per se." Asa ignored us discussing his, um, snake. "There was skin."

That shocked my mind out of the gutter with a jolt. "Skin?"

An evidence baggie, or snack baggie as Clay called them, had kept Asa's phone dry during his swim.

"Yards of it." He woke his display then turned the screen toward us. "Sliced to ribbons."

Tracy Amerson had never left the bathroom. Her remains, such as they were, unfurled from her stall.

"I peel apples that way." Clay dropped the humor too. "What the actual fuck?"

Thankfully, Colby was off in her own world, but still.

"Language," I reminded him. "Colby doesn't need to start cursing like a sailor."

"Sailors could take pointers from me."

Given his age, all that he had seen and done since his creation, he was probably right.

"Yeah, but who says *curse like a golem*? No one, that's who."

After accepting the cell from Asa, I swiped through the gallery while Clay looked on beside me.

"No bones, no organs." He leaned closer. "No blood either."

Up to this point, blood had been the only common denominator between the cases.

Then again, those had involved children. This was an adult, though teaching made her kid adjacent.

Asa was fastening the top button on his dress shirt when I glanced up at him. "Black magic?"

Nothing could be done for his wet hair, but I did finger-comb it and re-braid it for a more polished look.

"The bathroom reeked of it," he confirmed. "The entire bottom floor of the boat is foul."

"The police are on the way," Colby announced, peering out of Clay's pocket. "They're about to dock."

Holding open his jacket, I got an eyeful of her fuzzy head, headphones on. "How do you know?"

"Police scanner." She grinned up at Clay, telling me where she got the idea. "There's a nifty app for it."

Leave it to Clay to keep Colby from listening in on us by eavesdropping instead on police.

As he adjusted his jacket, careful of his passenger, a bittersweet pang struck me.

For the longest time, it had been Colby and me. Me and Colby. We had no one else who knew our secrets. Now we had Clay and Asa and Aedan.

I might have saved her, but she didn't pick me. Specifically. She hadn't measured me and found me worthy of her trust. She had been grasping for a lifeline, and I threw her one. For better or worse, she caught it.

These days, there was slack in that rope, and it made me as happy for her as it made me...wistful?

Fascination came with a heaping helping of *feelings*. Worse, those pesky emotions didn't contain themselves to matters of Asa and me. They dug into all the relationships in my life, forcing me to view them through a different lens. I didn't always like what I saw, but I was grateful for the clarity.

As if I could outrun my touchy-feely moment, I strode with purpose to meet with our warg contacts.

"How about aerial scout while we're on board." I pasted on a smile for Colby. "You don't need to see this."

"Too many birds." A shudder rocked her. "I'll close my eyes, okay? I don't want to go up there."

Since she was happy to play lookout before Asa volunteered, I knew she just wanted to be nosy.

"Then it's podcast time." Clay tucked her in tight. "I cued up one on how to cheat in Mystic Realms."

"It's not cheating if it's coded into the game," she protested. "It's totally legal, if you know the combos."

Once she settled in again, I touched Clay on the arm and mouthed *Thank you*.

"Anything for you, Dollface." He chucked me on the chin. "You know that."

With our littlest team member secure, we hit the dock to meet the Marine Police cruiser.

One of the rangers called out to Mr. Officer, who hung back to talk to him with an easy familiarity.

Mrs. Officer dipped her chin at the ranger but strode toward us. "What have we got?"

"Another victim," Asa supplied. "Her name is Tracy Amerson."

"Andreas Farmer's teacher." Clay fed her the connection. "She rode out with us today."

"Come on then." Mrs. Officer swore under her breath. "Let's get this nightmare started."

Nightmare was an apt description of the scene that greeted us in the cramped bathroom.

The photos and video hadn't prepared me for the putrid slap of air upon entering, a foul tang that didn't remind me of death or decomposition so much as it coated the back of my throat with fetid black magic.

Hard to tell without another sampling, given the leg's condition, but I felt certain the signature matched.

"What the hell are we looking at?" Mr. Officer was breathing through his mouth. "That ain't right." He pointed to the remains. "Whatever *that* is, it ain't right."

"Human flesh," Asa supplied, kneeling beside the body as if seeing it for the first time. "It was cut from the victim in a spiraling motion, crown to toe, with no discernable break in stroke."

"Are you serious?" Mrs. Officer cringed. "Like one of those spiralizers they sell for zucchini noodles?"

"Yes." He pulled on a pair of gloves and lifted a thready blonde lock. "The hair on the scalp is intact."

How he could tell was beyond me. From where I stood, I saw a heap of string. But I suppose it was uniform in length, if you pieced the sections together. Maybe he did that earlier, for him to sound so sure.

"We're dealing with a professional." I wedged myself against the sink. "They've had a lot of practice to peel it so perfectly. And by practice, I mean they're a practitioner." I indicated a nubby mass. "Even the individual toes and nails were preserved. I can't see the fingers in that mess, but I'm guessing they're the same. This is powerful black magic."

"I've never heard of anything like this." Mrs. Officer checked with her husband. "You?"

"No." He shook his head. "This beats all I've ever seen."

"We need to get the remains to a lab." I would have preferred Black Hat handle it, but the cleaners were the next best thing. "Tell your people to determine her species first. That takes priority over COD."

The cause of death would be a catastrophic use of black magic. Immunity to the spell was more pressing, and it reminded me. The park ranger was still MIA, but he must be here somewhere. Fort Sumter wasn't that large. The Vandenburghs would need to question him and verify his species to flesh out my theory.

Before I forgot, I told them just that, ensuring the ranger didn't slip through the cracks.

"How did the deckhand determine gender?" Mr. Officer squinted at the mess. "The hair?"

"Not the hair." Mrs. Officer aimed a pointed glance at Asa. "Guys grow theirs out too."

The vague gesture she made in his direction was enough to break me out in sweat. Though I didn't want to swat her hand and risk an incident, I was sure she would prefer a quick smack to amputation via *y'nai*.

Those little boogers were crazy fast and utterly bloodthirsty when it came to defending their charges.

The creepiest part by far had to be, not their penchant for amputation, but their ability to go undetected until the precise moment some poor sucker touched his or my hair and earned a free hand removal.

"Good question." I made a mental note to locate the deckhand and ask. "Tracy didn't leave the boat. We were heading back early to check on her when he called out, 'She's dead.'" I fudged my story to cover for Asa's earlier aquatic adventure. "She was already on my mind, so I jumped to the conclusion it was her."

There. Totally plausible. Not at all like we had been sneaking around behind their backs.

"We've all been there," Clay comforted me with a smirk. "Don't beat yourself up over it."

Right now, I was more interested in beating him up over helping me throw myself under the bus.

"The skin was moisturized," Asa murmured, rubbing a curled length between his fingers. "The texture..." He flipped it inside out to show us. "It reminds me of tanned leather." He flexed it. "It's supple, smooth."

"Are you saying the killer was *wearing* the teacher?" I pictured the mechanics, well, I tried to anyway. "It would be like wrapping yourself in an Ace bandage from head to toe. Except the seams would have to match exactly, and even then, one wrong move would unravel you, mummy-style."

This was my chance to get a solid read on a victim for comparison, and I took it without permission.

Crouching beside Asa, I traced a crease—a knee maybe?—and the stain of black magic inked my fingers. I rose while rubbing my stinging hands, burdened with the certainty no simple black witch had done this.

No wonder Charleston had a black witch deficit. This proved they had their own dark arts practitioners.

"We need to find out more about our victim." Clay eyed her remains with pity. "If Tracy has a spouse or significant other, they can tell us if she's been acting odd lately and when it began. We can cross-check that against our other cases, see how it fits."

"I estimate this happened four or five months ago." Asa glanced up then. "We need to see where that falls on the timeline."

"I would ask how you know," Mrs. Officer said lightly, "but there are things you expect from a daemon."

White noise filled my head, crackling in my ears. "How to make people jerky is one of them?"

The softness of my voice strung tension through Clay, who crept nearer to me.

"Yeah." She thought I was serious. "There's probably a recipe book in his mom's kitchen that covers it."

Between one blink and the next, I had her throat in my palm and her back against the wall. She kicked her feet and fought my grip. Her nails lengthened to claws that pricked my hand, but I held on.

"Let go of my mate," Mr. Officer snarled to my right. "You don't want this to get ugly."

"Yeah." I forced my fingers to ease their grip. "I wouldn't want to rile your animal instincts and risk you eating the evidence." However, I couldn't quite let go. "I hear dogs love jerky treats."

To give them a taste of their own medicine proved my point, but it left a sour taste in my mouth.

"Your wife started it," Clay said behind me. "Let Rue finish it."

About the time *finishing it* began to sound good to the roar in my head, warm arms encircled me.

"Let her go," Asa whispered into my neck. "You don't want to do this."

"Pretty sure I do." I sucked in a whistling breath through my teeth. "You can watch."

"You don't have to protect me." He slid a possessive hand over my hip. "I can take care of myself."

The weight of the bullet in my pocket told me otherwise, but this was a different kind of hurt. This wasn't a physical pain she was inflicting on him. It was a verbal wound piercing thick psychic scar tissue he might no longer feel, but it agonized me enough for the both of us.

"I'm...sorry," Mrs. Officer wheezed, her body fighting off a shift, her face a lovely shade of purple.

Eggplant? Chartreuse? No, that was green. Though she had a tint of that too. Aubergine? Yes! That one.

A biting kiss stung my throat, Asa jerking my attention from her to him. "Old prejudices die hard."

Malicious or not, ignorant comments like hers kept breathing new life into them.

No one assumed Asa was dae. Or fae. They pegged him as daemon, and he let them. It was safer for him if others thought he was the biggest bad in any room. But where he was concerned, that title fell to me.

These two knew he wasn't all daemon, but that was still the stick they wanted to measure him by.

"We have a job to do." I let her go, and she fell. "Even look at him again, and you'll regret it."

"Thank you." Asa gathered my hands in his then checked with the Vandenburghs. "Are we done here?"

"Yes," Mr. Officer answered, voice straining. "We all need a chance for our tempers to cool."

Rather than rush to his mate's side, he stood his ground. More posturing. Whatever. Let him puff out his chest. I could huff too. I could damn well blow them both down if they insulted Asa again in my hearing.

Mrs. Officer rose slowly, reclaiming her dented pride, and straightened her shoulders.

"Agent Hollis." Mrs. Officer rubbed her throat. "I forget how easy it is to speak hate, and I shouldn't."

She lowered her eyes in a symbolic gesture that scored her points. Alphas didn't do submissive.

As much as I wanted to snap *too little, too late*, I saw her trying. That was all any of us could do.

No one got it right one hundred percent of the time, and I was as far from perfect as Earth was from the sun.

"Wargs have been discriminated against for as long as we've existed. Most of the lore is wrong, and the assumptions about us are downright offensive." She didn't look at Asa, but she angled her head toward him while she spoke to me. "I've never met a daemon, and your mate has given me no reason to think badly of him or his species. I apologize, truly, for any harm I caused with my careless words." She coughed softly. "I'll do better."

"Thanks." I unclenched my fists enough for Asa to mesh our fingers. "We all make mistakes."

"Maybe I should have mentioned this earlier." Clay scratched his jaw. "Rue and Asa are in fascination."

Understanding pinched the alphas' faces, and they took a healthy step back from us both.

Huh.

Maybe we should print couple's business cards with *Ask Me About Fascination. Or I Might Kill You. Oops.*

"We'll be in touch." Mr. Officer and his mate kept their distance. "Text if you need us."

We exited the boat and hit the dock without being stopped again, and I scanned the horizon for a rescue ferry, but I didn't see one.

"We're not going that way." Clay pointed to the families sunning outside the fort's walls. "We're going this way."

Straight toward the spot where we last saw the silver fox and her boobies. I mean, buddies.

"You're not serious."

"Time to plug in, Shorty. No spying, okay? Listen to your podcast, and only your podcast, I'll buy you that flaming sword you've had your eye on." Once the bargain was struck, a bribe she couldn't resist, he smoothed a hand through his hair. "She looked friendly, and she has a boat."

"You don't know that she has a boat. Maybe she came with friends."

"Who must have a boat for them to be on an island, so the argument is still valid."

"You're splitting hairs."

"Wigs don't do split ends, and neither do I."

"You know what I mean."

"Look, I don't know about you, but I don't want to be stuck onboard while the police interview everyone prior to releasing them to their cars. The Vandenburghs are out. They're stuck here for the duration. What options does that leave us?"

"Fine." I held up my hands in surrender. "Try your luck."

"Luck has nothing to do with it." He shot me a saucy wink. "Give me ten, and then follow."

Ten minutes was a stretch. I doubted he needed five. Assuming his mark was still ashore.

I suspected the extra time was for Asa and me. Clay was right to force me to admit my behavior was out of line, but he was wrong if he thought I was sorry.

"Can I blame fascination for this?" I threw out the question as Clay sauntered off. "Or your faeness?"

"Do you think it's possible," Asa said softly, "that you care about me? That when others seek to hurt me, it wounds you more?" He stepped behind me and wrapped his arms around my middle. "It's okay to care, Rue."

"Care isn't a big enough word," I confessed, because he deserved the truth. "When people talk down to you, I just…" I mimed breaking a stick with my hands, "…snap. I don't know why. I can't control it."

"You protect the ones you love." He pressed his cheek to mine. "Fiercely. Passionately." A rumble moved through his voice. "Viciously."

Love?

Much bigger word than care.

Exhaling a slightly panicked laugh, I relaxed into his hold. "That last one turned you on, huh?"

"Yes," he growled, nuzzling me. "I am half daemon, after all."

In his voice, I heard we were okay, that he understood I was better with showing emotion through violence than with sweet words. Better than that, I heard that he was okay with it. I might be emotionally stunted, but I could read the room. He not only accepted the darkness in me. He *liked* it.

He liked *me*.

The *real* me.

I held nothing back from him. I couldn't. Fascination had infected me, turned me into a person with *feelings*. And worse? I expressed them. Frequently. Just with chokeholds and throat punches.

"Time's up," I croaked, pulling from his embrace. "We better go see what trouble Clay's got us into."

"All right." He fell in step beside me. "This ought to be interesting."

5

Given the size of the island, we didn't have to search long to spot Clay and a half dozen of his new bikini-clad besties. His broad wave in our direction confirmed he had secured a ride back to the mainland, and I had to hand it to him. He worked fast. The silver fox snuggled into his side, and a bevy of scantily clad ladies surrounded him, as if he were the first man to land on a planet populated only by women.

Goddess only knows what story he spun to earn their unwavering loyalty so quickly.

"Here they are now," he told the women, then boomed at us, "Come aboard."

Asa and I waded in ankle-deep water to reach the ladder then joined the others on the biggest privately owned boat I had ever stepped foot on. Dare I call it a yacht? Perhaps *floating city* worked best?

"You didn't mention your *friend* was a girl." His arm candy pouted. "Is she your daughter?"

"Yes," he lied through his teeth. "My daughter, Rue, and her boyfriend, Asa." She placed a proprietary hand on his chest. "These are my new friends, Marta, Tamsin, Shae..." he smiled down at the silver fox, "...and Glinda."

"How do you feel about sharing?" A woman with pink cheeks wet her lips. "You're such a lovely couple."

Was she asking me to let her seduce him? Or was she inviting us both to join her? And did it matter?

Nope.

Not even a little. The answer was no. It would always be no.

Hitchhiker I might be, but I wasn't paying for a ride back with sex.

"We don't share." Asa's palm warmed the back of my neck. "Thank you for the offer."

"You understand I had to ask." She slid Clay a glance. "Though I suppose it would get weird with your dad there." She must have read my shock. "He's agreed to join us tonight for our sacred moon rite." She held a hand to one side of her mouth. "We're witches."

If a single one of these women had an ounce of magic in them, I would eat Clay's wig. "Uh-huh."

"Usually, it's just us girls, dancing naked under the stars," Glinda, the only woman whose name I could match to a face, confided. "But Clay is too tempting." She smoothed a hand down his shirt. "We don't mind sharing at all, do we, girls?"

The girls in question cheered and whooped with glee, and Clay might as well have been my father for how traumatized I was by the deal he had struck. Even if I knew he would enjoy the heck out of being ravaged by "witches" on a remote beach somewhere, I could have lived the rest of my life without knowing about it.

"The things I do for the goddess." Clay squeezed Glinda tighter. "Ladies, I'm at your service."

"You will be," a brunette purred. "As soon as the sun goes down."

"How about that trip to the mainland?" I clapped my hands loudly. "Let's go, shall we?"

"We need to prepare for tonight anyway," Glinda declared. "Full steam ahead, Trish."

Seeing as how the engine woke to a dull purr on her command, I decided Trish was the captain.

Once we got underway, Asa and I found a quietish spot away from the pre-orgy festivities.

Forearms braced on the rail beside me, Asa cleared his throat. "Rue—"

"Nope." I shook my head. "We're not talking about it."

Quiet laughter moved through his shoulders. "You two really are like siblings."

"Siblings who don't need to know about each other's orgy plans."

Still chuckling, he smoothed a fingertip over the mistletoe necklace he'd given me where it rested, blown off center by the wind, against my left collarbone.

"That's not how it works." I wrapped his braid around my hand and used it to tug his face down to mine. "*You* are supposed to kiss me when *I* touch it."

"Hmm." The vibration moved from his lips to mine. "Is that right?"

"Touch it again." I chuckled softly. "See what happens."

"For the love of God," Clay begged, "do not touch it again. Whatever *it* is."

The ick factor in his voice was almost on par with the one that had been in mine earlier.

"Well, if it isn't the willing sacrifice." I squinted into the sun. "This was the boat you chose? Really?"

"I didn't choose the boat, the boat chose me."

"Mmm-hmm." The boat wasn't the one wearing dental floss as a bikini and seducing innocent tourists down to the beach, but whatever. "Before or after you met Glinda the Good Witch?"

"I'll have you know," he said in a haughty voice, "her last name is Lasky."

The three of us leaned on the railing, ignoring the catcalls and blaring music coming from the front.

"An unraveled person," Clay said, his voice heavy, "has got to be the weirdest shit we've ever seen."

I cleared my throat at his potty mouth and shot his pocket a pointed look he decided to ignore.

As far as he was concerned, he had purchased his privacy from Colby until we got home. A paid system I couldn't allow to continue without us creating an epic quest-worthy moth monster I would get stuck slaying so he could remain her white knight.

"Not even black witches go full-on mummy with their victims' skins."

The right spell achieved the same outcome without the hassle of hiding a body afterward.

An anecdote from one of the director's lectures rose to the forefront of my mind with hazy edges.

"There's a coven that steals souls to wear." I couldn't recall their name. "They're outliers, though."

They maintained an archive of souls who leapt at the chance to possess any witch requiring a disguise for coven business.

At the time, I remember thinking it was the coolest trick ever to have a closet full of victims to wear.

Now I saw it for the waste of life that it was, and I was ashamed to admit it had once impressed me.

"Witchborn fae," Asa murmured. "I've heard rumors they live in Atlanta, but I haven't encountered one."

The witch link might not have piqued his interest, but I bet he filed away all sorts of mixed-species trivia.

That foothold in the case helped me climb to my next question. "Do we need to pursue them as a lead?"

"I've got friends down that way. I'll put in a few calls, see what I can learn." Clay tamed his hair from his eyes. "We'll set Shorty on cyber sleuthing when we get back to the suites."

"Good idea." I gazed out at the dolphins leaping and playing. "She's been in the field a lot this trip."

Colby was used to the computer screen acting as a buffer. The distance helped her to compartmentalize. It gave her extra layers of separation between her and our victims. Not that she considered herself one.

No, I was the one forever battling the instinct to bubble wrap life for her, as if I could hide all its sharp edges.

"Colby will tell you if it's too much." Asa sounded certain. "She's a smart girl."

"She wants in too much not to take it seriously." Clay sent his pocket a fond smile. "Plus, she has us. We'll pull her back from the edge if she steps too close." He rubbed my shoulder. "It's better for her to help than be left at home feeling helpless."

A shudder rippled through me as a crystalline memory of the night I met Colby flooded my mind.

She had been afraid, so very afraid. I had killed the Silver Stag, but his spell was draining her. A soul couldn't survive outside its shell for long. She was dying all over again. Slowly. Painfully. As she clawed at any means to hold on to life, she begged me for help. To save her. *Me*. As if I knew how to save anyone.

For her, I had learned, but I still heard those pitiful, desperate screams in my dreams.

No, she didn't consider herself a victim.

And that gave me no right to continue seeing her that way either.

"It doesn't stop me from wishing there was another way," I rasped. "I didn't want this for her."

"Colby is special." Asa trailed his fingers down my arm. "She was never going to have an ordinary life."

Once upon a time, she would have, if the Silver Stag hadn't chosen her.

Clay's fan club descended upon him then, stealing him away, drinks sloshing over their hands.

Head resting on Asa's shoulder, I watched the crime scene recede to swirling blue waters. It should have been calming, but I kept fixating on the call from the girls, on the stranger in town, and I couldn't settle.

Samford only had room for one black witch.

And it was me.

The elevator took approximately fifty forevers to haul us up to our suites, and we broke apart to ready ourselves for the next steps. Daytime trips, like the one to the fort, required us to mingle with humans in sunlight, but the real hunting always happened at night.

Once I settled Colby in her room, I wrote her a to-do list then let her get to work.

It felt a little like assigning homework. Too bad she didn't get GED credits for these projects.

The guys were waiting for me at their tiny kitchen table, staring down at the busy intersection below. A line was forming for a popular restaurant across the way, and there was commotion over a homeless man canvassing the diners for leftovers as they exited the building.

"I have four hours." Clay watched the ensuing chaos. "Then I have to meet Glinda and her pals."

"You don't have to go," I pointed out. "You could bow out of their faux witch faux orgy."

"There will be nothing faux about the orgy." His eyes twinkled. "Want me to send proof?"

"Pics or it didn't happen?" I scoffed at the old joke. "No thanks and no evidence required. Seriously. Do not send any, or I will hurt you."

"That's why our friendship can weather any storm," he informed me. "Our foundation is bedrock."

I would have compared it to a flotation device, given the storm analogy, but that would have opened the door for Clay to walk through with a joke about boobs. He might be as old as dirt, but his sense of humor belonged on a guy waiting for his first chin hair to sprout.

"That, and we stay out of each other's business." I thumped his ear. "Mostly."

Head tilted, he squinted at me. "Do you really believe that?"

"No." I blasted out a sigh. "But it doesn't hurt to dream, right?"

Before I pulled out a third chair, Asa caught me by the hips and set me on his lap.

"Hey." I popped his hands. "I'm here to work."

"I'm aware." He trailed a finger down my spine, and I shivered under his touch. "I won't interfere."

There was no room for thought when he touched me like that, a gentle exploration of wants and needs that had never been met until me.

The mistletoe necklace should have been my gift. To him. He deserved a way to ask, without words or awkward overtures, for the affection he craved in a manner obvious to us both until we got the hang of this couple thing. But I never would have thought of it on my own. Not in a million years.

Even now, with a button to press in the event of a smooch emergency, I hesitated to lift the safety glass.

Every.

Single.

Time.

"Do we have any updates from the Kellies?" I strove for professionalism, but Asa's knee was applying pressure to an interesting place that tempted me to squirm. "Any news on who the leg belongs to?"

"Nothing yet." Asa skimmed emails on his phone. "It's yet to be matched to any of our missing persons."

Hopefully, that meant the lab was backlogged, not that we had a brand-new victim.

"We need to finish the background searches on the victims' parents," I told them. "See what pops."

"I'll wrap it up," Asa volunteered, tracing the waistband of my jeans. "I've already started notes."

I shifted my weight then regretted the accidental tease sparking heat between my thighs.

"Okay." I sifted through everything we saw today and prioritized my own list. "I'll focus on the teacher."

If there were any undiscovered connections between Tracy and the victims, we had to rectify that.

The Kellies were good. Better than good. Superb. But they worked tirelessly on all Black Hat cases. Any personal attention we gave this material bettered our chances of finding our killer before they struck again.

"I'll call down to Atlanta, chat with my friend." Clay got to his feet. "Maybe he'll have some ideas."

With assignments handed out, I climbed off Asa's lap, and we set up our own computers at the table.

Heads down, thighs brushing, we delved into Charleston's dark underbelly, searching for clues.

6

An alarm pinged on Clay's phone, and he rose so fast, he knocked over his chair. "I'm out."

Hours of research had passed in a blink, and I rubbed my dry eyes clear. "Have fun."

"I plan to," he assured me, doing a little shuffle step that made me cringe. "See you kids later."

Once he shut the door behind him, I reached for the bottle of water Asa had brought me at some point.

"Did you throw up in your mouth a little now, or was that just me?"

"You know what the dancing means?"

"I do." I shuddered. "Do you?"

"I'm aware."

When Clay started shaking what his momma—erm, creator?—gave him, I knew he was off to have sex. I wasn't sure when my understanding of it began, but I felt it was intentional on his part. He wanted a way to clue me in, back when I was younger, that he would be out scratching an itch and not to worry if he didn't come home until morning.

It was the golem equivalent to hanging a sock on the doorknob to warn away a roommate.

Why it bothered me this time, I wasn't sure. Unless it was his choice of partners. Faux witches might not have any magic of their own, but the truly devout sourced grimoires and other arcane trinkets to boost their nonexistent power. Mostly nothing came of that either, but there were always exceptions.

This one time a human and twelve of her besties decided to play coven on Halloween. At midnight. Under a full moon. But it turned out their yard sale grimoire was real. They got drunk on boxed wine, ate their weight in white raspberry truffles, and summoned a lesser god from another realm.

He ate them, got tipsy from their high blood alcohol levels, then slurred demands for more cream-filled treats (humans) in exchange for returning to his home without first rampaging ours.

At the time, I found the entire exchange hilarious, but I had grown since then.

Though I did still crack up remembering how the god had humped Clay's leg until he passed out drunk.

The god, not Clay.

"Let's hit the streets." I tugged on Asa's arm. "We can tour the crime scenes, see if we missed anything."

"And Clay says you're not romantic."

The barb struck home, but I didn't let it hurt. He hadn't meant it to, so I shook off the twinge.

"Keep sweet-talking me, and I'll take you to King Street to watch drunks vomit on the sidewalk."

Smile in his eyes, he followed me out the door and into what I had mentally dubbed *the cursed elevator*.

The endless ride down gave me plenty of time to check in with Colby.

>Asa and I are heading out for a few hours.

>>Cool.

>>Paperwork for cleaner database access has been filed.

>*Any word on the deckhand?*

>>*The Vandenburghs cleared him. The crew was combing the boat for a passenger who didn't disembark at the fort. They had her name on the manifest. She's a regular chaperone, so the crew recognized her. That's why the deckhand jumped to the conclusion it was Tracy Amerson.*

>*Huh. I should have thought of that.*

>>*The Vandenburghs also said all the rangers on duty were accounted for. Their interviews are logged into the database if you want to skim them. I read them, and they were about what you'd expect.*

>*Thanks for doing the legwork on this.*

>>*Well, I do have more than you.*

>*Ha. Ha.*

>>*Me and my legs are going to play with my friends.*

Most of her guild was back from their holiday breaks, and they were all eager to be together again.

>*Have fun. Call if you need me.*

>>*Do you think the daemon can play with me when you get back?*

Heart clenching that she would ask, I flashed the screen at Asa.

"Tell her yes." He touched her words with a gentle finger. "I would like that. Very much."

>*Game on.*

As we stepped out onto the sidewalk, a man leaned a woman against our building for a long kiss.

"Are you ever jealous of them?"

"Humans?" Asa paused to consider. "Or their ignorance?"

"Their ignorance," I decided. "They get to live these firefly lives, to burn bright and burn out, and they never have to know the truth. That monsters exist, and they like people with a side order of ranch."

A twitch of his shoulders told me I had startled a small laugh out of him, but he shook his head. "No."

"Not even a little?"

"If I were mortal, I would have been bones by the time you were born."

"I'm a black witch." I elbowed him. "Bones aren't a dealbreaker."

Okay, even as a black witch, necrophilia held no allure for me. Though it did beg the question of how sex with a vampire was categorized. They were dead humans, resuscitated by necromancers. Undead wasn't the same as alive, and...I was putting way too much thought into this.

"I'm not sure you qualify as a black witch." He led the way to our first destination. "Your smell..."

"No longer makes your eyes water?"

"I've never had a problem with your scent." He inhaled at my throat. "You've always smelled like home."

Asa had told me that once before, but not with the same tender inflection he used now.

The softness in his eyes made my throat close over any response I might have made.

"Come on," he said, tugging me along as if he hadn't just shattered me. "Our turn's on the left."

Charleston was bisected with public alleys scenic enough to rate their own walking tours. They tended to be bricked or cobbled, with high walls protecting the privacy of the homes to either side. Creeping fig clung to every available surface, and moss grew in thick clumps. The green film enabled vandals to scratch such timeless messages as *for a good time call* without damaging the walls themselves.

Our first victim's blood had been found down such an alley, one famous for duels in the late 1700s. The spot was so popular for settling matters of honor that a ghost tour guide (the city was lousy with them) hinted one of its archways once led to a cemetery for easy body disposal. I wasn't sure if that was true, but it did make for a good story.

"Hey." I put my hand on his arm. "Look."

A palm-sized wreath of dried white flowers lay on the cobbles, marking a crime the cleaners had erased beyond my ability to detect the faintest hint of the victim, Luke Reynolds, or his attacker.

Oleanders.

I wouldn't forget their heavy presence in the city again.

The craftsmanship on the wreath was superb, its intricacy reminiscent of Gullah sweetgrass baskets.

A quick check of the Bureau database told me it ringed the epicenter of the blood spilled here.

"An immortelle." Asa circled the token. "Whoever left the wreath considered this a grave."

"A remorseful killer?"

Drawn by instinct or intuition, Asa prowled ahead, scenting the area for clues as to who had been here.

Within the confines of the alley, I couldn't shake the sensation of being watched, but we were alone.

"Perhaps." He thinned his lips. "Do you think Colby could disable any security cameras in the area?"

"One way to find out." Hating to interrupt her game, I dialed her. "Do you feel up to being illegal?"

"I was feeling illegal earlier," she told me. "The urge has mostly passed."

"What did you do?"

"Installed a tracking app on your cell, hacked the security feeds the cleaners use to collect evidence, and programmed a backdoor so I could black out areas with a keystroke if you need mobile backup."

Torn between laughing and crying, I did the only thing I could do. "Good work, Agent Smarty Fuzz Butt."

"You're welcome, Agent Spit Muffin."

Asa, who could overhear every word, came dangerously close to snorting.

"Can you give us a ten-minute blackout window? I would offer to let you know when to bring everything back online, but your spy cams will tell you."

"They're not *spy* cams, they're..." Her sigh proclaimed she had given up on me. "Never mind."

"Tell Clay about it when he gets home. He can dumb it down for me later."

"You're lucky you're a witch." I could picture her shaking her head. "You fail at technology."

"You're not wrong." I checked on Asa and found him stripping to his boxers. "I have to, uh, go."

"Keep an eye out." Asa rolled his shoulders. "This won't take long."

Before my brain finished its nosedive into the gutter, I was scooped up by a wall of red muscle and swung in a dizzying circle.

"Rue," the daemon yelled in my face, setting my ears ringing. "I miss you."

Cases that fell within city limits forced him to let Asa take the lead, and he hated when we excluded him.

"I missed you too." I flung my arms around him. "Colby wants to play with you when we get back."

"I like Colby." His eyes lit with childish glee. "She help me kill bad orcs and rescue fuzzy kitten."

"That's great." I wiggled until he set me down. "Can you do me a favor and check out the crime scene?"

"Asa's nose not good as mine." He turned smug. "I help Rue."

"I appreciate it." I checked to make sure the hulking daemon wasn't drawing attention. "Just make it quick, please. This area has a lot of foot traffic."

Vulnerability softened his features, and a crease dented his forehead. "See you later?"

"I'll make snacks for you and Colby. I'll even watch you guys slay orcs." I smiled. "Promise."

With a nod, he began a careful examination of the area, filling his lungs and exhaling in loud gusts.

"Old blood." His nostrils flared wide. "Old bones too."

Much like Savannah, Georgia, and New Orleans, Louisiana, this city was built on the dead. It didn't vibrate under your feet here the way it did for me in those places, but I trusted the daemon's nose.

"Anything recent?"

"No new blood." He fixated on the area around the wreath. "No new bones either."

"The cleaners did their job well. Too well. We need more samples of the black magic used here."

A single touch would have allowed me to compare the peculiar offering to the teacher's remains, but, as I was often reminded, I carried my own black aura. I couldn't risk contaminating any new evidence when we had so little. A fingerprint wasn't a big deal to the lab. I was on file and easily eliminated. Same as the fingerprint they would find on the teacher's remains. Powerful magical signatures were harder to erase.

I had been greedy for answers on the boat. I couldn't be so careless a second time.

"This new." He crouched beside the token. "Same as leg."

A gesture of contrition didn't fit with the mental picture I was building of this killer. And the oleanders? I couldn't fathom how the symbolism applied here. Oleanders signified complicated relationships. Endless love. Destiny. Desire. Romance. Weird choice, when you think about how every part of the plant is toxic.

Years spent playing apothecary shopkeeper had me seeking meaning when there probably was none.

Other than oleanders were readily available and easy to harvest from the city-maintained garden beds.

"Okay." I checked the alley again. "Can you let me talk to Asa for a minute?"

"Caramel apple."

I waited, but he didn't elaborate.

"Okay, I'll bite." I caved before he did. "What about a caramel apple?"

"You have Asa back if I get caramel apple." His eyes gleamed. "With nuts."

Fighting the urge to chuckle at his blackmail attempt, which shouldn't have been as cute as it was, I agreed. "One caramel apple with nuts, *if* you give Asa back to me before we get caught."

A beat too late, I grasped that I had fallen into the same bribery trap as Clay had with Colby, and I could have kicked myself.

From the look on his grinning face as flames licked over him and flickered down him, he knew it too.

For a second, Asa stood there, regaining his bearings as he often did after a transition.

And then his boxers, stretched to capacity, fell around his ankles.

The messages etched in moss absorbed my attention, and I crossed to investigate, giving him my back.

"That has—" I felt certain, "—never happened before."

Pretty sure the Hulk would envy Asa's extensive Black Hat wardrobe. Particularly the stretchy underwear pioneered for shifters. His slacks also expanded to accommodate multiple girths, but the shirt and jacket got trashed each time. Shoes too. Had he lost any of those, okay, fair. But his underwear? Again? *Really?*

"He's jealous." Fabric rustled when Asa shifted his weight. "He wants to spend more time with you."

"We might have to let him out more in the suites." I made it sound like he was a pet tired of his crate, and I cringed from the comparison. "Between the price tags on the properties, and the bustling tourist trade, this area is under constant surveillance. Otherwise, visitors to the city might be tempted to claim a memento or carve their name into a hundred-year-old oak. I imagine everyone has private security of some kind."

Which explained the earlier creeping sensation warning me there were eyes on us.

Likely, there had been. Just electronic ones.

"He's too conspicuous," Asa agreed. "He knows that, but his impulses are harder to control."

"We'll do better," I promised him. "We'll start accommodating his need to surface."

That is, if we wanted Asa to keep his pants on.

Which, honestly, I wasn't sure qualified as a problem exactly.

Forehead pressed against the stucco-covered brick wall, I let the chill soothe my flushed skin.

I was a bad, bad person.

Terrible, really.

But I already knew that.

It was strange to want another person. The wanting was making me behave like a teenager with her first crush. Asa was in no hurry to rush our physical relationship, and I suspected—just as he knew I preferred violence to emotion—he worried I would use sex in place of emotion if he let me.

So, maybe it would be a good thing if he kept himself covered until we figured out that part.

"Do you have gloves?"

"Depends." I wet my lips. "Do you have pants?"

"Yes." I heard the smile in his voice. "I'm even wearing them."

Stifling a laugh, I jerked when something hit my shoulder. I caught it as it fell and almost dropped...

...his underwear.

"Thanks?" I balled them in my hand. "Is this like when guys tuck girls' thongs in their pockets?"

Amusement lit his eyes, and he raked his teeth over his bottom lip. "Look at the waistband."

I shook out the material and examined the ultra-elastic until I hit a rather large rip down one side.

"He tore your underwear." I traced the slice from his claw. "He wanted you to put on a peepshow."

The daemon must have been tickling Asa's subconscious with mischievous intent for him to take the unusual preventative measure of stripping down to his undies rather than only removing his shirt and jacket.

"He's eager for us to mate." Asa wiped a hand over his mouth. "He wants our bond cemented."

Avoiding that not-exactly-a-question, I asked one of my own. "Do you mind if I keep these?"

Eyes on the fabric, he cocked an eyebrow that implied all manner of things.

"Not for me." I fought down the heat building in my cheeks. "I want evidence to show him that explains why he isn't getting his caramel apple. Certainly not one with nuts."

As endearing as I found the daemon's shenanigans, I couldn't let him push Asa, or me. He had to learn there were boundaries, and that the three of us had to function as a unit. We had to cooperate with each other in order to get what each of us wanted from this relationship.

"Ah." Asa's eyes laughed at me. "You can keep them."

"I'm not a pervert for asking," I said, defending myself. "I'll throw them away after we're done."

"I didn't say anything."

Maybe not, but I heard him loud and clear.

7

Historic Charleston City Market stretched four chaotic blocks behind Market Hall in a riot of colors and scents. Underneath the four sheds original to the market, which opened in the 1790s, huddled dozens of tables bowed under merchandise. Most days it was bursting with handmade wares, packed with quirky vendors, and surging with delighted shoppers.

The walk over was scenic but with enough twists and turns to provide easy cover for our killer.

Add the deep shadows cast by live oaks and crape myrtles, and they would have been all but invisible.

A chime had me searching my pocket for my phone to find a text from Colby.

>>*Tracy Amerson was single. No kids. No close friends. No hobbies.*

The lack of a social circle could explain why the killer found her an appealing target.

>*And you know that last part how?*

>>*The internet is a magical place, full of wonder and mysteries.*

For little hacker moths, sure.

>>*No link between the victims either. Or their parents. Not that I saw.*

Asa had his own notes, so I would set them up to compare their findings.

>*Thanks, smarty fuzz butt.*

>>*I'll be slaying the orc scourge if you need me.*

Those poor orcs. Seriously. As far as I could tell, their lives were an endless massacre.

Reflecting on the file for Bryce Masters, our second victim, I recalled the scant details.

After a nice dinner with his extended family, his aunts, visiting for the holidays, wanted to see the sights. Happy to play guides, his parents indulged them with an abbreviated tour of City Market.

Eager to get home to his new kitten, Bryce ran ahead of his family, vanishing into thin air.

The next morning, dark blood soaked the pavement where he had last been seen.

The exact location fell across the street from the sheds, outside a store with a black dog on its logo.

"The blood was found here." I stood on the exact spot. "Are those…flower petals?"

"Crushed leaves and dung traces too." Asa bagged a crumpled sample. "A horse must have trampled it."

Carriage rides were popular in downtown, and several companies offered daytime and nighttime tours.

The various stables were nearby, so the market was an established part of their routes.

"Likely a grounds custodian or street sweeper tossed it after that."

"This is enough to test it against the wreath we have to see if they match."

Flowers left on graves that weren't graves by a killer who mourned the victims as their body count rose.

Proof they wanted to get caught? Genuine remorse they couldn't stop? A macabre token of thanks?

A text chime yanked me from my grim thoughts.

>>*The leg has been identified.*

There weren't words for how much I hated Colby had been the one to update me.

>*And?*

>>*It belongs to the first victim. Luke Reynolds.*

Had we been able to ask the parents, they might have told us their son wore his sister's hand-me-downs. Or they might have told us he was obsessed with the characters printed on the shoe and didn't care if he had to wear girls' shoes to get them.

I would never have an answer, and for some reason, that single detail haunted me.

>*Thanks for letting me know.*

>*I thought you were playing.*

>>*I set an alert on my phone for database updates from the Kellies. And the local cleaners.*

>*Smart.*

>*You should get back to your game. Those orcs need a good scourging.*

>>*Do you remember all the times you asked me if there was anything you could do to help?*

Help her cope with losing her life, her family, her entire self.

>*Yes.*

>>*This helps. Doing something helps. Stopping people who prey on other kids helps.*

I shut my eyes and forced myself to remember she wasn't a normal kid. She was a familiar. Before that, she had been fae. She would only pop the lid off any box I tried to cram her into, because she was more than the brave little girl I found in the woods that night, the one who begged me to save her.

>*Okay.*

That was all I could manage without pushing, and that always got us nowhere fast.

>>*Besides, all my friends left to eat dinner. I promise to go be a kid in like thirty minutes.*

Her friends spanned the country, and the globe, so they tended to switch up mealtimes so they could eat as a group then get right back to the serious business of murdering orcs, looting bodies, and, apparently, rescuing kittens who probably hacked up flaming hairballs or had spikes on their rough tongues for licking the flesh off their enemies.

>*We'll be back soon.*

>>*I'll be in our room.*

With that exchange done, I filled in Asa, which never got weirder. I was so used to the guys overhearing my phone conversations, they didn't need me to spell out the information. But texts were one medium where paranormal hearing wouldn't slip you a cheat code.

"Do you think all the victims were dumped in the harbor?"

"All the victims were bled out *where* they were taken, but not *when* they were taken. In each instance, the killer circled back. A ritual element, perhaps? From there, the killer must have relocated the bodies to a secure area where they could cast the carving spell without interruption. The skins require time to cure. The killer likely disposes of the bodies while they're waiting. I can see the harbor as a dumping ground. It's close, easily accessible, and it all but guarantees discovery."

Most killers who evaded capture for this long did so by avoiding those kinds of simple mistakes.

This one? I couldn't pin down. The wreaths, if they were genuine tokens of regret, hinted the killer might have given us the leg on purpose. But if Tracy was now our template, had the kids been unraveled too?

Why put so much effort into small bodies? Who could wear them? Surely not the killer.

Unless…

Had the killer pretended to be a child to lure the other children away from safety?

Always nice to discover new breeds of monsters. As if I didn't already have enough trouble sleeping.

"Hmm." I reached back in my memory. "The third victim's blood was found on Morris Island, right?"

"Near the lighthouse." He checked the files on his phone. "At the mouth of Charleston Harbor."

"We'll have to charter a boat if we want to see it for ourselves."

The odds of a wreath surviving out there this long were slim, but I bet there had been one.

"That can be arranged." He watched me. "There are tours that go out that way."

"Let's find out if our victim took one." I kept circling back to our earlier points. "If so, we can book with that company and get an idea of how those last few hours went down."

One good thing about the bountiful tourism? It made finding a lift—land or sea—fast and cheap.

"Easily done," Asa told me then pulled out his phone and began texting. "Colby added it to her to-do list." After logging the unhappy pinch of my lips, he resumed typing. "Which she will start on tomorrow."

"Thanks." I shook off my weird mood. "You didn't do anything wrong, it's just I hate dumping on her."

"We have other resources, and we can use those any time you believe Colby is taking on too much."

A good reminder, given her drive to prove herself was as bad, or worse, than mine.

"And where," I asked him, voice gone soft, "does that leave us?"

We had documented the two sites searchable on foot, but Morris Island required daylight.

"Restaurants are still open, if you want to grab dinner."

"Eat in public?" Hand to chest, I staggered back. "Like a normal couple?"

We tended to order in, if I didn't cook. Aside from the occasional diner breakfast, we didn't have time to sit around and wait on food. On a case, it was all *go, go, go*. Except like now, when it was *wait and see*.

"Okay." I stuck out my hand. "I spotted a place a few blocks over that looks interesting."

"Lead the way." He linked our fingers. "We can pick up something for Clay to reheat later."

"Good plan."

Halfway back to the restaurant, I detected a faint scent that was *not* the ricotta gnocchi à la Bolognese in the article I read on best eats in the city. Dark, coppery, and bitter. Not black magic, but a similar profile.

This was the odor from the Battery, from the skin, from the wreaths. Only fresher, more pungent.

Breaths coming in fast, I cut my eyes toward Asa, but he only tightened his grip on my hand in response.

The earlier impression of being watched intensified until my nape stung like second-degree sunburn.

"What is that?" The urge to glance back twitched in my neck. "You smell it, right?"

"We interrupted a feeding." He nudged me toward the restaurant. "Go get us a table."

As in, he would investigate the obvious threat while I munched on warm breadsticks.

Pfft.

Not happening.

Apparently, I wasn't the only one with loose connectors in my brain.

"We better hurry." I checked my phone. "We've got an hour before the restaurant closes."

An expression caught between exasperation and affection softened his features. "All right."

"I'm not as big or as bad as I used to be, but I can hold my own."

"I know."

"Then why try to ditch me?"

"You know how you wish Colby didn't have to see the things she does?"

"Yes."

"I wouldn't wish this—any of this—on you either."

Much as Colby had said to me, I found it no less true in my case. "It helps, making a difference."

Good deeds accumulated going forward might never outweigh the bad things scattered behind me, but I had to do what I could to balance the scales. I expected no afterlife, no eternal reward, but Colby was linked to me through the familiar bond, and I would do my best to earn her a spot in whatever hereafter suited her.

Asa pressed his warm lips to my forehead, then we turned and began retracing our steps.

The creature, whatever it was, must have been startled by our passing and carried away its prey.

A familiar pattern darkened the asphalt, marking the attack, but the wet pool was only six inches across.

Asa crouched near the blood and took a sample from a tiny kit he kept in his jacket pocket.

"The killer was here." I was getting ahead of myself, and I didn't care. "We walked right by them."

About the time I was ready to throw back my head and scream at my own stupidity, I smelled it.

Viscera. Magic. Death.

A yowling lament raised the hairs on my nape, and then, six yards away, I saw it.

A cat.

Well, sort of.

The creature moved wrong, its gait loose and wobbly, and its skin wasn't right. Its orange fur was striped with red, like slashes from a giant paw. Each step jarred its body, causing a slinky effect as its pelt bunched and released over its spine. Except I saw through the bands of flesh to the alley behind it. It had no bones. With its hide slipping and sliding over air, it was a small miracle it held a recognizable shape.

"I was running low on nightmare fodder." I ventured closer, Asa beside me. "Thanks, cat."

The cat meowed, as if it understood, as if it had vocal cords, which only added to its freak show vibe.

Gaze pinned on the target, I asked Asa, "Can you tell if this cat slinky matches the blood?"

Flames leapt over his skin, and the daemon bared his teeth at the animal, hissing as it drew closer.

"It match." The daemon kept his eyes locked on the animal. "Bad kitty."

The kitty in question slowed its rolling gait, gave its skin time to catch up to the rest of it, then sat.

"Hello." I watched the beast for signs of aggression. "Do you mind if I ask you some questions?"

Like why its magic smelled like our killer, similar but not quite the same.

Then again, this was an animal. Not a human like the other victims we had encountered so far.

The difference in species, and the amount of magic required to peel the skin, differed greatly.

"It kitty." The daemon spoke to me as if I were a child. "It not talk to Rue."

In my experience, it was better if you treated any unidentifiable creatures as an equal in intelligence until they proved otherwise.

"Rue?" A sugary feminine drawl filled the air. "That your name, darlin'?"

"Yes?"

"You don't sound sure." Husky laughter swirled around me. "Are you, or aren't you?"

Briefly, I wondered if this was how Alice felt when dealing with the Cheshire cat.

"I'm Rue." I dredged up a polite smile to cover how creepy I found its form. "And you are?"

"Jilo." The cat twitched a whisker. "You can call me Jilo."

"Pretty name." I rubbed my index finger over my thumbnail. "So, you're a cat."

As far as interrogation methods go, it was a weak lead-in, but she had thrown me off my game.

"Good Lord, no." She laughed, louder this time. "This is how I've chosen to appear to you."

"Don't trust bad kitty." The daemon sniffed the air. "Stink like death."

This wrapper wasn't supple leather like the teacher but a fresh kill, and it reeked of the dark arts.

No wonder we hadn't encountered any freshies. They would have been simple to pick out by their smell.

"Yes, well, that is how avatars are made." The cat rolled its eyes. "Would it make you feel better if I told you the cat was a stray with cancer, that it would have died anyway? Probably in agony? That I spared it that terrible fate?"

The daemon stared at the cat with less ire. "Poor kitty."

"I'm not saying that's true," she teased, "but I did wonder."

"You lie about kitty?" The daemon's head snapped back like she had slapped him. "Why?"

"He's not bright, is he?" The cat flicked her tail. "Tell me the pretty side of the coin is intelligent."

"Kitty." I blocked the static tickling the back of my mind. "You might want to watch your step."

The cat lifted its dainty nose, inhaled like it had lungs to fill, then sneezed.

"You're in fascination." She unsheathed her claws. "No wonder you're so overprotective."

People heard the daemon and assumed he was simple, but his mental capacity wasn't diminished, it was immature. Asa fought that side of himself for so long, the daemon hadn't developed alongside him. The daemon was a big kid. A big, violent kid who would do anything to protect those he loved from harm.

Ignoring her prying statement, I willed her to get to the point. "You murdered a cat for a reason."

"Other than I was hungry?" She bared her fangs. "You seem more competent than your counterparts, so I've decided to help you."

The word *counterparts* had me picturing Marty and the other Black Hat agents, whether she meant them or the Officers Vandenburgh.

Either way, Jilo had been stalking us. The three of us. Determining by our actions whether we merited her assistance.

Guess this meant we really were being watched earlier.

This, if we could trust her, might be the breakthrough we had been waiting for. "Oh?"

"One of our own has gone rogue." She licked her paw, sort of. Her tongue was more of a twisty ribbon. "Her actions have attracted too much attention to our way of life."

That was putting it mildly. "What are you?"

"A boo hag." She rose, and her skin did that slinky thing again. "Ever hear of us, black witch?"

"No." I reflected on the witch-adjacent lore I had learned but came up empty. "What's a boo hag?"

"A creature of meat and bone and blood and magic." She began to pace, careful to keep a safe distance. "We prey on those who meet our gaze in the shadows, though we kill few. For most of us, it's enough to steal breath from our prey while they sleep. They wake up tired, we go to bed full. It's a win/win."

"Mmm-hmm." I doubted their victims saw it that way. "But this rogue has other ideas."

"There are rules, and rules must be followed."

"That's what I hear, but I wouldn't have a job if that were true. What are we talking about here?"

"If the person wakes, we must kill them to protect our secret."

"None of the victims that brought us here were sleeping."

They had been wide awake, enjoying the outdoors with their

families, which lent weight to the idea the killer had been posing as a child to lure them in.

"Everyone's got to sleep sometime, darlin'."

Paras had elevated the simple loophole to an artform, and this one I should have seen coming. A perfect example was Andreas Farmer. He disappeared at Fort Sumter, and I suspected he had never left. That he was held there, somewhere, then bled out before dawn. Perhaps the killer waited until he succumbed to fearful exhaustion first. But why hold that one rule inviolate while flaunting common sense precautions?

"We both know you do more than kill them."

"Not always." She laughed. "Only sometimes." She flicked her paw. "Mostly for special occasions."

"After you peel off the wrapper and suck out the filling, what happens to the rest of the candy bar?"

"There are strong rip currents," she said conversationally, "if you know where to look."

"I see."

"You can't throw stones, black witch."

"Of all the evils I've done, I've never committed a sin against a child. Can your people say the same?"

"It's taboo, even for us, which is why I decided to lend you a paw with your little investigation."

History lesson aside, this was sounding more and more like a waste of time. "Can you give us a name?"

"I could, sure, but it won't help you. We're not fae. Names hold no power over us."

Maybe not, but they held last known addresses, previous employment, and criminal records.

"Can you tell us where to find the rogue?"

"What good would I be otherwise?"

When she didn't share, I pressed her. "Can you tell us how to trap them?"

Boo hags were, as best I could tell, part skin shifter and part black arts practitioner.

That combination could prove deadly without first determining the faction's weaknesses.

"That ain't happening." She scoffed. "I tell you how to trap her, and it's the same as how to trap me."

"Okay." I held back a tidal wave of annoyance. "What can you tell me?"

Aside from the killer's gender, which she let slip, she had given us nothing apart from her species.

"What you ought to be asking is what can I do for you?"

"Did I hallucinate the last five seconds of our conversation?"

"You asked me to *tell* you." The cat whipped its tail. "I'm offering to *show* you."

Flames ignited on my periphery, leaving Asa wearing a tattered jacket and shirt.

Thankfully, the daemon behaved during transition, and Asa's pants remained on.

"There he is," Jilo purred. "You're easier on the eyes than your other half, I'll give you that."

"My other half, as you so eloquently put it, enjoys playing games. He's quite adept with numbers."

The bravado drained out of the cat, who barely dared to twitch so much as a whisker.

"That's why, earlier today, I exchanged a handful of dollar bills for pennies, nickels, and dimes."

Jilo took a step back, ears pinned to her scalp, her fur bristling. "*No.*"

Out of his pocket came a fistful of gleaming coins. "Do you like numbers too?"

Hissing, spitting, swearing, the cat spun to flee.

She didn't get far before Asa flung those shiny discs bouncing across the asphalt in haphazard directions.

"One, two, three..." the cat yowled with fury, batting dimes into a pile, "...four, five, six..."

Confused, yet more than a little impressed, I asked Asa, "What am I watching here?"

"Boo hags are obsessed with counting. They're compelled to do it. They have no choice."

"Talk about an obscure kryptonite."

Much sadder than pimento cheese.

"Local lore recommends leaving a straw broom propped outside your front door for protection. To enter your home, the boo hag must count every bristle. Marbles in a jar on your nightstand works too. So does a hairbrush on your dresser. I read you can leave a sieve or a colander hung on your doorknob as well."

"The tourist trade is bullshit," Jilo muttered under her breath. "Utter and complete bullshit."

"The same ghost tour guide who mentioned confederate tea jokingly warned his group how to protect themselves while in the city," Asa explained her anger. "I had never heard of a boo hag, so I decided to do a little research."

"Your hearing is ridiculous," I told him. "I didn't catch anything past the poison."

That was one daemon power I wouldn't have minded inheriting, but I had plain old witch ears.

"It was a quiet night." He slanted me a smile. "And the guide projected his voice well."

"Mmm-hmm."

"Your game won't occupy me for long," Jilo snarled, "and then I'll come wring your pretty neck."

"Do you know how to kill a problematic boo hag?" Asa angled his chin my way but kept his gaze on the cat. "Leave out a sufficient quantity of an item. They can't stop counting once they've started, as our friend here has proven, and if the dawn finds them, they vanish into smoke."

"You're dead." Hatred and avarice burned in the cat's eyes. "You hear me? *Dead*."

"I'm out of change." Asa reached into his pocket a second time. "However, I do have this." He held up a sachet like the ones tucked into our suites' closets. "I wonder how many lavender buds are in this one?"

"Godsdamn your red hide." A yowl ripped from her throat. "What do you want from me?"

"Your word that you will assist us in solving this case—"

Paw twitching in frantic taps, she spat, "You already had it."

"—and your vow you won't kill us after the fact."

Fury vibrated the beast until its strips of fur slid off to puddle like overdone noodles on the pavement.

Beneath it pulsed a creature so red it was black. No skin. All raw meat. Which put the whole spiralizing thing into perspective. Wisps of black magic curled from it, rendering it translucent in places.

And the smell...

Even my stomach briefly considered emptying itself before it remembered this wasn't the worst thing I had ever seen.

Top ten? Yes. Top five? Eh. Not quite that emotionally scarring, but still plenty traumatic.

"You're questioning my honor?" Jilo was not amused. "What does a daemon know about honor?"

"I would ask the same of any unknown entity," Asa said, and it was true. "We're here to perform a service to the community. We want to fix this problem and then go home. Preferably, all wearing the skins we arrived in."

"Fine," she spat, "but you're making me regret my Southern hospitality."

Fine wasn't the same as *I won't kill you horribly*, but Asa didn't force her to revise her statement.

A text chime on my phone drew my attention to a message from Clay.

>>*Where are you guys?*

>*We're making new friends and bad decisions.*

>>*Double standard much? You can make new friends, but I can't?*

>*Yours was more like a quadruple, if I recall correctly, and I'm not naked.*

>>*Ah. That explains why you're texting. You're not having any fun.*

>*Ha. Ha. We're wrapping up now. See you back at the rental.*

With that mature exchange over, I pocketed the phone and returned my full attention to Jilo. Even that short break from looking at her head-on had me jolting when I saw her again. I was definitely not having any fun with her. But I could play nice if it got us one step closer to our killer.

8

"Meet us here tomorrow night," Asa made it an order for Jilo. "Then you can *show* us."

"All right, all right." She finished collecting the change. "What time?"

"Dusk." Asa took my hand. "Any later, and we'll come hunting."

"Might be later," she warned. "Full dark is a requirement for my continued existence, unless you would like me to take a human avatar for the occasion. Their skins are thick enough to protect us from limited sun."

They haggled over a time, eventually settled on one, then Asa ripped the lavender sachet at one corner.

"Apologies." He tossed a handful of buds in her direction. "I want to ensure a safe exit."

Grumbling under her breath, she began to count again, but there wasn't any venom in it now.

Still, Asa kept a brisk pace in the direction of Hassell Street, and I matched it, eager to escape Jilo.

With his clothes in tatters, dinner out wasn't happening.

So much for getting my sticky sorghum pudding fix.

Clay might stock an eclectic kitchen, but I doubted even he had those supplies on hand.

"You've been keeping secrets."

"I wasn't certain boo hags existed." He held up a single lavender bud, turning it this way and that. "The idea a monster could be defeated by counting struck me as farfetched." He rubbed it between his fingers, releasing its fragrance. "I'll email you my notes on what I've learned about them so far."

"Have you checked the Black Hat database?"

"The only new information it had to offer was that boo hags are an endangered species."

"No wonder they're almost extinct." I shook my head. "Counting? Really? Such a lame weakness."

Asa stifled a laugh and returned the bud to his pocket. "Do you think her offer of aid is legitimate?"

"A death here or there, a coven might—" I hesitated. "What do you call a collective of boo hags?"

"A grume."

"Okay, a grume might dismiss the occasional death as accidental, but the predation of human children is specific. It draws attention that requires Black Hat to expend serious resources to keep those stories out of the news. That won't last. It can't. Even magic has limits. So does the tolerance of the other factions in the area, who won't want the boo hags' carelessness to spark a witch hunt that exposes us all."

"We need to get ahead of this."

"How do you propose we do that?"

"We need to file paperwork for dredgers, see if we can recover some of our victims."

"Are you sure we want to invite scrutiny on such an active harbor?"

For the grume to maintain its low profile, the boo hags must have tested their dumping grounds before committing to them.

Originally colonized by the English in 1670, Charleston had relocated to the peninsula by 1680. By 1740, more than half of South Carolina's population were African and West Indian slaves. Forty percent of all slaves brought to America came through Charleston Harbor.

And they brought their folklore with them, giving familiar names to new iterations of old monsters.

So, yes, boo hags had plenty of time after the Gullah immortalized them in stories, in *warnings*, to figure out how to dispose of their victims without tipping off modern descendants to their ancestral truths.

Yet the leg washed ashore. In a tourist hotspot. One also popular with locals.

Discovery was guaranteed, which meant it couldn't have been accidental.

"We may not have a choice."

"Jilo mentioned currents." I replayed the conversation in my head. "She never specified the harbor."

"No," he said, after a moment's pause, "I don't believe she did."

"We pegged the harbor for ease of access, but we should have considered the practical aspects."

"The grume is surrounded by water." He followed my line of thought. "One of them must own a boat."

Hadn't I been thinking that very thing after our trip to Fort Sumter?

We should have investigated that angle sooner, but it would take ages without a name for a title search or a description of the craft, and we had no way to get either without Jilo's cooperation.

"The grume itself could have purchased one for the sole purpose of dumping bodies in deeper waters."

With all the charters offering deep-sea fishing, no one would blink over one more sports fishing boat.

"We need to ask Jilo."

"We can try." I unclenched my jaw. "We didn't have much luck with that tonight."

"Whatever aid the grume provides its members in times of crisis, the killer no longer has access to those communal resources. Perhaps for the first time, they're cleaning up after themselves, and they may not be doing it well. Or the sloppiness might be intentional. We've theorized the killer wants to get caught."

"Disposing of body parts within sight of popular tourist attractions is a surefire attention-getter."

Back at the suites, we found Colby swaddled in her blanket, locked in battle with Clay against a dragon.

Pretty sure neither of them noticed our return.

That was how tight we kept security around here.

Flames licked the ceiling on my periphery, and the daemon picked Clay up by his shirt collar.

"My turn," he announced, tossing Clay onto the floor. "I play now."

Colby spared a snicker for poor Clay and welcomed the daemon with a fist bump.

"Traitors." Clay shoved to his feet. "The both of you."

"Come on." I tugged his arm. "I'm starving. I'll cook while I update you."

There was no point in asking if there was food in the kitchen. The surprise would be in what he had chosen to stock us with this time, and what I could do with it before most of us shuffled off to bed.

Before I forgot, I made extra salty popcorn, sprinkled chocolate-covered raisins over the top, and fulfilled that part of my bargain with the daemon. The gaming, I would have to watch in snatches while I cooked.

Clay waylaid me in the kitchen, launching into a highlight reel of his night, and I girded my loins for TMI.

"You'll never guess what I learned."

"That's a loaded statement if I've ever heard one, and I'm begging you not to pull the trigger."

"The faux witches? They held a skyclad ceremony out on Folly Beach. Lots of tequila involved." He noted my eye roll. *"Anyway."* He nudged my shoulder. "They discovered a washed-up body." He waved a hand. "Tripped and fell over it, but that's beside the point."

For a second, I debated smacking him with a frying pan for holding out on us. *"Tonight?"*

"They tripped and fell onto other things tonight, if you catch my drift."

Perhaps sensing he was seconds away from tasting my cast iron displeasure, he held one hand in front of his face as a shield then cracked the fridge and passed me a foam bucket marked as local oysters.

"You don't get hangry. You get *mean*. Does that make you hean? Mangry?"

"I know you keep your signed photo of Giada in the bottom of your favorite wig box."

Giada De Laurentiis, famous chef/TV personality, and current object of Clay's culinary obsession.

"Leave Giada out of this." His gaze darted toward his room. "It was four or five days ago, okay?"

"Thank you." I found an oyster knife in a drawer and handed it to him along with a towel. "What else?"

"They ran to get help, but when they came back, the body was gone."

"Why didn't they...?" I caught up to what he had been saying. "They were naked, so no phones."

"No phones, so no pictures. No one wanted to stand watch, so they all ran back to their vehicles."

"What I'm hearing is, there's no proof any of this happened the way they claim or even at all."

The best we could hope for was a record of the call to the local PD, which the Vandenburghs could verify for us. A boozy firsthand account without evidence didn't amount to much but was better than nothing.

"The faux witches found one item to mark where the body had been." He ducked into the living room then returned with a paper bag he crinkled for effect. "The police told them it was nothing. A kid probably lost it in the sand." He placed the evidence on the counter, thankfully far from the food. "Most of them decided they had watched *Jaws* one too many times and must have tripped over their own feet."

"Tequila," I murmured, not without sympathy.

"*But* Glinda couldn't let it go, and she asked to keep it."

I had a bad feeling what I would see when I looked in that bag, and I wasn't proven wrong.

A shoe.

A *girl's* shoe.

A girl's shoe last worn by a boy.

"It's a match for the first victim." I recognized the characters. I was starting to think I would never forget them. A side effect of conscience? "Luke Reynolds vanished at night. His blood was reported in the alley the next morning. Let's say the killer has a secure location for casting the unraveling spell. The skin must cure prior to use, so she brought Luke's body to Folly Beach for easy disposal while she waited. Then she wore the skin to lure in the next victim. Rinse and repeat."

"The previous victim luring the next to their death. That's dark."

"That's the timeline Asa and I hashed out, but if your source is telling the truth, then we got it wrong somewhere. There's no way they wouldn't notice the corpse was missing its skin."

"Taunting humans by planting evidence? Or us?" Clay sighed. "Either way, it wouldn't be the first time."

"We'll go tomorrow," I decided. "See what we see."

After he filled in a few other details I could have lived without, mostly involving his new friends and their spectacular figures, I described our run-in with Jilo and supervised his shucking.

"I'll take naked witchy wannabes over a spiralized cat any day."

"Me too," I admitted. "Did you learn anything else?"

"They're the only openly practicing coven in the city." He chuckled. "They were very proud of that."

"Goddess bless," I muttered. "What a mess."

"What boo hags practice falls firmly within the dark arts realm, no question, but it's got a familiar vibe." He helped me dredge the oysters in a flour, cornmeal, and herb mix. "Do you think they're related to black witches? Maybe they branched off along the evolutionary line."

"I was wondering that too." I checked the temperature on my oil. "What are you thinking?"

"The director has only sent you on cases involving Black Hat rogues."

"And this doesn't have that feel?"

"Not every case can be a giant conspiracy against the Bureau, but…"

"Maybe we're in a lull. The calm before the storm." I dropped my first round of battered oysters in the pan, raising my voice to speak over the hiss and crackle. "Or maybe we landed a perfectly normal case."

Okay, fine, so the slinky cat alone meant normal had flown out the window a while ago, and it wasn't coming back anytime soon.

"The director pulled you back in," he argued, washing his hands, "and we still don't know why."

"He's spooked, Clay." I could tell him that, and he would get it better than anyone. "He's afraid."

The mention of that fear had my thoughts casting back to Samford, to the girls, to my own weaknesses.

"He's fought off coups before," he countered. "What's special about this one? Why involve *you*?"

"Other than he still believes I'm his heir and that we'll skip off into the sunset together one day?"

"You found your grandmother." He lowered his voice. "That should have freaked him the hell out."

"Language." I popped his hand with a spoon. "And yeah, you're right. I expected a bigger reaction too."

But he wasn't sweating the fact I knew Calixta Damaris's location. As former High Queen of the Haelian Seas, and his former lover, one kept locked in a silty cage at the bottom of a swamp, I had expected more.

More cursing. More threats. More yelling.

Either he knew enough about the magic containing her to be confident I alone could set her free, and then only if I sacrificed myself for it, or she was small potatoes compared to the threat stalking his heels.

Now, if he had any inkling Delma's ashes were in a safe full of arcane artifacts at my house, and Granny wasn't *quite* as secure as he assumed, then he might flip his lid.

Unless or until I decided to reopen that can of worms, I was content to let him think the mother of his child remained a nonthreat.

Which begged the question...

What was worse than a raging former Haelian queen bent on reclaiming her throne over her ex-lover's dead body?

9

The next morning, I regretted my life choices. Fried oysters were delicious, but when you cooked them at home, the smell lingered for days. I wasn't sure we could crack a window—I bet the sills had all been painted shut—but I would ask Clay to check.

A faint vibration warned me I had an incoming call, probably what woke me in the first place, and I searched the mattress until I found my phone.

"Hollis," I grumbled, turning over and pulling the cover up to my shoulders.

"I can't get over your Special Agent Hollis voice," Camber teased. "It's nothing like your shop voice."

"You sound sleepy," Arden yelled in the background. "Did we wake you?"

The worry forever knotting my gut these days lessened to hear them safe, home, and cracking jokes.

"Possibly." I snuggled deeper into the mattress. "Anything the matter?"

"It's past noon." She sucked in a gasp. "Maybe I should apply to become a police consultant."

"Sure beats waking up at six in the morning." Arden sighed loudly. "Must be nice."

"You're traveling with your *boyfriend* too." Camber cackled with glee. "Or is that why you slept in?"

"Hi, Asa." Arden snickered. "Is that a banana in your pants, or are you just happy to see Rue?"

"Why would he sleep with a banana in his pants?"

"Performance anxiety?"

"Girls," Aedan chastised from nearby. "Update Rue then let her wake up in peace."

"Spoilsport," Camber grumped. "Okay, so we did have a reason for calling you."

"Okay?" I smiled at the familiar bantering, not minding when Aedan joined in at all. "What is it?"

"We're doing inventory," Arden supplied. "We're out of winter rosebuds again."

"Do we reorder?" Camber sounded doubtful. "We never sell them, but they're always out of stock."

"I'll set some humane traps." Aedan stepped in to save the day. "We'll probably just catch mice."

"Mice with a winter rosebud addiction?"

That was Camber.

"It can't hurt to try." Arden, of course, pitched in with Aedan. "How about we give it a week?"

"Fine," Camber grumbled. "We better get back to it. Talk to you later, sleepyhead."

"Bye, girls...and boy."

"You guys go on," Aedan was saying. "I need to talk logistics with Rue."

Static crackled as the shop's cordless phone came off speaker.

"If you really do set traps," I began, "please don't let the customers find them."

"I'll set them out after we close then pick them up before we open." His tone warmed. "There are plenty of field mice at home to fill them with before the seven days are up." A familiar creak told me he had sat in the chair at my desk. "Is this something that should concern me?"

"It's on my to-do list, but it's low priority. Whatever takes them isn't hurting anyone or anything else."

There was a distinct possibility my presence in Samford had attracted pixies, who were drawn to magic.

As long as they kept their raids isolated to the rosebuds, I was fine with supporting their snacking habits.

"I hate to add another item to your to-do list, but I have more to report on the feral hog."

"That's not reassuring." I rubbed my eyes. "What's up?"

"The store smelled funny when we opened. It was hours old, but I can't shake the feeling it was the same guy from yesterday. That faint black witch aroma is everywhere, especially in the office."

"You think he broke in?"

"I see no evidence to support it," he admitted. "The door was secure when we arrived, and there were no scratch marks on the lock or dents in the jamb."

"Trust your gut."

Thanks to running from a homicidal older sister most of his life, he had uncanny instincts.

"My gut says the guy came back sometime last night, walked around the store, maybe checked the office, and left. He didn't take anything that I can tell. That's what prompted the inventory, but I thought you would want to know."

"You were right to call. Just keep a closer eye on the girls, okay?"

"I will," he said softly, and I didn't have to be there to know he was staring at Arden as he made his vow.

Goddess save me from the male of the species.

Before I blurted something totally hypocritical, I ended the call and tossed my phone on my nightstand.

Arms stretched over my head, I smiled when Clay strolled into the room and flopped onto my bed.

"I heard back from my buddy in Atlanta."

"Good morning to you too."

"He emailed me a file I forwarded to you from the Office of the Potentate of Atlanta pertaining to the witchborn fae case. He says the coven was wiped out, and their source of power destroyed."

"Jilo did claim the killer was a boo hag."

"Hey, anytime we mark through another option, I call that a win."

While it was fresh on my mind, I filled him in on my call from the girls, and Aedan.

"Now that's more like it." He rolled onto his back, arms propping up his head. "Is it weird I'm relieved?"

"How does a black witch in Samford link to boo hags in Charleston?"

"There must be a connection. Otherwise, we wouldn't be here. *You* wouldn't be here."

Whatever had frightened the director, I assumed that was the target at which he would aim me.

But what if I misread the situation? What if I wasn't the arrow? What if I was...the bait?

And if I was a trap, then who or what did he expect to catch with me?

"Don't count your chickens before they hatch." I rubbed my stomach. "I could really go for cheese eggs with a side of bacon."

Knowing me, Aedan should have chosen a better code name for the black witch.

"Ace went to round up breakfast." He studied me. "How's life on the road with your man?"

"It's only been a couple of days, so pretty much business as usual."

"Except when this is over, you can't escape."

"I fell off the radar for a decade, Clay. I can vanish again any time I like."

It would gut me, and Colby would never forgive me for breaking up our little unit, but I could do it.

"I'm talking reality of the daily grind," he pressed on. "Not escape hatch hypotheticals."

"Okay?"

"We'll follow you home, follow you to work, follow you home, follow you to work, on and on and on."

"I'm confused." I tread carefully. "Are we talking about me living with Asa or me living with *you*?"

"We're not a package deal." He picked at my comforter. "You don't have to put me up too, you know."

The reason for our heart-to-heart dawned on me, and I hated Clay felt he even had to ask.

"You're family." I took his hand. "For a long time, you were the only friend I had in the world."

"You're grown now." He kept his head down. "You and Ace might want privacy one day."

"One day, we might." I held on to him tighter. "If that day comes, then we'll knock down a wall and build on to the house. Give you your own soundproof golem-in-law suite. Colby's been after me to build her a dedicated game room forever. It would be more of a favor to me, honestly."

"Just don't let me overstay my welcome."

"Impossible." I lunged at Clay, startling a laugh out of him, and wrapped my arms around his neck.

"Working up an appetite?" Asa poked his head into the room. "Breakfast is ready when you are."

Evil grin on his face, Clay clamped one massive hand over my linked ones. He shrugged me over his shoulder, which flung me onto his back, and stood. I had no choice but to endure the piggyback ride.

"I'm too old for this," I complained, smiling against his nape. "I'm not some bony kid anymore."

"If I'm not too old for this, then you are, by default, fine." He headed into the kitchen. "Let loose every once in a while. It's good for the soul." He grunted. "Though, I'll be the first to admit, this might not be good for the back."

"I will end you." I leaned forward, bit the back of his silky mahogany wig, and mumbled, "Take it bath."

"Are you telling me I stink?" He lifted an arm, sniffed. "I'm fresh as a daisy. No pores, remember?"

"Take it bath," I tried again, yanking my head to tug on his hair. "Or elsth."

"You have sharp teeth." Asa stepped up beside us. "They're better than a pair of clippers."

Frozen on the spot, Clay attempted to turn his head, but I didn't let him get far. "Rue."

On my periphery, Asa pulled out a chair and angled it beneath me.

"Have you ever cut hair before?" Asa pretended to consider Clay's nape. "Your lines are quite straight."

"That's it." Clay let go, but Asa caught me with the chair. "You better be joking, or you're both dead."

"*Oof.*" I shifted my weight to one side and rubbed my tailbone. "He's in a mood today."

Asa didn't say anything, which made me wonder how much he had overheard before interrupting us.

"He's right, you know." Asa unpacked several containers, along with bottled milk. "You don't have to put us up at your house. We can find our own lodgings in town if it would make you more comfortable."

"Are you two trying to get kicked out?" I spun the question around on him. "Far as I know, neither Colby nor I have given any indication we mind having you guys underfoot. As a matter of fact, she loves it."

"What about you?" He set a box in front of me. "You can't allow her needs to dictate your entire life."

Despite the phrasing, which raised my hackles, I understood what he meant.

"I like it too." I toyed with the lid to my bottle. "I thought we were all happy."

"I want to make sure I'm not pushing you into an awkward situation with me just to keep Clay close."

"Clay thinks he's a third wheel. You think you're a third wheel." I glowered at him. "There are *four* wheels on a car, not that I'm down with comparing my loved ones to rubber donuts, but whatever."

"I apologize." He sat beside me and gathered my hands in his. "I'm not sure how to do this."

"I don't know what *this* is," I confessed, withdrawing from him, "so you're in good company." I did the unthinkable and forced out more words in the shape of my feelings. "I'm happy waking up and knowing you're down the hall. I like when we stay up late and fall asleep together. I enjoy having people to cook for, people who understand me and Colby. It's nice having a slice of normal, where we don't have to pretend to be anyone other than who we are." And since I was pretty sure I was having an allergic reaction to those emotions, I followed up with, "What am I looking at here?"

"One egg over easy with cheddar and coffee-rubbed bacon on a biscuit donut with fresh hash browns." He let the matter drop. "There's mocha dip in the bag."

That combination short-circuited my brain. "What did you get?"

"Croissants stuffed with breakfast sausages with rosemary maple dip. Also with hash browns."

Water flooded my mouth at his description. "And Clay?"

"Cheesy hash browns topped with one egg over easy, black bean pico, jalapeño honey chutney, and cactus-glazed pork."

A moment of silence passed where Clay rejoined us, peeked into each box, and slapped Asa on the back.

"This smells incredible." He grabbed a milk. "You really are more than a pretty face."

While I had them both at the table, I pushed my chair back and stood at my place.

"You're both staying with us until you tell me otherwise. Colby and I want you in our lives, and in our home. We're cramped, yes, but I'm willing to build on. I wasn't kidding. I will hire a contractor tomorrow. I know a guy in Samford. He'll give me a deal." I held each of their stares. "Are you in, or are you out? I need to let Colby know either way."

"You wield the kid like a weapon. How can I pack a bag now?" Clay shoveled in a mouthful of food. "I had one foot out the door, and then you had to go and move the steps."

"Clay," Asa chastised. "Be serious."

"I was gut punched when you left the last time, Dollface." Clay broke his plastic fork in half. "I thought we were a team, that we would have matching tombstones with Thing One and Thing Two on them. Then you were gone. No goodbye. No forwarding information. Hell, not even a fucking note." He jabbed his finger on the table for emphasis. "You. *Left*. Me."

"Clay..."

"I was mad for a long time, but I made my peace with it. Mostly. I moved on." He started breaking off each tine. "About that time, the director sent me to fetch you. Like it was nothing. Like you had gone out to get a carton of milk and dawdled at the store talking to the cashier. And it hit me all over again, that he didn't see me as a person. I was a thing to him. A useful thing. A helpful thing. But a *thing*."

And I had made him feel the same way. Like he was a means to an end. Like he meant nothing.

Before he could finish, I circled the table and flung myself at him for a second time. "I'm sorry."

"Yeah, well, now I know why you did what you did. I understand. It's just... I love you, Dollface. You're the kid sister I never wanted, and now I'm an uncle. I have a family. With you and Colby." He gripped my arm where it circled his neck. "I don't want to lose that again. I don't want to cease being a person. I want to stay with you and Shorty, maybe not in your house, not forever, I mean. But I could buy a place in town or adjacent acreage and build my own home where Colby could have a room for nights when you and Ace want privacy."

"That sounds great, Clay." I wiped the tears off my cheeks. "But not for a while yet, okay?"

The part of me that craved connection to others reveled in having my own mini coven under my roof.

But mostly I wasn't ready to let him go, not when I had barely gotten him back.

"Yeah." He pried me loose. "Maybe not yet."

Time would heal his wounds, however much I regretted inflicting them, and we had plenty of that.

Back in my seat, ready to attack breakfast, I eased my hand under the table and squeezed Asa's fingers.

This was a sore spot between Clay and me, and Asa didn't deserve to get caught up in the fallout. They were a solid team, and they were friends, but Clay was right. He and I were family, and I should have done better by him. These days, I would have, but that was the whole point. I wasn't the same person now as I was then.

Happy to turn the conversation, I settled in to give a Samford update. "We have a situation back home."

By the time I finished retelling the story, Clay was chuckling so hard, he almost shot milk out his nose.

Fork poised above my hash browns, I tossed him a napkin. "What's so funny?"

"You know how much fun I've had with you and Ace and this fascination thing?"

When I stabbed my food, the tines pierced the Styrofoam. "Yes?"

"I get the feeling you might experience it from the other side in a few years." He made the noise again, a guffawing blast of amusement. "It's going to be hilarious when you realize how weird the food thing is from a spectator point of view."

"Nope." I stabbed again. "They're not going to fixate on each other."

Beside me, Asa wore an amused smile, soft around its edges. "They don't always have a choice."

"Let me pretend I have some control over this small corner of my life, please?"

"No fascination for Arden," Clay chimed. "Bad daemon for even looking at her."

"No fascination for Arden," Asa agreed and then he went and ruined it. "Until she's healed enough to decide for herself."

"I'm going to pretend," I grumbled, "that was a unanimous vote for *no*."

Obviously, I wasn't prejudiced against daemons. I was in fascination with one, and I was a quarter myself, but I was also a witch. Their world was my world. I grew up aware of them, and them aware of me. Arden had no idea what or who Aedan really was, and learning that truth would rock her world.

Worse yet, she would drag Camber into the fray with her.

They were joined at the hip, as close as sisters, and I had no doubt how it would go.

The girls' horizons would expand, and they would find out, sooner or later, who and what I was too.

And they would hate me. For lying. For what had happened to them because of me.

I wasn't saying I didn't deserve the reckoning, I did, but I never expected it to actually come.

A peculiar rustling noise had me leaning forward in my chair to check the floor behind Clay.

"Colby?" I shot to my feet. "What's wrong?"

"Just tired." She yawned. "Didn't sleep well."

For a moth to walk such a long distance, this went beyond tired. The kid was exhausted. Wings dragging on the hardwood, antennae drooping down her back, legs wobbly. One more step, and she might face-plant.

Good thing she sized up to make the trip shorter. Otherwise, we might have stepped on her.

A shudder rippled down my spine at the thought of her crushed under a shoe on accident.

Abandoning my food, I rushed to scoop her up and carried her to an open spot at the table.

"Sit tight." I busied myself mixing sugar water and filling a saucer with pollen granules. "Eat." I plunked them both down in front of her, but she was already asleep. "Colby." I jostled her awake. "Sweetie, I need you to eat something, and then you can nap, okay?"

"Mmm-kay."

Slowly, she took tiny bites and sips until a glimmer of her usual spark returned to her features.

The guys exchanged wary glances over her head, alarmed she wasn't feeling well.

Colby was a soul given form. I hadn't realized she could get sick. It had never happened before.

Unable to resist, I stroked her back while she ate. "Did you stay up late playing Mystic Realms?"

"Yep." She grinned at that. "I found the invisibility helmet."

"I thought it was an invisibility cloak?"

"Do you know how dangerous it is to walk around in a cloak? They get caught on everything."

"I can't say I've put much thought into it, but I see your point." I stroked her head. "How do you feel?"

"Better now." She stretched out her wings. "I should go." She yawned. "Raids don't plan themselves."

With less oomph than usual, she glided off the table and sailed out of the room.

As much as I wanted to snag her from the air and coddle her, I knew she hated being babied.

"She put in a lot of hours yesterday." Clay stared at the doorway. "Not all work, either. Her guild decided last minute to pillage the forgotten city to steal that helmet. It was a six-hour quest with no pee breaks."

"How do you keep all that straight?" I was already lost. "Do you play the game that much?"

"I watch the highlights on Colby's channel." He winked at me. "Saves me time."

Living forever was often much more appealing in the abstract than in practice.

Clay kept a strict schedule, dividing his days and nights, though he never slept. Structure had kept more than one immortal sane, and it was working for him. That meant even though he could stream her recent footage in a night, he restricted himself to a certain number of hours to give the impression he couldn't hold his eyes open for another minute.

He had done the same thing for me, his insomniac partner, with baking. Carved out a portion of his night to lure me into a hobby that could occupy me the way Mystic Realms broke up the monotony for Colby.

To this day, I wasn't sure if Clay figured my being a witch meant I would be a natural fit with cookbooks and recipes. (I did own grimoires and mix the occasional potion.) Or if he simply wanted to share a hobby he enjoyed by cultivating that same deep love in me.

Now that I thought about it, this might be another secret to his longevity. He picked up hobbies left and right, a sponge that soaked up everything on a given topic then wrung itself dry to start all over again.

Mystic Realms was his new religion to give him common ground with Colby, but he was already staging his exit by training the daemon to take his place.

"What's on the agenda for today?"

"A trip to Folly Beach." I lifted my cold breakfast, which was still amazing. "I want to check out the area where the first victim's body was or wasn't found by the faux witches."

That Asa didn't ask me for the particulars told me Clay had shared them with him.

"We're free until tonight." Asa poked at his food. "We have to meet Jilo then."

"That ought to be fun." Clay seemed to mean it. "Never met a boo hag. Or a talking cat."

"Mind if I try?" I didn't wait for Asa to respond. "Your hash browns look crispier than mine."

"Only if you'll trade me coffee-rubbed bacon."

"I'm not sure that's an equal exchange." I nibbled my sandwich again. "This bacon is life altering."

Faster than I could blink, Asa leaned over and helped himself to a huge bite.

"You're right." He savored the flavors. "That is life altering."

Before I could fuss, he loaded a fork and shoveled hash browns into my mouth.

The reason I asked for them over his sausage-stuffed croissants became clear the second the food hit my tongue. He had eaten some of the hash browns. I must have noticed and filed it away, and our weird daemon quirk urged me to complete the loop by sharing food with him.

Mouth full, Clay answered around his fork when his phone rang. "Kerr."

At his hand wave, Asa and I tuned in, with me straining to hear what came to them easily.

"Found some bones," a low voice grumbled across the line. *"Picked clean."*

"Where?"

"Folly Island."

"We're on our way."

"Make it quick." The caller grunted. *"Had to pull one out of Fran's mouth."*

"Thanks, man." He pocketed his phone and rubbed his temples. "There's no such thing as coincidence."

Since Clay knew everyone under the sun, I asked, "Who's Fran?"

"She's part turkey vulture, and yes, that is a weird-ass shifter designation."

All I needed was for her to fall in love with roadkill to be in one of my romance novels.

He was clinging to life. She was swooping down to eat him. Then their lives collided, literally.

Yeah.

I might need to dial it back on the improbable shifters if I was blurbing their stories in my head.

"I'll check on Colby." I handed Asa the rest of my sandwich. "Then we can go."

"I'll give the Vandenburghs a heads-up," Clay offered, "see if they want to join us."

While the guys planned our trip, I ducked into her room and found her snoring on her pillow.

Knowing how she loved to sleep with it, I searched for her green blanket, but it was nowhere in sight.

I wrote a quick note and left it beside her, telling her where we had gone and ordering her to check in the second her eyes opened. Then we locked up and headed for the beach.

10

No surprise, Clay decided to ping his new friends, the wannabe witches, to ask for a ride.

Based on his pinched expression, and their lack of greeting, I decided it wasn't going well.

"Huh." He ended the call. "I must have dialed a number wrong." He shrugged. "Fat fingers."

Asa drove while I rode shotgun, but I kept twisted in my seat to give me a view of Clay.

"The number has been disconnected." He stared at the phone. "How...?"

"Maybe it was a burner phone?" I adjusted my seat belt. "They might prefer to handle their rendezvous anonymously." Hard to do with a floating city as their bachelorette pad, but still. "After the night is over, toss the cell and clean the slate."

"Their coven is out in the open." Asa called my attention back to him. "Their practices might not be."

The last thing they needed was practice if they were weekend orgy hosts, but I knew what he meant.

"I feel so dirty." Clay dropped his phone onto the seat. "I thought what we had was special."

He was only half teasing. Getting dumped bothered him. Probably for the same reason it bugged me.

They offered him and his friends a ride, then invited him for nakey beach time where they shared a story that might connect with our current case. Now his only means of contact with them had been cut.

Call me crazy, but that struck me as suspicious.

"We can hunt them down through their public front," Asa decided, "if it comes down to it."

"Touch base with the Kellies," I told Clay. "Ask them to verify the police were called and a report filed."

People did all kinds of weird things. People lied. We couldn't trust these women had told Clay the truth.

They might have wanted to impress him and thought pulling out their most gruesome story would do it.

Poor things.

They had no idea that nothing they had seen or ever would see held a candle to his life experiences.

"Okay." He palmed his phone. "We'll need to drop the shoe off for testing too."

One good thing about the cleaners being involved was we could scrape that off our plate onto theirs.

"It's a twenty-minute trip to Folly Island." Asa fiddled with the built-in GPS. "We can drive it."

"Oh." I leaned back, happy for an easy fix. "I figured the whole 'island' thing required a boat."

"Not in this instance."

With that settled, I began light snooping into this public coven in the event we needed to talk to them.

What I discovered was an intrepid marketing scheme for an upscale holistic spa experience.

Witchy Ways wasn't claiming to be a coven. Not online anyway.

But that was their cutesy name for the staff, who were, of course, *like family*. From what I could tell, their big deal was riding out to tourist hot spots, welcoming new friends onto their floating island, then sailing them back…to the spa.

From there, they passed out free vouchers for an event called "skyclad moon worship" to help open your pores or chakras or whatever buzz word fit the mark. I was skimming by that point. Not that a site would advertise any *extra* services, but I saw no reviews to indicate the sales staff also initiated orgies.

Which meant…

Twisting in my seat, I stared at Clay until he glanced up at me. "How are your nonexistent pores today?"

Suddenly, the ceiling held the mysteries of the universe, and he was a devout student of its glory.

"You Googled them."

"I did."

"Then you know."

"I do."

"I'm an idiot." He pinched his fingers together. "I was *this* close to investing in a pyramid scheme, Rue."

As much as I loved Clay, he was vain. (Mostly about his hair.) That made him ripe for scamming by pretty faces with flattering words. The wannabe witches played into that vanity, thinking they could con him to buy their branded skincare or whatever they were hawking in bulk. Maybe sell extras to his friends, for a profit. As if he needed the money. Or the product. He had been molded, carved, every detail was exactly as his creator imagined. And though he never saw himself as such, I thought he was perfect as is.

It made me want to show them what a real witch could do.

But that was the old me.

The new me would simply flip Colby's switch to *annihilate* and watch her topple their enterprise via bad reviews that exposed their shady practices. As much as she adored Clay, I wouldn't have to work hard to convince her this quest was a worthy one.

"I don't follow." Asa checked on his partner in the rearview mirror. "What do nonexistent pores have to do with a MLM scheme?"

"I thought the women were interested in me." His shoulders drooped as he leaned back. "They were only interested in my money."

They must have been at Fort Sumter that day to scout for marks and picked Clay out of the batch.

"You let me think you were out there having some kind of wild sex party when you were listening to a sales pitch." I thinned my lips. "Why lie about that?"

"I didn't lie, exactly." His gaze drifted back down to mine. "I just let you believe I still had *it*."

"*It?*" I understood after I spoke the word and held up a hand. "Never mind."

"It's been a long time for me, and after we ran into my ex, it got me thinking." He rubbed a hand over his mouth. "I went to the beach for the free show, which is definitely *not* mentioned in the brochure, but when I kept my pants firmly in the zipped position, that's when Glinda pulled out the story about the body to hook me."

Oh, I was sure he was into it plenty. But he would have never unzipped for a bunch of strangers.

People could be cruel, humans more than most, and he wouldn't have exposed himself to ridicule.

"Wait." I scrunched up my face. "Why would she randomly volunteer that specific information?"

Big conversational leap from moon worship to murder.

"I might have told the ladies I was a special agent with the FBI to get us a ride back to Charleston."

That line worked on a certain subset of people, and he *had* been dressed for the part when they met.

Sadly, that lent more credence to Glinda's story. Pity. I was hoping for a reason to question her.

With my foot on her windpipe.

"I don't see why you're so put out." I shoved his knee. "You're not the only one not getting any."

A choked noise reminded me Asa was listening in. Perhaps I shouldn't have chosen this as my feel-good argument to boost Clay's self-esteem. Too late. I was in it now. Might as well follow through.

"You're in a relationship." Clay pointed at Asa. "Sex is right there, if you want it."

"You don't have to be in a relationship to have sex. You must have told me that a million times."

"And you didn't listen," he reminded me. "I would say you were waiting for an emotional attachment—"

"—but I don't do feelings, I do what feels good."

Oh, how I regretted starting this conversation. For so many reasons. Most of which revolved around Asa having a front row seat for a discussion on how little I cared about sex, how rarely I'd had it, and my lack of interest in it—and relationships—overall. Not exactly the endorsement you want when you're looking to seduce a partner.

Against all odds, Asa slid his hand into mine where they fisted on my lap.

Maybe he thought mutual inexperience was a good thing. Or maybe he figured if I knew the basic mechanics that we could puzzle out the rest together. That, or he felt sorry for me.

Right about now, I know I felt sorry for me.

Emotions were stupid, and you shouldn't have to involve them in every single decision of your life.

The three of us called a silent truce, Clay and I licking our wounds, and no one said another word until we arrived at the beach.

The Vandenburghs were leaning against their cruiser, deep in conversation, when we arrived.

"Afternoon." Mr. Officer smiled at us, professional to a T. "The remains are this way."

Mrs. Officer nodded, but she kept her mouth shut as if she was afraid what might fall out of it next.

We walked about five minutes before I spotted wooden stakes driven into the sand and wrapped in the familiar yellow of crime scene tape. Inside the square, small bones rested in a jumble.

"The remains were in the water too long for me to pick up any traces of black magic." Mrs. Officer, comfortable talking about work, led the conversation. "I was hoping one of you could confirm it."

Of the three of us, only one of us had any hope of identifying a scent a warg nose couldn't parse.

"Is the beach secure?" I scanned the shore. "We need to make sure what happens next won't be seen."

"We've got about a mile of clearance, unless someone has a telescoping lens on a boat too far for us to make out from here. That's about all the guarantee we can offer."

"That will be fine." Asa began removing his shirt and jacket, which he handed to me. "I'll be quick."

Flames engulfed him, roaring for seconds longer than usual, and the daemon emerged with a low growl.

Both wargs stumbled back a step, and Mrs. Officer put her hand on her service weapon.

"You even think about pulling that on him," I said cheerfully, "and I will slap your heart between two pieces of white bread and call it lunch."

That caused more panic, which was satisfying, but it also made my stomach rumble with false hope.

"Please tell me you'll add lettuce, tomato, and mayo like a civilized person."

That earned Clay, who knew I wouldn't waste a good heart on cheap condiments, a scowl from me.

"Rue like me." The daemon slung an arm around my neck and ruffled my hair with his fist. "She threaten mean dog people for me."

Another chortle lodged in Clay's throat, and I couldn't decide who was on worse behavior today.

"Yeah, yeah." I swatted the daemon's hand. "Gloat later. You're exposed here. It makes me nervous."

To appease me, the daemon swaggered to the bones and began his examination.

"I've never seen anything like that." Mrs. Officer gawped at him. "Is he…dangerous?"

"You saw him give me a noogie." I finger-combed my hair. "Clearly, he's a rabid killing machine."

"I wish transformation was that simple for us." Her husband stepped in to smooth over the bump. "He can change at will?" He snapped his fingers. "Just like that?"

"Just like that," I confirmed, in case they got any ideas the fae-er version of Asa was an easier mark.

"I can't imagine how it must feel to transform in a blink." She dug her nails into her palms, as if to leash her tongue. "His control is remarkable."

"Does it hurt?" Mr. Officer smiled when the daemon raked the sand with his claws. "It feels like I'm being torn limb from limb. Every time." He barked out a laugh. "Probably because I am." He chuckled. "It never gets easier."

"Ask him yourself." I waved the daemon over when he started wandering. "They have a question."

"For Rue." He thrust out his hand and dropped a perfect seashell on my palm. "Pretty."

"It is pretty." I admired it from every angle. "Let me put it in my pocket so I don't lose it."

Nodding his permission, he glanced at the wargs. "What question?"

"Does it hurt when you shift?" Mr. Officer let curiosity get the best of him. "Do you even feel it?"

"No shift." He looked at them like they were crazy. "Am me all the time."

"This is not how you looked when you arrived," Mrs. Officer explained delicately. "That's what we meant."

"Oh." He thrust a handful of hair into my hand. "You pet." He screwed up his face. "I explain."

From beside me, Clay snickered, barely holding in a snort.

The daemon was spoiled rotten, and I had to start enforcing rules for good behavior.

Somehow.

I let too much slide in the name of cuteness.

And there was nothing more adorable than the daemon looming over us all, rubbing his chin with his thumb and finger, pretending to entertain deep philosophical thoughts on the duality of his nature while he conned me into stroking his hair.

"I me," he finally said. "Asa me too." He tilted his head. "We same." He held up a finger. "But different."

To keep from chuckling, I bit the inside of my cheek. "There you have it, folks."

Neither warg appeared to understand what he meant, but I was used to the line between them blurring.

"Can you tell if black magic was the cause of death?" Mr. Officer recovered first. "Or something else?"

"No black magic smell." He tapped his nose. "Fishy smell."

"Thanks for trying." I returned his hair to him. "Can we have Asa back, please?"

How I phrased the question earned me speculative stares from the wargs, but I was good at ignoring people I didn't want to justify myself to, especially when it came to Asa and his secrets.

"The remains were in the water for too long." Asa accepted his shirt and shrugged it on. "I can't help."

"No problem," Mrs. Officer assured him. "We'll bag them up and get them tested."

After a brief inner debate, I asked, "Mind if I try?"

"Not at all." Mr. Officer watched me kneel and extend my hand. "You can tell by touch?"

"Sometimes." I knew it was a bust before I made contact. "Looks like this isn't one of those times."

Clay passed me a wet wipe from his pocket, and I cleaned my hand as I stood.

"While we're talking black magic," he interjected, "have you had any dealings with the local boo hags?"

"The grume polices their own. There are so few hags left in Charleston, they tend to travel in pairs and avoid other paras. They do kill humans, but nothing outside their allotment as a predatory paranormal species." Mr. Officer thought about it. "There haven't been any verified hag kills in the past fifty years."

"They clean up after themselves," Mrs. Officer explained. "That doesn't mean they weren't killing."

"They just didn't leave a mess behind," Mr. Officer agreed. "Hard to track that kind of activity."

That was the whole point. Healthy predators hid their tracks. Only the sick earned Black Hat attention.

"You think the grume is behind this?" Mrs. Officer crossed her arms over her chest. "No one on the force was around fifty years ago. The whole not-aging thing means we rotate pack members throughout the Southeast to keep the faces fresh. We wouldn't even know what to look for, really."

Good behavior would explain why the officers hadn't suspected boo hag involvement from the get-go. It also lent weight to Jilo's claims and validated her reasons for stepping forward to help us solve this case.

"We've received a tip that might be the case," I allowed, "but we don't have evidence to back it up yet."

Aside from Jilo's slinky cat routine, I meant. But that didn't prove another boo hag was responsible. Only that she wanted us to believe a former member of the grume was behind the murders. That seemed unlikely, if the Vandenburghs doubted their involvement enough to avoid mentioning them as possible suspects.

"Let us know if that changes." Mr. Officer frowned. "We might be able to help."

"We'll keep you updated," I only slightly fibbed. "We'll know more soon."

As in, as soon as the sun went down, and we met Jilo.

On that note, we left the wait for the cleaners to the locals and piled back into our SUV.

Not that Black Hat was big on teamwork outside the team to which you were assigned, but I wrote a quick report I sent to Marty to pass along to the other agents and to the director.

The problem with pairing up so many different species with such similar pasts was you formed packs. Or covens. Or clans. And those got territorial. Since no one had actual territory, they fixated on cases assigned to them. They guarded them with predatory glee and attacked anyone who attempted to steal them or had the bad luck to be assigned to the case as backup, thus forcing them to "trespass."

Things got violent when that happened, more often than not. So it was meanspirited of me to envision them floating in hot tubs, eating pizza, and watching sports or skin flicks to avoid work.

Even if they did that exact thing.

As one of the few females who rated the initiation to Black Hat, the boys' club spent my formative years attempting to shock me. The joke was on them. I had been so lost to my own addictions by then, I didn't care what they said or did or watched. I had my own movies playing in my head.

Blood. Meat. Violence.

Power.

Even thinking it made my mouth water.

Some things never change.

But I had.

At least now I could tell it was wrong to catch the beat of a person's heart and salivate.

"Colby hasn't checked in yet." I thumped my phone against my thigh. "It's not like her to sleep so much."

"This is her first real case, and she's dedicated to solving it." Asa cut his eyes to me. "Perhaps she's been sneaking in extra screen time to work angles past her curfew?"

The Bureau lifestyle carried a weight of responsibility no child should be forced to shoulder.

Maybe it was that simple.

Stress.

Stress made people tired, right?

"We're keeping an eye on her." Clay thumped the back of my seat. "She's going to be fine."

His refusal to allow for any other possible outcome buoyed me, and I was grateful for his faith.

"What's next on the agenda?" Clay leaned forward between Asa and me. "Where do we go now?"

"We're going to walk the streets," I decided on a whim. "See if we can pick up that black magic smell."

It would also keep me from obsessing about the feral hog back in Samford until we met with Jilo.

Asa appeared to consider this. "Do you think it will lead us to where the boo hags nest?"

"It's better than twiddling our thumbs. Mine are starting to get blisters."

11

"Do you want to stop by the suites and check on Colby first?"

The question drew my focus to Asa and away from the postcardworthy view of Rainbow Row.

"That would be great." I sagged in my seat with relief as he cut the wheel. "Thanks."

The guys idled at the curb in front of the defunct restaurant while I ran upstairs and let myself in.

The wards hummed as I exited onto our floor, telling me all was well within.

But, since I had trust issues, I didn't let that stop me from calling for her from our entryway.

"Hover much?" Colby yelled from her room. "I feel a breeze from your helicopter parenting from here."

Relief swamped me until I felt sick with it, and tears prickled the backs of my eyes for no good reason.

"You were supposed to text me." I shook off my worries. "It's your own fault I'm coming in for a landing."

"How was I supposed to know?" She glided out to meet me halfway, sailing lower than usual. "I was asleep when you left."

"I wrote you a note." I pointed to her laptop on the bed. "I stuck it right there where you would see it when you woke from your nap."

"Maybe it fell on the floor?" She scrunched up her face. "Sometimes I flutter in my sleep."

The gentle breeze produced by her wings was more than enough to send a sticky note flying.

"Maybe." I rounded the bed, but I didn't see any yellow squares on the hardwood. "Nope."

A thread of indignation wove through her voice. "I would have done it if I saw the note."

"I'm not accusing you of lying." I patted my shoulder for her to land. "I would never do that."

A kid she might be, but she had never given me a reason not to trust her.

"Then what happened to the note?"

Good question.

Unfortunately, I had no answer.

Giving the wards side-eye, I confirmed no breaks, tears, or kinks in coverage.

We had ourselves a genuine locked-room mystery.

"I don't know." I kissed the top of her head. "Grab your stuff."

One thing was for certain, I wasn't leaving her alone while things were vanishing without a trace.

I was too afraid she might be next.

"I get to meet the boo-boo?"

"Boo hag, and it looks that way." Unease crawled over my skin. "Chop-chop. We're on a schedule."

Happy for any activity that put her in mortal peril, she gathered her things and met me at the door.

"I'll carry that." I tapped my head. "Hair-bow mode, activate."

"Activated." She shrank to her smallest size and nested in my hair. "This will be so cool."

Given how much Colby hated cats, being a moth and all, she might find the boo hag's latest vessel more traumatic than greeting a human wrapper. I wasn't sure if they could reuse a skin after they discarded it, so Jilo's appearance would be a surprise for us all.

I really hated surprises.

The worst thing about investigating a crime were the lulls that boiled down to waiting for the killer to make another move to give you a clue that might inch you closer to catching them. Nothing makes you feel inepter than when your shortcomings cost people their lives.

The weight of unseen eyes pressed down on me, heavier than before, and I couldn't shake the sensation we weren't the only ones out hunting the streets.

This part of the job was much easier earlier in my career when I didn't care who lived or who died. It was a challenge to overcome, a puzzle to solve, a feather in my cap, but that was it. Unless it involved power boosts or raw, pulsating meat, I couldn't have cared less.

We discovered no flashing arrow signs pointing toward the killer's secret hideout during our walk, which would have been nice. Colby tucked in my hair left me feeling exposed on the street, and paranoia she was being targeted—*again*—left me twitchy.

On the plus side, the fresh air perked Colby up quickly.

The old saying *canary in a coal mine* flashed through my mind with peculiar insistence.

How secure was our rental? How safe was she there? Or any of us for that matter?

"You okay, Dollface?"

Aware Colby was listening in, and equally aware she couldn't participate in this conversation and maintain her cover, I filled him in.

"The note I wrote Colby is gone. She never saw it." I hesitated. "Her blanket is missing too."

"That's not good." A soft curse slipped under his breath, and I pinched his arm. "She loves that thing."

Within minutes of opening that gift from Asa, it had become more than a present. It was her security blanket, a talisman against the bad dreams that once plagued her.

"Fingers crossed she left it in your room or Asa's." I rubbed my forehead. "She's never without it."

As a matter of fact, we cranked the AC up at home to accommodate her preference to remain bundled.

"We'll find it." He stared at the back of Asa's head. "That, or Ace better knit like the wind."

The ancient practice of Tinkkit was a craft few fae mastered, and the result of the knitting was a gift with intent. I was fuzzy on the fine points, but I wasn't sure if Asa could make another identical blanket. The pattern and fabric, he could duplicate. The magic protecting Colby's sleeping mind? I was less sure the same endowment could be given twice.

"You brought a friend," a low voice drawled from overhead. "Hello, golem."

Head tipping back, I scanned the tree above us for a set of red eyes and found their hungry glow.

"Hey, Jilo." I offered a wave. "This is Clay." I gestured to the branches. "This is Jilo."

"Hello, boo hag." Clay grinned up at her. "How's it hanging?"

"Eh." The leaves rustled. "Could be better." A squirrel zipped down a limb. "These two made last night a freaking misery." The creature flicked its bushy tail. "Not a fan. Of either of them."

"I'm the nice guy." He spread his hands. "Ask anyone."

"He is the nice guy," I confirmed. "Until he's not."

"That hurt." Clay slapped a palm over his chest. "I think it's a mortal wound."

Jilo chuckled, low and throaty, and the squirrel leapt onto his shoulder. "Poor dear."

Had I not already admired Clay, I would have respected how he allowed a spiralized squirrel to land on his shoulder without a) screaming b) swatting it off or c) swatting it off and then stomping it flat while screaming.

"I hear you're our tour guide for the night." He kept his smile movie star bright. "Lead the way."

The squirrel stroked its paw down his cheek, and somehow he didn't flinch.

"You're cute." She winked at him. "Big and muscly. Just the way I like 'em."

"What did you want to show us?" Asa kept a hand tucked in his pocket, a clear threat. "We don't have much time."

"The night is young." She curled her tail around Clay's neck. "Let's not rush, shall we?"

About to toss my cookies, which took a heck of a lot, I jerked my chin to set Clay walking.

"My partners," he began, "mentioned you have a rogue on your hands."

"Partners as in work?" She bit her lower lip. "Or partners as in play?"

Unsure how Clay would react, I was seconds from telling her we three were in a deeply committed relationship to rescue him from her clutches. I doubt Asa would have fussed much. He had to be just as creeped out as me.

A flash of amusement twinkled in Clay's eyes, and I got the uncomfortable idea he was enjoying this.

Between his ex and the naked pyramid witches, he had taken hits to his confidence, but a squirrel?

Even if she took a human form, she would be wearing dead—

Nope.

Not going there.

Not thinking about it.

Clay was a grown man who could handle himself.

And I was a grown woman willing to handle him right back into our SUV if he got that desperate for companionship.

"What did you want to show us?" Asa repeated, flexing his hand in time with his steps.

After our trip to the beach, he could have had any number of tiny items in his pocket for her to count.

"Ugh." The squirrel darted down the front of Clay's body and shot off in the dark. "Come on, losers."

We followed the bushy tail until Jilo skidded to a halt outside a cemetery.

A slight twitch on my head announced Colby had gone lax, her legs sprawled in my hair to hold on while she slept. That she was napping through an opportunity to examine a boo hag told me she still wasn't back to her usual self, and that worry distracted me.

"We can't have children." Jilo rubbed her paws up her arms. "That's why our faction is dying."

"I'm sorry to hear that." Clay beat me to the platitudes. "On both counts."

"We're predators of a bygone era," she lamented. "There shouldn't be more of us. We can't support a larger grume than the one we have without drawing the kind of attention that brought you to us. But, sometimes, one of us lingers in a role and gets ideas."

"Play human too long," I guessed, "and you start to dream human dreams?"

A husband. A home. A child.

"The dream is enough for most." Jilo's tail drooped slowly. "They target husbands and play wife. Or wives and play husband. Or mothers and play with the children until..."

"...the wrapper expires?"

"Wrapper?" She had the grace to wince at my word choice. "Yeah." She fidgeted. "It's not healthy."

"Does anything of the original owner remain?"

"No." She jolted. "Can you imagine?"

About as well as I could picture wrapping myself in a bandage made of human skin.

"Are you implying," Asa cut in, "that the rogue is kidnapping human children as surrogates?"

"We have our own creation stories." Jilo's nails clicked on the cement. "The same as everyone else." She flicked a tiny wrist. "I won't bore you with details, but there are some who believe it's true. Every word." A beat lapsed while she cleaned her whiskers. "Even the parts about the first boo hag, Sorie, who craved the companionship of another creature like himself so desperately that he split himself in half, creating a child in his image." She scratched behind her ear. "That child matured, followed in her father's footsteps when she too became lonely, and thus began the propagation of the species."

"Asexual reproduction?"

"More or less." The squirrel leapt from the street onto the wrought iron fence. "It's a myth."

"Then how were you born?"

"I wouldn't say *born*." She wrinkled her nose. "We lack the plumbing for that."

"Okay." I played along. "Made? Created? Burst into existence?"

"If I knew that," she said wryly, "we wouldn't be a species on the brink of extinction, would we?"

"Yet you told us about the myth." Asa drew nearer. "You think your rogue attempted it?"

"Oh, sugar, plenty of folks attempt it. We're dying out, and times are desperate, but there's no record of anyone surviving. Either half. If they make it that far. Most don't. It takes grit to rip yourself in two."

"If your rogue was successful," Asa said, studying her, "why would the grume turn out a miracle birth?"

"Marah..." Her dark eyes glistened when they met mine. "She broke off too much and not enough."

Clay tried for a sympathetic ear. "What does that mean?"

"We can't contain them. They're too hungry."

"There are two of them." I gave that revelation space in my head. "Are they both preying on children?"

"Marah hunts for Sorie." Her voice went soft. "That's what she named him. *Sorie*. After the story."

Again, Clay stepped in with an empathy I couldn't fake. "Why target kids?"

"To be allowed to live, he must learn control." Her fingers curled into tiny fists. "Children are a bite-sized meal. They're good practice for teaching him how much to eat and when to stop. Except it doesn't work like that. He's always hungry, and she's always feeding him. She can barely eat without Sorie begging for her scraps. Marah's control is thin. She's going to snap, and when she does, she'll devour this city."

Thinking back to the body at Folly Beach, I asked, "Is Marah using the unraveling spell on the children?"

Whatever the grume called it, it wasn't that, but Jilo caught on to my meaning fast enough.

"She uses their…wrappers…as lures for the next victim. That, and her avatar as an educator."

"She was posing as Tracy Amerson." I heard the pieces click together. "How long was she the teacher?"

"Six months." Jilo grimaced. "We thought it might help, being around children all day, but it only made her more desperate for her own offspring. We didn't realize what she had done until the second human child went missing."

What she implied, that Marah was hunting within the school system, left me hollow and aching for those parents.

But it wasn't as simple as Marah bringing home a new student each time her offspring got hungry.

One of the victims was from out of state. He wouldn't have been enrolled in her jurisdiction.

There was more to this, things Jilo wasn't telling us, but we needed as much from her as we could get.

"The teacher's remains were found on the boat we took to Fort Sumter," I told her. "We were viewing the site of the fourth abduction when a cry went up from the crew. Her skin was found in the bathroom."

"Who is Marah now?" Asa jingled his pocket. "We need to know how to find her."

"I don't know if she's taken a new avatar." Jilo jerked her head up to glare at him. "Threaten me all you want, daemon, but I'm already sticking my neck out to help this much."

Before this escalated, I drew Jilo's sharp gaze to me. "What did you want to show us?"

"There's a tunnel accessible through the Thurman family mausoleum." She rested a hand on the bars. "Originally, it was used by pirates to smuggle liquor into the city. Now it's a stronghold for those who are willing to follow Marah's example and attempt to create offspring."

Given my unease the past few days, I had to wonder if more boo hags than Jilo had been tailing us, watching us, weighing the threat we posed to them and their plans for a rebirth of the species.

"You want us to clean house." Clay beat me to it. "You'll give up the problem that brought us here, but you want her acolytes wiped out to avoid a repeat visit from us."

"They haven't fractured themselves yet." Jilo wiped her nose with a tiny paw. "But they will, as soon as they work up the nerve. They view it as their duty. Preservation of the species. But it's a death sentence. For all of us."

"Are they guilty of any crimes?"

"They hunt humans, if that's what you mean, but they're not unthinking killers." She slouched. "They will be, though. One day. If they go through with it. Hunger will rob them of their sanity. They will feast to grow strong enough to survive, and leave a trail of bodies in their wake. And we can't stop them. Boo hags can't kill one another."

Asa beat me to the problem, no doubt because he had been turning it over in his head for days.

"You have no way to distract them until dawn," he said, "without falling into the trap yourself."

The phrase *mutually assured destruction* came to mind, since a handful of coins scattered on the pavement would do as much to Marah, and her offspring, as it would to Jilo.

"No one wants to end up a martyr," she lamented. "There's no glory in death."

"We'll discuss what you've told us." I soaked up Asa's warmth. "But we'll need a plan before we barge in."

The smart thing to do was familiarize ourselves with the terrain, and I had an idea of how to do that.

We said our good nights to Jilo much earlier than expected and meandered back to our rental.

Up in the suite I shared with Colby, I woke her and set her in front of her laptop. Annoyed to have missed the good stuff—her words, not mine—I asked her to dig up blueprints for the cemetery.

The originals might not be available online, but there was a good chance ghost hunting enthusiasts had mapped it for their own communities. Those would be marked with paranormal hotspots, which might help us pinpoint any other areas the boo hags were hanging around in, in addition to the Thurman family mausoleum.

Humans got it wrong most of the time, but sometimes they got it right to an alarming degree.

"One hour of work," I instructed Colby. "Then it's game time."

"Mmm-hmm."

Already, she was distracted by the hunt. For a moth, she had serious killer instincts.

And the lovely people at Witchy Ways would get a taste of it soon enough.

The guys were lounging in their suite, so I joined them to discuss the drama that had fallen in our laps.

"We got played." I sat with one thigh on each guy's leg and

wiggled until they scooted over to make room for me. "Jilo has a hit list and seems to think we're hired guns."

"To be fair," Asa said, curving a possessive arm around my middle to draw me closer, "we are."

Grumbling to avoid having to agree with him, which made him laugh, I curled against his side.

"Reminds me of that movie," Clay said, "where police from the future go back in time to kill their worst criminals before they commit their crimes."

"They kill innocent people because of the damage they might one day do?" I frowned. "That's grim."

"Yeah." He propped his jaw in his palm and his elbow on the armrest. "But it makes you think."

"We can't wipe out an entire grume—subgrume?—without Black Hat authorization." Asa ran his fingers through my hair. "Unless they move against us, or are connected to the case, they're innocent in the eyes of the Bureau."

As innocent as serial murderers could be, anyway.

Black Hat was fickle that way. The problem here was not that we had killers on the loose. That was every day that ended in Y. The issue was the targets were human, and children. A combo guaranteed to wreak havoc on the paranormal community if the situation wasn't neutralized quickly.

"I don't like it." Clay shifted his weight, and the couch protested. "Jilo was too helpful, leading us right to Marah's lair. And then, oh! I forgot. There's also a community of future problems living under there too. You should kill them all. Just to be safe. Thanks."

"I don't like it either," I admitted. "We aren't authorized to use that kind of force willy-nilly."

"We need to approach Marah with caution." Asa twirled a wavy lock around his finger. "Jilo can communicate with us, even when she's an animal, so there shouldn't be a language barrier."

"The choice of squirrel was interesting." Clay kicked his feet up on the coffee table, which wobbled. "Was she trying to approach us in the least threatening—if creepiest—way possible?"

"Or—" I leaned into his theory, "—was she playing at being a vegetarian?"

There was a whole movie franchise about vegetarian vampires. The comparison wasn't that off base.

"All we have is Jilo's word that the others are responsible for the killings." Asa gave my scalp a tug. "The story she spun is convincing, and it would explain the teacher, who didn't fit the profile for the other victims, but it's too easy."

"Yeah." I breathed in his green apple and cherry tobacco scent with a happy sigh. "None of us almost died, which means this is far from over."

"Why don't we call Marty with a hot tip and let him search the tunnels at dawn?" Clay laughed evilly. "He could report back on the structural integrity of the place, and if he got spiraled, it could only improve his personality."

Snorting a laugh, I struggled to keep my eyes open. Must be a fascination thing. Snuggle your honey, and you pass out from bliss or something. Or, knowing daemons, the oils in our skin combined to create a supernatural melatonin.

The guys kept laughing, but the sound came from a great distance, their tinny voices echoing.

Adrenaline crashed through my brain, snapping it into overdrive, but my limbs hung, weighted and useless.

Asa was *right there*, but I couldn't call out to him.

"Rue?" A heavy hand landed on my shoulder. "Dollface?"

"Did she fall asleep?" Asa tensed beneath me. "She never naps."

"This isn't natural," Clay agreed then shifted his attention back to me. "Can you hear us?"

Locked behind my lids, my eyes darted with frantic messages they couldn't read.

Nothing worked. Not my arms, my legs, fingers, toes.

I was paralyzed.

And then…a warm burst of magic seeped into my veins, growing hotter until the lassitude melted away.

Slowly, as if wading through molasses, I forced out a single word. "Colby."

Sunlight glinted off the gleaming coffee table to stab me in the eye with its cheery brightness.

"Hey." Asa cupped my face in his hands. "You're awake."

"Am I?" I cuddled nearer to him. "You're on the floor."

The rest of our surroundings filtered in, dust motes whirling through the beams of my waking mind.

I was stretched out under a blanket on the couch in the guys' suite. Asa was sitting on the floor with his side pressed against the couch, a foot away from my face. He had, I realized, been standing guard while I slept, which was odd. I didn't even remember…

"Colby." I jackknifed off the couch, kneeing the side of his head in the process. "Where is she?"

Panic shot me to my feet, and I sprinted for her room before he could confirm she was there.

"In here," Clay called after identifying the stampeding elephant as me. "She's with me."

Pivoting too fast, I smacked into a wall, bounced off, then reversed direction.

"What's wrong?" I yelled as I burst into the room. "What happened?"

I rushed to where she lay, cat-sized, on a pillow with a blanket up around her shoulders.

A blanket.

Not *her* blanket.

Fresh panic glazed my spine as I hit my knees beside the bed and stroked her downy fuzz.

"She was working on whatever project you gave her, and she conked out. She missed a guild meeting, so one of her friends shot me an in-game message to ask if everything was okay. I didn't see that until *after* you passed out in Asa's lap and mentioned Shorty."

"How long has she been asleep?"

"Same as you." He flashed me his screen to show the time. "About sixteen hours."

"Has she stirred at all?"

"After she got her eight hours in, I started waking her at the top of every hour to force sugar water down her. That seems to help, but she falls back asleep after."

"That's why I passed out." I turned it over in my head. "She was so exhausted, she wiped me out too."

The familiar bond ran both ways, but there were precautions in place on my end, as the anchor.

For her need to have been so great that she short-circuited those protections, her energy stores must have dipped to dangerous levels. A terrifying thought when she was a pure soul, pure energy.

"This isn't a natural ailment." Asa leaned in the doorway. "It can't be."

Hearing our voices, Colby fussed in her sleep, reaching for and then discarding the comforter.

"She keeps asking for her blanket," Clay said, tucking her back in, "but we haven't found it yet."

"She brought it on the trip." I saw her with it a few times. "She had it when we left the hotel."

"Did she leave it in the SUV?" Clay sat up on his side of the bed. "I didn't want to leave her to check."

"It was here." I was sure of it. "In this rental."

"Someone has been in our rooms." Asa drew the only logical conclusion. "How did they get past the wards?"

"Good question." I leaned over to kiss Colby's forehead then stood. "We need to figure that out, but first, we're going to break whatever hold this has over her before it digs in any deeper." I singled out Clay. "Give me five minutes, then bring Colby to the kitchen."

Thoughts spinning, I didn't notice Asa following me until I bumped into him while retrieving my kit.

"How can I help?" He steadied me. "Tell me what to do."

His concern for her touched me, and I was grateful he was holding on to his skin. The daemon must be freaking out right about now. He and Colby were growing closer, and the daemon loved his people hard.

"Run to the store." I shoved him toward the door. "Buy as much salt as you can find."

Without hesitation, he palmed the keys and left, giving me just enough time to draw a simple circle using what salt remained in the shaker from the kitchen. From my kit, I pulled rosemary, thyme, oregano, and rue.

My namesake.

The alias I chose as a ward against evil was the last ingredient I mixed with the other herbs in a mortar.

As I tested the consistency, deciding the fragrant mix was correct, Clay entered the room.

"Put her in the circle." I waited until he withdrew to sprinkle the herbs in a tight ring butting up against the salt. "Don't let her flutter until I finish."

One flap was all it would take to blow away my work, which would cost us time Colby might not have.

"Got it." He placed a gentle hand on her back to pin her wings against her sides. "Come on, Shorty."

Her antennae jerked, but she didn't open her eyes or raise her head.

"Stay put." I ran to the nearest closet and emptied it of lavender sachets, ripping them open on my way back. "It's not as good as fresh, but it ought to do." They could have been in there for years, but the spell would perk up any remaining oils. "One more ring ought to do it." I chewed on my bottom lip, debating, then remembered. "There are bath salts in the welcome basket."

Between the two baskets, I had enough to build a thick outer ring. Better yet, there were lavender buds and cornflower petals mixed in, giving the blend an extra boost.

As I adjusted it to my satisfaction, Asa strode into the room with two canvas totes full of salt.

Kosher salt, truffle salt, sea salt, coarse salt, fleur de sel, table salt, red, black, and smoked gray salt too.

The gourmet assortment coaxed a low whistle out of Clay. "Did you knock over a chef or something?"

Sure enough, the bags, jars, and boxes within were marked with logos from various trendy restaurants.

"Several." Asa ignored Clay and handed me the goods. "Is it enough?"

"This is perfect." I pressed a quick kiss to his lips. "Thank you."

The rest was messy work, but it was simple. I poured out every grain of salt onto the table in rings that grew larger as they fanned outward, until the entire surface held the design.

"This will purge her," I told them. "Depending on what's wrong, it might not be pretty."

A simple spell would break under the pressure I was about to apply, but there was nothing simple about how fast she had been drained to unconsciousness.

"Clay, you can let go now." I waved them both back. "You won't be able to reach her through the wards, so don't try. You'll get a nasty burn for your trouble, and you still won't touch her."

The guys moved into position, one at either of my shoulders, ready in case this effort drained me. Given my reserves were low too, I didn't mind the hovering.

Withdrawing my wand, I closed my eyes and focused on the familiar bond I shared with Colby.

Inside the salt rings, she was stronger, her light brighter, and I didn't waste more time with indecision.

Murmuring a spell under my breath, I tapped my wand against the table and pushed energy into the tip until a dozen miniature wards sprang to life around Colby. A pang in my chest, reminiscent of a pulled muscle, warned me I might have done my job too well. The familiar bond wasn't happy about the barriers between me and my power source, but I fought down the panic threatening to clog my throat.

A heartbeat later, my ears popped, and Colby's eyes flung open.

Too bad mine chose that moment to close.

12

"I'm tired of being the weak link," I mumbled, unwilling to open my eyes again. "Give me a heart."

Arms too limp to bend, I wiggled my fingers, waiting for warm meat to hit my palm.

"You're not the weak link." Asa's familiar hands stroked my face. "And I would carve out my own first."

"Don't say things like that." I cracked one eyelid. "It makes me feel unaccountably violent."

"I like when you're unaccountably violent on my behalf."

"I know." A smile tickled my lips. "You shouldn't encourage me."

"Colby is fine." He gave me what I wanted before I could articulate the question. "She's bored, but fine."

"How long was I out this time?"

"Three hours." He planted a hand on my shoulder to pin me to the couch. "Go easy."

During the brief time Colby had been my familiar, I had already gotten used to the boost she gave me. A typical white witch didn't pack much of a punch. Given I had been trained in black magic, which required a heck of a lot more power to fuel spells, I had been downright puny during the Silver Stag copycat case.

This was a good reminder that, without Colby to draw on, I was still punching far above my weight class.

After clasping forearms with him, I gave a tug. "Help me up?"

Slowly, he lifted me into a seated position. I managed that without dizziness, so he eased me to my feet. The room attempted to spin at its corners, but I trusted Asa to keep me from eating hardwood.

With him by my side, I walked into the kitchen to check on Colby, still safe within the salt rings.

"Rue." Her wings jerked once. "How are you feeling?"

"Like a balloon that got popped," I confessed. "How about you?"

"Like I had the best sleep of my life." She bounced her shoulders. "I could fly for *days*."

"That's great." I couldn't fight my smile. "But your wings are clipped for the next few hours."

"Why?" Her antennae stiffened. "I'm not tired anymore."

"See, here's the thing." I rubbed the back of my neck. "You weren't sick. You were a snack."

An inferno burst to life at my elbow, and the daemon bellowed in fury.

"Who hurt Colby?" He swung his head in search of the culprit. "I make them a snack."

Lip curled, fangs on display, he punched his open palm with his massive fist.

"You don't make them a snack." Colby palmed her forehead. "You feed them a knuckle sandwich."

"I not feed them." The daemon frowned. "I kill them." He tightened his hand. "With my knuckles."

A laugh slipped out of her before she could catch it, but she blamed the herbs for making her sneeze.

"Hold on, big guy." I rubbed his shoulder. "There's no one in need of a beatdown." I paused. "Yet."

"Rue sure?" He punched his palm again. "I ready."

"There's a saying about people who have been preyed on by boo hags," I explained, drawing from what I had read of Asa's file on them. "It's kind of odd. They say you were ridden by one."

"Pet." The daemon thrust his hair at me. "Then tell story."

"Brat." I really had to quit caving to his demands. "I glossed over it the first time I heard it. It sounds…"

I rolled a hand to indicate Clay should fill in the blank for himself, since the daemon held a kind of innocence that wouldn't extend to the sexual innuendo, and I wasn't enlightening Colby either.

"Then I thought it must mean people who were spiralized," I continued. "That the boo hag wore them."

"You don't think that now?" Clay wiped a smile off his face, but its imprint lingered. "What then?"

"Jilo mentioned stealing breath." I kept stroking the daemon's hair while he hummed low in his throat. "It's called being ridden because a boo hag will straddle your chest while you're asleep, lean down, and steal your breath. Except it's not your breath, like she said, it's your soul."

"Colby is soul." The daemon lowered his arms. "Boo hag eat Colby."

With the Proctor grimoire still playing hard to get with information on Colby, I wasn't sure how a *loinnir* was made. And yes, I realize that's crazy talk since I had created one. But, in our case, it was a spur-of-the-moment decision made in desperate haste.

When I pondered her substance, I always pictured one of those handblown glass swans with the colored liquid in them. A fragile but beautiful exterior with an ethereal substance within. A beautiful creation that one careless move could shatter into a million pieces.

It was wrong of me, I know, when she was so much stronger than anyone gave her credit for.

But she was also my little moth girl, and on bad days, when cases dug under my skin, I looked at her and didn't see the brave spirit but heard the broken sobs as she begged me to save her.

"Colby is safe within the wards." I checked with her. "How are you hunger-wise?"

"I'm never going to eat again." She sat back to show us her distended belly. "I'm ready to pop."

"Can you make it three or four hours?"

"I don't know." She considered the rings flowing out from her. "I might die of boredom by then."

"I've got an idea." Clay held up a finger. "Gimme a minute."

While he was gone, I negotiated with the daemon for Asa's return.

All it cost me was the caramel apple, with nuts, he didn't get last time.

Clay came back with the coffee table from the living room. He set it in front of the table, then placed a chair on top. On the seat, he propped her laptop open on Mystic Realms. Beside it, on his computer, he opened a YouTube channel on cheat codes and secrets then hit play.

"How about this?" He clicked a few keys. "You can talk to your friends and plan your next quest."

"Epic." She rubbed two sets of hands together. "Thanks."

Hooking my arm through Asa's, I tugged him closer. "Chopped liver and I are heading out."

Clay shot us a hard stare. "So am I."

"No." I smiled, and it was predatory. "You're going to wait right here for our uninvited guest to arrive."

"Okay." His answering grin promised violence. "Maybe I could use a few pointers too."

For Colby to fade so fast, the boo hag must have been a nightly visitor since we arrived in Charleston. Or, at the very least, since we switched from the hotel to the rental. Yeah. That felt right. Fewer witnesses here. We occupied an entire floor, and the building under us was empty. As far as we knew.

That didn't explain how a boo hag got past the wards, but I had an idea of where I made my mistake.

"Asa, we need to check the restaurant." I tossed Clay a lavender sachet. "If you get in trouble, rip that open and toss the buds."

"Sounds easy enough." He eyed the pouch with curiosity. "What did you do to it?"

"Nothing."

"Lavender is to boo hags what silver is to wargs?"

"Boo hags can be defeated by forcing them to count until the dawn takes them," Asa explained. "Colby will be safe behind the ward rings. You're the one in danger. Use the lavender. Whoever shows can't count that many buds before you find something else to throw at them."

Intent, imbuing an object with purpose, must be what forced a boo hag to stop and count specific items. A broom left outside to ward them off did exactly that. Marbles by the bed? A brush on the nightstand?

Normal people could use common items, no magic required, to defeat boo hags. Pretty large loophole, if your prey is plain vanilla human. Small wonder so few boo hags remained with such an easily exploitable weakness.

"Good to know." He tossed the bag and caught it. "I'll break out the spices if our boo hag's a prodigy."

The pantry was stocked with basic seasonings, minus the salt I had stolen. It was a solid backup plan.

"Looks like it's just you and me." I fisted Asa's shirt and hauled him down for a kiss. "Let's go."

A growl pumped through his chest, and the glamour concealing his gleaming horns flickered for a beat.

With my kit depleted, and my link to Colby filament thin, I wasn't the best choice for this.

But the joy of the hunt sang in me, echoed in Asa, and our hearts pounded as we left Clay and Colby behind.

Holed up in the elevator, its descent eternal, I sucked in a sharp breath when my back hit the wall.

Asa pinned me to the metal with his hips, speared one hand through my hair, and yanked my head back. His mouth closed over mine, bruising in its intensity, and our hearts synced. I slid my hands under his jacket, relishing the hard muscle flexing under my palms.

When that wasn't enough, I traced the ridges of his abdomen with a clawed finger, careful not to shred his shirt. I stroked the metal buckle on his belt with my thumb, and his groan turned my knees to jelly. I was about to investigate the zipper on his pants when a lethargic *ding* interrupted us.

Lips slick and swollen, Asa cleared his throat and slid his arms out from under my shirt.

I didn't remember that part.

Pity.

A scrap of serviceable cotton hung from his fingertips.

"That," I said with utter confidence, "is my bra."

Upon closer inspection, I saw he had sliced through the band with a frantic claw.

"I'll buy you another one." He folded it and put it in his pocket. "That one suffered from defective manufacturing."

"Obviously." I tried my best not to laugh. "They don't make 'em like they used to, huh?"

In the polished metal walls, I studied his flushed cheeks in reflection, but he didn't look sorry.

If anything, he looked determined, and he hadn't taken his hand out of his pocket.

A pleasant heat unfurled through me, and the temptation to go for another elevator ride itched under my skin. But we had a job to do. And, in the small eternity required for the doors to open, I got myself under control.

The space before us loomed dark and dusty. The ghosts of grease and smoked meats haunted the place. The furniture had been removed, leaving a massive empty room with restrooms off to one side and a kitchen in the other direction. There must be a storage area, maybe a smokehouse too.

Drawing my wand, I prowled into the room and began clearing it with Asa a step behind me.

"Rue—"

Flames ignited as the daemon stole Asa's skin again and emerged with a snarl.

"Rue follow." He waved me on. "I show Rue."

Through the kitchen, he marched, passing me a lock of hair over his shoulder in clear demand of pets.

Given how hot and heavy Asa and I had been minutes earlier, I couldn't fault his other half for asking for an equal share of my affection. In his preferred currency, of course. But dang it. The promise of an apple had only bought me about ten minutes with Asa. I was hoping for more.

Kisses.

Touches.

Defective clothing...

Without missing a beat, the daemon aimed straight for a steel wood-and-charcoal-fired pit. One of Clay's cooking shows might have called the flat top a fire table. The oven, or fire box, was tucked to the side. There were baskets for smoking vegetables too.

A rig like this cost a fortune. It must have been custom, probably built by a local craftsman. Either the previous owners hoped it would enjoy a second life with the next people to lease the space, or they simply couldn't afford to pull it out and take it with them.

"Eerie." I touched the grate. "Everything else is gone, but this is pristine with all its attachments."

"No." He caught my wrist. "Look." He lifted the metal. "See?"

"Charred bone shards." I curled my fingers into my palms. "Jilo didn't mention hags like barbeque."

Indelicate as it might be to say so, human flesh was mild, not gamey. It might not pass for chicken, it was a bit dry, but turkey? Smoked turkey? Yeah. I could buy that. Only once decomposition set in did human remains distinguish themselves from other rotting meats. No wonder we hadn't picked up on it sooner.

Pretty sure our killer had been incinerating the remains of their victims, with magical help, to avoid tweaking our noses, which left me lost as to why we had one set of physical remains.

Had the body sighting and the leg been a wild-goose chase? Had Marah been daunted to work alone? Had she panicked and dumped it before securing this place?

Most importantly, how in the heck did we end up staying above her new killing grounds?

Something smelled fishy, and it wasn't the harbor.

What had Clay told us? That a cashier at the biscuit shop gave him the tip to rent this place? A cashier whose father happened to own prime real estate in the heart of downtown? A cashier he met *after* the desk clerk at the hotel we ditched passed on a coupon for that very shop?

Dollars to donuts, the desk clerk was a boo hag. The cashier at the biscuit shop too. The father? He may or may not exist. For all we knew, the person who owned the property was killed for it. That might have been last week or last year. We had no way to know without more information. The rest? It was likely backstory to fit the boo hag agenda.

One thing was for certain.

Boo hags had tracked our every step in this city. Easy to do when a motley crew of well-dressed creatures descending upon downtown would have heralded Black Hat's arrival to anyone watching.

Using their victims as camouflage, they had led us around by the nose, and we never even noticed.

"No scent left." His forehead creased. "Think it human."

"Yeah." I sifted his hair through my fingers in a nervous gesture. "Me too."

With my free hand, I snapped pictures and recorded a video for our records.

Then, to keep him in the loop, I texted Clay.

>*Pretty sure we've got human remains in the fire pit.*

>>*Want me to bring down the hot sauce?*

Gallows humor used to fly over my head. I was too literal with it. Now it made me roll my eyes.

>*Have you touched base with your biscuit shop girlfriend?*

>>*I meant to ask her out, but then the witches happened, and I swore off women for all eternity.*

Eternity, in that context, might last six months. Last time, it stretched maybe six weeks.

>*I think she was ridden by a boo hag to maneuver us into position.*

>>*I'm not saying you're wrong, but that's a lot of moving parts.*

>*Think about it. The desk clerk at the hotel gave you the coupon, pointing you toward Bridge's Biscuits. Bridge's Biscuits is a breakfast joint. They're only open from eight to twelve five days a week. Limited hours means limited staff.*

>>*No matter when I went, she would have been there.*

>*Exactly.*

>*She sees you, swoops in, and spins a story about her dad owning this amazing property you could rent for a steal. With the killer using downstairs for body disposal, upstairs was likely kept empty. That left it ready for us to move in, and it put us right where they wanted us.*

And if that hadn't worked, they would have tried a different angle.

The possibilities for machinations were endless when you can be anyone to suit your narrative.

>>*Dammit.*

>>*Why can't anyone love me for me? Or at the very least my extensive wig collection?*

>*Text her. See if she responds. Then report back.*

All my failures paraded behind my closed eyes while I waited with my phone in my hand.

>>*Hey, I found that weird spell book of yours in my tent.*

I did a double take before I noticed it was Aedan, and not Clay, touching base.

>>*Did you leave it there? I must have missed it. Am I supposed to protect it while you're gone?*

That goddessdamned grimoire was up to its old tricks again.

I was an idiot for not destroying the book after the first glimpse of its contents.

No more excuses. No more bargaining. No more delays.

A black witch was sniffing around the shop, and it decided to pay Aedan, an employee, a visit?

Nope.

Not happening.

Arcane objects craved fulfillment of their purpose, and I was not letting it hitchhike to a new master.

>*Pick up the book and toss it in the fire pit.*

The outdoorsy Christmas gift from me wasn't fancy, but it was sturdy, and it ran on propane.

>>*Are you serious?*

>*As a heart attack.*

>>*Are you sure you don't want to do it yourself when you get home?*

Once the daemon cleared the rest of the space and declared it empty, he gave me back Asa.

>*Burn it then dump the ashes in the creek.*

The sticky front door jammed my shoulder when I shoved through it out onto the sidewalk.

>*I would ask you to video chat with me while it roasts, but we're following a lead. Film it for me?*

>>*Sure. Yeah. I'll do that.*

>*Good.* I exhaled through my teeth. *Thanks.*

Asa let me walk off my mad on the way to the parking deck, and I vented to him the whole time.

"Do you feel better?" Asa palmed his keys. "More importantly, do you think it will work?"

"I feel...ready to tear out the pages and use them as toilet paper if it doesn't."

"Then let's hope it does." He stepped back as the liftgate engaged. "The last thing you need is for its magic to clog your septic tank."

From the SUV, we loaded backpacks with gear for mausoleum spelunking.

"What's in this?" A gallon of sand was my guess. "It weighs a ton."

"This and that." He pressed a hefty metal flashlight into my hand. "Keep this at the ready."

"Hags aren't repelled by light." I tested its unexpected weight. "I could crack a skull with this."

"We don't know what condition the tunnels will be in." He took a flashlight for himself. "If we have to fight our way out, we need to see what's around us." He hesitated. "Your power is diminished with Colby cut off from you. That means we rely on your magic as little as possible."

"Until we need it."

"Until we need it," he agreed with grim acceptance that told me how worried he was for me.

"I made it ten years as a white witch without drawing on Colby, and I didn't die once."

"While I respect that—" he stroked my cheek, "—I'm of the opinion once is one time too many."

Black witches were hard to kill, and I had enough accumulation in me to keep me alive unless someone relieved me of my head. Probably. Healing grievous wounds took years or decades, but it could be done. There was a slight chance someone with my pedigree might even survive having their heart taken.

But I was in no rush to find out how much immunity my lineage offered now that I practiced white craft.

Especially when the risks I took with my life gambled with Colby's as well.

>>*Biscuit shop girl's number has been disconnected.*

"Aedan again?"

"Clay." I shook my head. "The number the cashier gave him has been disconnected."

The pattern emerging left me convinced we were being played. We just had to figure out by who.

13

As fate would have it, we had to wait for a ghost tour to finish at the cemetery before we could break in. There was probably a metaphor in there if you squinted hard enough, but I was too antsy after Aedan's texts to find it. This case deserved my full attention, but my thoughts kept drifting back to Samford, to the black witch, to the grimoire.

"I've never understood the fascination." Asa stared through the ornate bars. "It's macabre."

"Maybe so, but it's a win/win if everyone plays their cards right."

"What do you mean?" He walked with me to the front gate. "I can't imagine the churches are thrilled."

"A lot of tour companies in cities like this pay for exclusive access after dark. That money goes into preserving the cemetery, or graveyard, and restoration projects for tombstones, mausoleums, and statuary."

"What's the difference between them?"

"Graveyards and cemeteries?" I waited for his nod. "Graveyards are attached to churches."

That was the simple answer.

"Hence the *yard*."

"Hence the yard," I agreed with a grin. "A cemetery is public burial ground not affiliated with a church."

I was starting to feel like a guide myself. How fun would that be? To preach haunted history for a living?

"So," I kept going, "tourists get their ghoul on, tour companies get to make a little extra for having the right access, and churches and cemeteries get help paying for maintenance they can't afford to keep up their curb appeal for future residents."

"How do you know about this?"

"When I was a newbie agent, Clay took me on a *lot* of ghost tours. It was a fun way to learn our region." Most agents were assigned to an area. Only specialists or consultants got sent to the greatest need. "It was also a good way to learn the hotspots in town while surrounded by the safety of a dozen humans."

Any paranormal creature would think twice before making a move in front of so many eyewitnesses.

Basically, it was the perfect setup for Clay to teach me the ropes, protect me, and entertain me.

That was how I learned about the symbiosis of ghost tour companies, tourists, and churches.

Though the same logic extended to historic homes, landmarks, and other cash-strapped organizations.

"The coast is clear." I grinned at Asa. "Let's get our boo on."

Given how busy the streets remained after dark, and the routine nature of tours in the area, I wasn't too concerned with giving us away to any boo hags lurking inside the mausoleum. I imagined, after a while, muffled by the thick marble walls, the outside chatter got to be white noise.

A touch of my wand to the lock popped it open, and we eased inside the gate, shutting it behind us.

From this point on, we would remain as quiet as the graves surrounding us as we crept toward our goal.

The Thurman mausoleum was easy to spot, as it was the largest and most central one in the cemetery.

Stained marble, abundant moss, and rusted metal gave the place an air of neglect.

There were, however, footprints on the steps leading up to the wrought iron door.

Asa came up beside me, and I unlatched the ornate lever holding the tomb shut without so much as a scrape. It swung open under my hand, and, to my utter shock, the tunnel ahead was brightly lit.

No cheap camping lanterns here. They had electricity. Wired in a *long* time ago, based on the fixtures.

A prickle of unease raised the hairs down my arms as Jilo's intel replayed on a loop in my head.

This didn't fit the story she pitched us.

What loomed ahead wasn't some low-rent hidey-hole. This was an old nest with amenities that suggested it was in frequent use and had been for years. Long before our first victim went missing.

Asa and I exchanged a wary glance, and then the daemon claimed his skin in a crackle of eagerness.

Unlike the stale restaurant from earlier, the air here was fresh. Clean. Helped along by strong currents that blew hair into my eyes. Either they recirculated their oxygen, or the tunnel was open at both ends.

Wand in hand, I took point, aware the daemon was not happy with me acting as his shield.

With him plastered to my back, I wasn't sure I was walking ahead so much as he was pushing me from behind. The only reason he didn't hook an arm around me was he understood I required a certain range of motion to use my magic.

Whoever oversaw this nest took their housecleaning duties seriously. The ceiling was cobweb free, the walls polished, and the floors had only a day's foot traffic to dust them. The lights overhead glowed in a neat row, unbroken by burnt-out bulbs.

The tunnel veered left, and the daemon edged around me to take the turn first.

"Hello."

The broken silence was deafening, or maybe it was the sudden thunder of my pulse in my ears as I stepped forward to find a young woman with a Civil War-era saber held against the daemon's throat.

"Hi." Cold rage echoed in my voice that the walls threw back at me. "Mind lowering your weapon?"

"Mind lowering yours?" Her gaze flicked to my wand. "I don't want to hurt your mate, but I will."

The mate comment sailed past me, muffled by the roar in my head. But I forced myself to calm down, to think past the caustic bubble in my gut that craved flesh between my teeth. This woman was rational, more rational than me at the moment, and that didn't fit with Jilo's summation of the problem either.

Next time we saw her, Jilo had some 'splainin' to do.

"Okay." I slid my wand into its pocket in my pants. "Let's talk."

"For future reference, it's rude to barge into someone's home. Next time, just knock."

"I apologize for our rudeness." I had to bite my tongue to get out the words. "I'm Rue."

The woman lowered her blade and didn't fuss when I yanked the daemon to me.

"Marah."

We shook hands like civilized people, made easier by the fact she was wearing one of her human kills.

Maybe not so civilized after all, when you really thought about it.

"We have a sitting room for visitors, if you want to work things out there." She smiled up at the daemon. "I have cookies." She chuckled. "They're not a bribe from the dark side, but they do have chocolate chips, pecans, and toffee pieces."

"Like cookies," the daemon reminded me. "Rue talk?"

"I'll bake cookies for you when we get back," I promised. "Probably not a great idea to eat them here."

Marah gave no sign of insult at my thinly veiled accusation that she might poison us, or, based on what we saw in the restaurant, feed us a new flavor of people cookie.

Seriously, when had those gained such popularity?

"Okay." The daemon thrust a handful of hair at me. "We talk."

"Right this way." The woman gestured us to follow her. "It's not much, but it's home."

The tunnel flared out into a twelve-by-twelve block laid out like a living room. Beyond it loomed the first security measure so far. A thick metal door with dented rivets and a patina of age guarded what must be the entrance to their inner sanctum. An old smuggler's route indeed. I wondered if it opened on the sea.

"We sit." The daemon claimed a plush sofa and patted the cushion beside him. "Sit, Rue."

Rue sat.

Right beside a large basket stuffed with glossy leaves and bright white flowers.

Oleanders.

The sprigs already twisted into the beginnings of a wreath like the one we found in the alley.

"I don't have to ask why you're here." The woman sank into a chair. "Jilo has been telling tales."

"Black Hat has rather grim views on murder sprees that bring attention to paranormals."

On occasion, it paid to be upfront. Especially with a murderous faction of people peelers.

After this debacle, the boo hags needed to know Black Hat existed, that we were aware of them, and we allowed their continued existence. On our terms. Which I was all too happy to enforce.

"Black Hat." She sat up straighter. "You're really one of them?"

"Afraid so." I leaned forward, elbows on knees. "Tell me about the spell on Fort Sumter."

It was a shot in the dark, but I hit the target with startling accuracy based on the jerk of her shoulders.

"Our grasp on magic isn't so different from yours. We did what we could to mitigate the damage."

She meant to imply she and I were alike, that black arts bound us, but I had broken free of those chains.

"Does that include having one of your people take a desk clerk at the hotel we stayed in our first night in Charleston? The same hotel where the rest of the agents have set up camp for the duration? Or a cashier at Bridge's Biscuits? What about her? Her 'dad'? Park rangers? Teachers? Spa owners?"

"We don't exactly track one another's avatars. What would be the point? We can scent our own kind."

Ah, the vague answer of a seasoned politician. Always open to interpretation.

"The wreaths were your handiwork."

She wanted me to know that. Appreciate it. Maybe even to thank her for it.

To memorialize the victims spoke of regret, but it struck me as staged for our benefit.

"Yes." She dipped her gaze to her basket. "A token of remorse."

"I've heard Jilo's side of things." I tuned out her attempts to humanize herself. "Tell me yours."

"There's a creation myth," she began, and settled in to tell her story. "The first boo hag, Sorie, was…"

The cadence was practiced, as if she told it often, and she didn't deviate from Jilo's tale by a single word.

Curious how she would spin it, I asked, "How does that tie into Jilo?"

"She believed the story was true." Marah tucked her legs under her. "She was convinced it was the way to save our kind. We only had to be brave enough to try." She made herself smaller. "We refused to risk even one life with so few of us left, so Jilo swore to do it alone. I don't know the specifics, but she did it." She dug her fingers into the arm of her chair. "She always was a little on the nose. She named him Sorie. He is an all-consuming hunger that is never sated, no matter how many times she kills and feeds him. He is proof of her beliefs, and she is willing to let the grume face a different kind of extinction to keep him."

Based on her stricken expression, she meant death by Black Hat, which was, after all, why we were here.

"Sorie caused the divide between you and Jilo." I tamed my temper to say, "You cast them both out."

To wreak havoc on their own.

"We are forbidden to harm one another, so our only recourse was to cast them out. It broke our hearts, to lose that spark of hope for a new generation, and our old friend, but we had to protect ourselves. We knew someone would come, eventually, when we quit cleaning up behind them. We've been waiting."

...when we quit cleaning up behind them.

Our killer at turns appeared both eager and reluctant to get caught, and I was starting to see why.

There were two different factions within the grume working against one another for different outcomes.

But which was which? Who was harboring Sorie? Who was ensuring he and his progenitor got caught?

"You expect me to believe Jilo is evil, but trust that you're sunshine and puppies."

"Like puppies," the daemon informed me. "Puppies soft."

Afraid the next descriptor out of his mouth might be *crunchy*, I kept going before he did.

"According to Jilo, you're a baby-crazed boo hag who tore herself in two to create Sorie. She claims it's you, not her, who has killed enough humans to garner our attention." I drummed my knee. "Forgive me, but it sounds like you're two buddies who had a falling out and now want to get the other in trouble."

"The best lies mirror the truth."

Leaving us with two similar stories from two opposing sides that each contradicted the other.

I didn't trust either of them. Jilo or Marah. There had been too much death for me to pick a side.

"You're the one who greeted us. Does that make you this grume's leader?"

"Yes," she said after a moment. "I suppose it does, but we don't view it that way."

"Then why does Jilo want to pin this on you?"

"Jilo believes that if she kills me, she will be welcomed home. She blames her excommunication on me." A flicker of grief washed over her. "She refused to leave, so I had no choice but to physically remove her and ban her from the nest." Steel entered her gaze. "The others support me. They won't take her back."

"Sounds like you've got it all figured out then."

The heavy metal door I noticed upon entering swung open to reveal two young men holding hands.

"Marah?" The taller one pushed his companion behind him. "Is everything all right?"

"They're guests," she assured him. "You have nothing to fear."

With a curt nod, he sidled along the wall to the exit then shoved the other man out ahead of him.

"You'll have to forgive them." She stared after the pair. "We can't afford to trust anyone these days."

"I know exactly what you mean." I rose, and so did the daemon. "We've got all we need, for now."

"We'll be here, if you decide to visit again." She spread her hands. "We're homebodies."

The daemon gave himself over to Asa, who reached in his pocket and flung a handful of BB gun pellets.

"Forgive me." Asa touched the small of my back. "Our experience with Jilo has taught us caution."

"I understand." A brittle smile crimped Marah's face as she hit to her knees. "One, two, three…"

With firm pressure, which I didn't mind at all, Asa guided me out the way we had come. "Iron?"

"Steel." He kept a brisk pace beside me. "I couldn't risk a purer metal." He flexed his hand. "It doesn't appear to have affected Marah either way, but I thought it worth trying."

Iron burned the fae half of him, and a wound inflicted with it could kill him if his attacker had good aim.

Boo hags must not have that problem, which, if they did branch off witches, made sense.

"Are you hurt?"

"I'm fine."

"Ah, yes. *Fine*. I was fine once. I almost died from it."

A huff of laughter was my reward as he hustled me out of the mausoleum into the balmy night.

I let him keep pushing until we reached a well-lit area, then I twisted the hand I held to inspect it.

"Blisters." I flipped a stern glance up at him. "Why not admit you're hurt?"

"I'm not." He skimmed his other hand under my hair. "I'm mildly inconvenienced."

"Next time, give me the pellets. You stick to lavender buds or coins, got it?"

"For you?" His eyes glittered. "Badly, I'm afraid."

"You would live longer if you didn't." I searched his face. "I'm always almost getting you killed."

"You're worth the risk." He let me glimpse how much he believed it. "How do I make you see that?"

"Take me for an eye exam?" I attempted to laugh it off. "Sign me up for LASIK?"

A heavy sigh parted his lips, and he stared at me like he might shake me. "I love you."

The ground pitched under my feet, as if I were about to tumble off the edge of the world as I knew it.

"What?" I couldn't hear over the tectonic plates realigning within me. "I missed that."

"I love the woman you were, the woman you are, and the woman you will be."

Tears scalded the backs of my eyes and flooded down my cheeks in a tide I couldn't stem.

"I hate having feelings." I threw my arms around his neck. "I really do."

"I'm aware." He pressed his smile into my neck. "And I accept that about you."

"Good." I sniffled into his shirt. "I'm pretty sure I love you too."

"I'll take it." He laughed, nipping my ear. "As long as you mean it."

"I'm wearing a bracelet made of your hair, I sample all of your food, and I don't complain when you space out knitting and forget to make out with me."

"I promise to work on my memory." He rubbed his cheek against mine. "As long as you remember *one more chapter* isn't a proper greeting."

"Okay, okay." I held on tight. "We'll work on giving each other space to do what we enjoy."

"I like watching you blush when you read whale shifters finding love with plankton shifters."

"I like listening to you knit," I admitted. "The clacking noises are soothing."

"How about we work on giving each other clearer cues when we want more than joint hobby time?"

"Deal."

"Starting now." He adjusted his grip to cup my nape and pulled me closer. "I'll go first, if you like."

A groan tore out of me as the burn for him in my gut struggled against my common sense.

"Bad dae." I wriggled free. "You're not going to distract me with your mouth."

"I have these too." He held out his hands, palms up, and his eyes grew dark. "Did I change your mind?"

Asa loved me. He wanted me. And I...panicked like a cat tossed into bathwater.

"This is why Clay didn't want us getting involved." I clasped one of his palms, spun on my heel, and hauled him after me. "I'm a bad influence on you. You're a bad influence on me. One of these days, we're going to strip naked in a hag nest and do the nasty in front of a live audience if we don't get this under control."

"Is that a possibility?"

"Performance art?" I snorted. "Been there, done that. There were no T-shirts. Because we were naked."

"Interesting."

"It's really not." I decided it was easier to talk about intimate situations with him behind me. "I can't imagine wanting to share that with another person, or a whole group of them, if it meant something." I felt obligated to joke, to lighten the truth. "Don't get me wrong, the cheering is very motivational, and you do learn a lot when you're surrounded by instructors convinced the harder you orgasm, the bigger the percussive magical burst at the end, but it's hollow. Transactional."

"What I meant was, you're a private person. It's surprising you would agree to put yourself on display."

"That's the difference." We cut a sharp corner. "You know Rue. You didn't know who I was, you don't have a clue how bad it can get. I'm an addict, Asa. Don't fool yourself. I'm recovering, but I can always backslide. I could be that person again. The exhibitionist. The temptress."

The power-hungry maniac willing to punch through ribs to reach a juicy treat.

"Addiction makes a mockery of who we are and twists us into the worst versions of ourselves." I exhaled. "I don't know why I told you any of that. It can't be appealing to hear me talk about how willing I was to trade sex for power."

The joint in my shoulder popped when he quit walking while I simultaneously kicked into a higher gear. Before I could yelp, he spun me around, into his arms, and lowered his mouth to mine in a claiming I felt down to my black soul.

"You don't have to be perfect." He kissed a line across my jaw. "You just have to be mine."

Tears scalded the backs of my eyes at his easy acceptance of my past, and I wanted to shake him awake, force him to look at me, to see the reality of me, but I also wanted to blindfold him. I wanted him to keep his idealistic view of me, to light up whenever he saw me, to always believe the best in me.

Worst of all, I wanted him to know me. Past me, present me, future me. I wanted him to understand. And I wanted him to want me anyway. To keep loving me, despite it.

"And, Rue?" His teeth closed over my carotid, and I stuttered a gasp. "I won't share you."

"Forever is a long time," I rasped, hating how I always fought to contradict him.

"Not nearly long enough. Not for me." He licked across my collarbones. "Not for *us*."

A shuddering exhale moved through me as my head spun and knees wobbled under me.

"When you take me, and you will, it will be you and me." He bit hard enough to bruise. "Always."

When you take me...

A whimper passed my lips that he devoured, and again I saw the gleam of horns in the streetlights.

Shoving away from him, afraid he might have been seen, I whisper-screamed, "You're horny."

"Yes." His teeth glinted. "I am."

"No." I gestured to his head. "Horny."

"I am."

"You don't get it." Throwing caution to the wind, I gripped one black curve. *"Your horns are out, Asa."*

A full-body shudder rocked him when I traced the ridges with my thumb to make my point.

"I thought you liked them," he panted, breathless. "I did it for you."

"Oh." I dropped my hand. "I thought you were really into the moment and your glamour shorted out."

"I was into it." His chest pumped hard. "Which is why I elected to seduce you with my horns."

"You *flashed* me." I slapped a hand over my mouth, ridiculously giddy. "I can't believe you did that."

The pinch of his forehead warned me he wasn't sure if I was laughing at his gall or mocking him.

Happiness fizzing up in me, I flung my arms around his neck. "I liked it."

Not just the horns, either, but the idea he wanted to seduce me.

"Are you sure?" He searched my face. "You don't have to spare my feelings."

Gently, I pulled his head down to mine, then lower, until I flicked my tongue across the warm onyx.

Asa's knees buckled on a gasp, and he caught himself against me, his heart a runaway train.

Never in my life had I felt more powerful.

A rush of tenderness swept through me, swirling through my stomach in a hot swell of emotion.

For once, I didn't fight it as I peppered his forehead with kisses. "I am very sure."

"I can tell," he croaked, forcing his legs to support his weight. "I'm sorry I doubted you."

"Come on." I allowed myself to rake my fingers through his loose hair. "We should get back."

The three of us had to put our heads together and decide what game the boo hags were playing.

Plus, I wanted to check on Colby, make sure she was holding strong within the wards.

When Asa wobbled like a newborn colt, I wound a fistful of hair around my hand and led him. If the daemon could see us now, he would laugh himself silly. That, or he would pitch a tantrum and demand his new favorite thing.

Wash, brush, braid. All of it.

Truly, I had created a monster.

And I didn't mind.

Not one bit.

14

An eternity passed on our ride up to the second floor. I could say this much for the elevator. It was nothing if not consistent. Snails everywhere would envy its lethargic but steady pace and its refusal to be rushed.

A rank odor hit me when the doors slid open, and the bottom dropped out of my stomach.

I didn't check with Asa. I didn't call out for Clay. I *ran*. Straight to the kitchen where I left Colby.

"Hey." Clay waved a potholder-clad hand at me. "I made eggplant parmesan and garlic crostini."

"I read him the directions." Colby fluttered her wings. "He almost cut off a finger on the mandoline."

"Chefs don't share their secret ingredients," he told her out of the corner of his mouth. "Now hush."

Colby mimed zipping her lips, but she couldn't hide her smile.

She was back to her old self, and I was sick with the relief of it.

Unable to relax yet, I informed Clay, "I smelled black magic in the hall."

"That's rude." He tossed his mitt at me. "I spent hours on this masterpiece, and I didn't invoke the dark arts for help even once."

"Unless you baked a chocolate boo hag soufflé for dessert, we've got problems."

"Rue." Asa touched my shoulder. "Look."

A Dutch oven sat on the floor, the kind with a glass lid, and blackness whirled within it.

"What is that?" I stepped closer as red eyes blinked open. "*Who* is that?"

Based on what we learned tonight, I had a good idea, but I wanted to be sure.

"Wakey-wakey." Clay nudged the pot with his foot. "Time to spill your secrets, or I spill this rice."

A low growl vibrated the lid with a metallic clink, but the hag didn't speak.

"How did you catch it?" I peered at the dark mass. "Is it trapped in there?"

"I was about to boil pasta when our guest here attacked the wards on Colby. I dumped a handful of kosher salt crystals in the water, and the boo hag dove in to count them before they dissolved. I slapped a lid on, and I've been adding various things to the pot to keep it occupied since then."

That a boo hag could be compelled into a pot of boiling water for the sake of counting was hardcore.

Too bad it hadn't dissolved along with the salt, but that was probably hoping for too much.

"We visited Marah," I told Clay. "We heard her side of the story."

A low hiss rattled the lid, as if steam were escaping from the vent, but it didn't speak.

Instead, it threw itself against the sides, roaring and thrashing. "*Hungry.*"

The petulant tone warned a tantrum was coming, all but confirming who Clay had caught.

"I will set this pot in the window at high noon before I feed you my daughter."

A coiled spring wound tight in my chest, until my heart nearly burst with the enormity of my declaration.

I tap-danced around my relationship with Colby for both our sakes, but apparently all the *feelings* Asa was stirring up had me in a claiming mood on that front too.

Too chicken to check Colby for her reaction, I focused on the hag. "Who are you?"

"Sorie."

Confirmation wasn't half as sweet as it ought to have been, given how I suspected he crossed the wards.

"Why are you here, Sorie?" Asa stood at my shoulder. "Who sent you?"

"Momma told me the light would make me strong. She said take little bites until it was all gone."

Momma.

Marah claimed Sorie was Jilo's offspring. Jilo claimed Sorie was Marah's offspring.

Who was the mother? Split personality? Whatever.

"She left you in an empty suite, didn't she?" I pressed. "You were hiding in one when we arrived."

"He didn't cross the wards," Asa realized. "He was already within them."

"She told you to stay in your room," I kept going, putting it together, "until Colby fell asleep."

Then he crept down the hall to feed on her, with none of us the wiser.

"Hungry," he whined in a little-boy tone. "Momma will be mad you didn't feed me."

"Who is your momma?" Asa towered over Sorie's temporary cell. "Who made you?"

"Momma," he wailed in hiccupping sobs. "I want my momma."

"This isn't going to work." I patted Asa's chest. "Can you do another salt run?"

"No need." Clay jerked a thumb toward the kitchen. "I had a shopper snag every shaker in five miles."

"Excellent." I pushed the red-tipped bangs on his black wig out of his eyes. "Good thinking."

"Handsome *and* smart." Clay struck a pose. "I'm a total package."

"Mmm-hmm." I had a thought and grabbed a whole bag. "Asa and I are going down together."

"Language," Clay whisper-screamed. "Keep it PG. There's a kid present."

A tingle in my cheeks warned me they wanted to flush, but I refused to give Clay the satisfaction.

"Do you mind doing the honors, Asa?" I indicated the pot with my chin. "We need to move fast."

Sorie was growing more agitated as we interrogated him, and I got a funny feeling his momma wouldn't be too far behind if she sensed her offspring in distress. Maybe now we would finally get some answers.

But to do that, we had to get Sorie outside the wards so his mewling could draw his mother to us.

"You're on Colby detail," I told Clay then eyed her. "You're on Clay detail. Don't let him get in trouble."

"Rue?"

Her soft voice shot ice down my spine, and I couldn't bring myself to look at her.

"We have to go." I smiled in her general direction. "We can talk in a bit, okay?"

"Okay."

With Asa holding the pot, and me loaded down with salt, we hit the elevators.

"Colby might not consider you her mother," Asa said into the quiet, "but she views you as a mother figure."

"I don't know why I said it." I mentally kicked myself. "She's so prickly about her family, with good reason. That's why we don't do labels. She's not ready for them. I know that." I growled. "I know that, and I said it anyway." I thumped my head on the metal. "I'm blaming this on your fae juju, just so you know. It's all your fault. The verbal diarrhea is contagious and infects all aspects of my life now."

"I'm sorry." Asa brushed his elbow against mine. "I can't help it."

"I don't want to change you," I said, knowing he needed to hear me say so. "I need the nudge, truth be told." I shifted the weight in my arms. "Otherwise, I might have let you get away."

"I never tried to escape."

Stupid warmth unfurled in my chest, making it hard to breathe. "No common sense."

"Not where you're concerned, no."

"Momma," Sorie whimpered, shattering the moment. *"Momma."*

Three years later, the elevator doors glided open, and we stepped back into the restaurant.

"Where do you want to do this?" Asa reexamined the space.

"Does it matter?"

"Center of the room." I removed the handheld besom broom from my kit and knelt to sweep away the dust while I cleansed the space of negative energies with a chant under my breath. "Okay, set it here."

Careful not to track dirt into the space, he did as I instructed then pulled away to watch my back.

Tuning out my hormones, I settled in to create a multi-ring ward like the one I set for Colby. This one packed less of a punch, but it wasn't meant to protect Sorie. Just keep him from escaping until Momma graced us with her presence, and we put this twisted case to rest.

When instant gratification proved unforthcoming, Asa and I sat with our backs against a wall in a small salt circle of our own. Enough to protect us from a sudden attack but one easily broken from our side.

"Jilo and Marah are both full of crap." I pursed my lips. "What do you think is really happening here?"

"Jilo experimented on herself to prove reproduction is possible. Perhaps it's dedication to preserving the species. More likely, she wants to usurp Marah and claim the grume as her own. She's betting on a dying species siding with whoever can guarantee their survival, and Sorie is her proof they can still propagate."

"I would have expected Sorie to be female, since he was torn off a female, but he's clearly male."

"Perhaps his mother wanted him to embody their originator in all ways," he mused. "That would explain why she fixated on boy children. If it was merely portion control, as Jilo suggested, any child would have sufficed, but all the victims are male."

"He was the bait." I turned the idea over in my head. "I thought it was her, but this feels right."

As soon as the mark wandered out of sight of his caretakers, she swooped in for the kill.

"If he wore the victims," he agreed, "it would have reinforced his gender identity."

The idea of learning from a skin made me question whether Jilo had been lying when she said nothing of the owner remained after death.

"Why did we have to stumble across the one faction that can't handle its own housekeeping?"

"We didn't," he reminded me. "We were brought here for our housekeeping skills."

"So, Jilo can't outright kill Marah." I got back on track. "Or her supporters."

"The same goes for Marah," Asa countered. "She can't kill Jilo or her supporters."

"Marah has a good thing going." I turned her potential motives over in my head. "She's the leader of the grume. It's small, so low maintenance. There are few candidates to choose from to replace her. They live in a secure location in a city where they can hunt safely. She has everything she wants. Why risk dying to create offspring when she's content in her role? She's accepted the boo hags' fate. Jilo, clearly, has not."

"Their feud doesn't explain how the killer knew to target Colby."

That question had plagued me since the moment I pegged a boo hag as responsible for her ailment.

"In either scenario, Black Hat was drawn here to take out the competition, whether it be Jilo or Marah." I drew my knees to my chest. "Thanks to the company uniform, we're not what I would call inconspicuous. The boo hags wouldn't have had to work hard to locate a hotel hosting a paranormal predator convention." I let my gaze go unfocused as I pieced it together. "They were still there, watching, waiting, when the four of us got in. Boo hags feed on breath, on soul. They would have noticed Colby's light and fixated on her, the same as a vampire would pop a dental erection if they smelled fresh blood."

"The next morning, the desk clerk gave Clay the first push with the coupon for Bridge's Biscuits." He pursed his lips. "They've nudged us back in line any time we strayed too far from the path."

"Do you think the grume owns Witchy Ways?"

"What makes you think so?" Asa angled his head toward me. "Glinda?"

"Hear me out." I lined up my ducks in a row. "The spa is a legit business that could fund the grume. Their MO of preying on tourists works in both senses. New customers keep them flush. Fresh food prevents the grume from eating the locals and drawing too much attention. Plus, it explains the boat. It's good for work and play." I had to admit. "If you're going to be given a burial at sea, you can't go out much fancier than that." I lifted a finger. "*And* that much socializing gives them access to a steady flow of potential wrappers."

"You make a compelling—"

A grating whine filled my ears, followed by the clatter of shattering glass from a distant window.

"Incoming," I murmured, leaning forward. "Let's see who we've got."

Black mist seeped through the jagged cracks, flooding the far corner of the restaurant.

"Momma?"

Asa tensed beside me, ready to rise, but we couldn't identify the swirling particles yet.

"Baby." A hulking mass of raw bones and meat solidified before him. "Are you okay?"

The long-limbed creature was as familiar as it had been disturbing the first time we saw it au naturel.

For better or worse, we had our answer.

Sorie's momma was—drumroll, please—*Jilo*.

The lesson here?

Never trust a spiralized cat.

"I'm stuck." He sobbed louder than ever. "I can't get out."

"Who did this?" A roar shook the building. "Tell Momma, and I will kill them."

"Funny," I said from my spot on the floor. "I made the same vow earlier."

The tendinous beast that was Jilo pivoted toward us, vibrating with maternal rage.

"That creature upstairs is not a child," she spat, "and you are no one's mother."

"Not to cast stones at glass houses, but that's not your kid. That's a corner you tore off yourself."

A full-throated scream sent dust motes dancing when it sank in she had no recourse for the truth.

"Sorie is the first child spawned of boo hags in centuries," she growled. "His life is worth any price."

"What about the lives of your victims?" I set my jaw. "Don't you think their parents felt the same?"

"Humans multiply like fleas on a dog. They can spare a few for his sake."

"And Colby?" A dangerous calm settled over Asa's features. "How would you justify her death?"

"You don't understand." Her hands curled into fists. "That much pure energy would transform Sorie. The wait would be over. He would reach maturity in hours. With him by my side, proof he is the future of our species, I can go home." Her eyes shone fever bright. "No one would choose Marah over me then. There would be a reckoning." She toned the venom down a notch. "I would teach the others how I did it. How I made Sorie. We could rebuild our numbers, take back our city. We could own the night again." Her fangs gleamed sharply. "Those damn ghost tour guides with their bullshit blabbering would be the first to go."

An ear-shattering boom rattled the jagged glass in the windows, and doors smacked against the walls.

Agents dressed in black suits poured into the restaurant with guns, claws, axes, and fangs out.

"Keep your seats, ladies." Marty swaggered in with a wink for us. "Let the real men finish the job."

"You've got to be kidding me," I muttered. "How did he know…?"

\>\>*You're welcome.*

The text from Clay left me confused as to what he meant. Marty? He sent Marty to back us up? Why? Clay must have tipped him off about our plan as soon as we left for him to arrive with the cavalry so fast.

\>*What am I thanking you for, exactly? Asa and I could have handled Jilo and Sorie on our own.*

\>\>*I decided to speed things along so you can get back to the girls sooner. I know you're stressed about the black witch in town. And Colby. This way, we all get home faster. Just sit back, and let Marty do what Marty does.*

\>*I owe you a chocolate pound cake with raspberry glaze.*

\>\>*I'll hold you to that.*

"There's our killer," Marty barked, drawing my attention from my phone. "Grab it, boys."

Jumping to my feet, I pled with the idiot to save himself. "Marty, that's not going to—"

Like bees on a hive, the agents swarmed Jilo, who misted to avoid attack then solidified to strike.

The two men nearest her smacked the wall after a swat from her massive hand. She kicked three more and stomped a fourth under her heel. The wet crunch was nauseating, and it triggered the daemon.

"Protect Rue." He bulled around me, tucking me behind his wide back. "Stay put."

Bullets and magic shot through the air, along with screams and challenges, but Jilo kept swinging.

"What did Asa bring?" I kept a palm on the daemon's shoulder. "What can we use against her?"

I had a few things, but they doubled as spell prep ingredients. If things got ugly, I would need those.

"Here." He dumped a handful of warm metal into my palm. "Found in gift shop."

What I held resembled the BBs from earlier, but they were stuck in a glob.

How was this supposed to help?

One and done.

Unless...

I pinched one of the outer beads, and it came away between my fingers, but it resisted the whole way.

"Asa is brilliant." I stepped up beside the daemon, who grumped at me. "You are too."

While he preened, I tore off beads as fast as I could separate them and hurled them into the room.

A screech rent the air when Jilo noticed the glint of metal and was forced to begin counting each dot.

That was when Asa's true brilliance revealed itself.

Each time she put a bead in her hand, it stuck to the others.

Two became one.

Three became one.

Four became one.

Each time she added to her ball, she was compelled to restart her counting.

"Stop shooting." I waded into the center of the room. "Hey, you, put down that sword." I flung my arm toward the furious creature. "Can't you see you're not winning?" I craned my neck to see Marty. "Where did you find these goons?"

"These *goons* are going to apprehend this beast, and then the director will sing my praises for a change."

"Are you serious?" I kept picking and tossing the beads. "The director can't carry a tune in a bucket."

"Marty dumb," the daemon told me behind his hand. "He not know better."

"I heard that." Marty curled his lip. "Keep hiding behind your girlfriend, daemon scum."

Marty's head snapped back before it registered I had thrown a punch. Cupping his bent nose, he toddled backward until he fell on his butt. Blood dripped down his jaw and soaked into his collar.

"Rue like me," the daemon informed Marty. "She not like you." He kicked Marty in the chest and sent him sailing across the floor into the wall. "I not like you either."

Ignoring Marty's howled promises of vengeance, I clapped my hands to gain everyone's attention.

"You see what I did there? With the beads? Keep her counting. It's the only way to trap her. If you can occupy her until dawn, she goes *poof*, and she's no longer our problem." I indicated the pot. "There's another one trapped in there. I sealed it in. Leave it alone, and it will leave you alone. When the sun comes up, push it into the light, and it goes bye-bye."

The argument could be made that Sorie was an innocent. That, in his own way, he really was a child.

But he had fed on Colby, almost killing her, and those mitigating factors? No longer mattered to me.

I was a better person than I used to be, but Colby was Colby, and deep down, I was still a black witch.

"Before we go—" I scanned their faces, "—any questions?"

"Did you really slaughter an entire coven for claiming you were one of theirs?"

The young male witch asking made my heart hurt with how much he wanted it to be true.

"They put my name on their roster and my face on T-shirts." I stared him down. "What do you think?"

The same bleak hope that he had met a legend come to horrific life gleamed in his eyes. "Yes?"

The daemon cut me a very Asa-like look, as if he could guess where this was heading.

"They advertised their affiliation with me," I said slowly, to make sure it sank in. "They basically drew a bull's-eye on their backs then took out ads for people with good aim to fire at them. Eventually, someone did. I don't know who. I don't care. Not my problem if a group of people share a death wish."

"Okay." He bounced to a new topic. "What about—?"

"Does anyone have a question about this case? About the monster in this room? The one that almost killed you all?" I checked with the others, most too afraid to meet my eyes. "No? Good. Follow my instructions. Administer first aid to Marty, if you feel like it. Let him bleed out if you don't. Otherwise, Asa and I have somewhere to be."

Inches from the door, the witch stepped into my path. "Can I go with you?"

"Apologies, Elspeth." A vampire I half recognized glided over to us. "He's rather enthusiastic."

"So I see." I frowned at his trainee. "Maybe Black Hat will scuff his shine a bit."

Otherwise, he would die rushing into battles he couldn't win for the sake of writing his own legend in his head. One thing was for sure. No one here would be gripping a pen in his honor if he kicked the bucket.

"I worked my whole life to get here," the witch told me with obvious pride. "I'm ready for this."

A chill seeped into my marrow to think he had walked the fine line between recruitable and irredeemable with enough panache to get sworn in at such a young age. Though, with me as an idol, he had tried to beat my record of thirteen, I was sure.

Eager to ditch my fan club of one, I marched out the door. Behind me, the daemon ignited, caving to Asa between steps as he followed me out onto the street.

Hands smoothing his poor clothes into a semblance of order, he asked, "What did you have in mind?"

"Marah invited us for a visit, remember? We'd be rude not to call on her before we left town."

The cemetery gate stood open in invitation, which was not a great sign, but we beelined to the Thurman family mausoleum with a blossoming sense of dread. The ornate entry door was locked, the path closed.

"Marah knew we would be back." I switched on my phone's flashlight. "See that?"

The back wall had been bricked up with a powerful spell since our last visit, and magic ebbed to me from where I stood.

"No wonder she extended us an open invitation."

"They warded it." I placed a hand on the cool wall, and my pride took a hit. "I can't break it alone."

And the next to last place on Earth I would bring Colby—the first being the director's office—was here.

"Look." Asa crouched beside a black envelope with a blood red wax seal. "There's a card."

When the paper hit my palm, I tore it open with more violence than necessary.

"Rue," I read out loud. "I have no doubt you'll return to confront me and demand more answers, but the truth is, you won't be happy with any I give you. You must understand we tried to help Jilo control Sorie, but his hunger would have ruined us. Can you imagine the fallout, had she wrested control of the grume? A plague of newborns would have swept across the city, devouring any human in their path. I did what I thought was right. A woman like you, with your power, in your vocation, must understand the choices we make to ensure those under our protection remain safe at any cost. Truly, I am in your debt."

Paper crumpled in my fist as her words sank in and took root.

"Yours in friendship." I wanted to punch something. "That's how she signed it."

"We need this." He pried the wadded letter from my fingers. "Marty will need it for the case file."

"Let's head back." I kicked the brick for good measure. "See if he's still alive."

Sadly, Marty was still breathing, but there was always next time.

Although, thanks to Clay's foresight, he was also accepting handshakes for solving the case.

In taking credit, he agreed to accept responsibility for the paperwork, and we got a pass to go home.

Already, I was tapping my foot, eager to get back to Samford and check on the girls and Aedan.

Clay let himself into my room and leaned against the doorway, watching me pack my bag.

"You did a good deed for Marty." I folded my last shirt. "You're such a kind soul."

"I thought of all the help he gave us, the support and guidance."

Clay faked innocence. Badly. "How could I not reward him? I thought —You know what? Marty earned this. He deserves this."

"I appreciate your quick thinking." I sobered. "This black witch thing sets my teeth on edge."

No good ever came of a black witch paying a visit, myself included. Unless I had been stress baking.

"I don't like it either." He ruffled his hair. "We'll all feel better once we're home again."

A buzz in my pocket had me reaching for my phone. "Hollis."

"Hey." Arden exhaled in a gust. "I don't want you to panic or anything—"

Heart galloping, I clenched my hand around my cell. "What's wrong?"

"We've blown a fuse at the shop," she carried on, oblivious to my panic. "Aedan is checking the breakers, but there's a burnt smell in here. Do you want me to call the electrician? Maybe he crossed a wire when he came out to do repairs after..." The Silver Stag copycat wrecked the shop while kidnapping Arden and Camber. "Anyway, I wanted to let you know and get your approval for the charge."

"Tell you what." I eased my grip as sensation returned to my fingers. "Keep the shop closed tomorrow."

Clay shot me two thumbs up for quick thinking.

"Aedan can meet the electrician," he said loud enough to carry. "You and Camber take the day off."

"Hey." I swatted him. "Bossing her around is my job."

"That is what bosses are for." I heard the smile in her voice. "How do you want me to handle this, Rue?"

"Aedan can meet the electrician." I stuck out my tongue at Clay. "You and Camber take the day off."

"Ah, the joys of being the new hire." She chuckled. "I'll get the ball rolling."

The call ended, and I almost fell face-first onto my bed to scream my relief into the pillow.

"See?" Clay chucked me on the shoulder. "Our luck is already turning."

The idea of driving to my house and falling into my own bed instead of a borrowed one, decompressing for the night and *then* facing the next catastrophe—while the girls were home safe and the shop was locked up tight—was almost enough to bring a tear to my eye.

Tears, much like sleep, would have to wait. "Any word on Marty's plans for the victims' parents?"

"The CPD will be knocking on doors tomorrow, but without bodies, the parents will hold out hope."

"If boo hags were dinosaurs, I would be rooting for the asteroid."

"On the topic of extinction," he said grimly, "the director ruled the guilty parties have been punished. He won't support any further actions taken against the boo hags. He feels it sets a bad precedent if we wipe out their entire faction." His jaw worked. "Even if they deserve it, in my humble opinion."

"Marah got what she wanted, and she got away with it."

"Not every story ends with an HEA."

"Since when does any case we work end in happily ever after?"

"I can't think when you put me on the spot, but I'm sure there was one."

"Mmm-hmm."

"Speaking of science fiction..." Clay rubbed his hands together. "What if Colby and I make a pit stop?"

Unsure if he meant dinosaurs or HEAs, I figured I would let it go. Probably safer that way.

"What kind of side trip?" I straightened the kinks out of my back. "Why aren't we all invited?"

"There's a convention in Atlanta. Mostly games and comics. We could catch the last day's presentations, get her some exclusive codes for Mystic Realm bonuses for attendees only, then head back." He checked the hall then eased in and shut the door behind him. "I can't help but notice you and Ace getting closer. I found his torn underwear in your pocket when I was doing laundry, and Ace has a ruined bra on his bed. Maybe the two of you could use some time alone to explore this new...intimacy...without fear of interruption."

For a full minute, I debated whether he was responsible for the power outage allowing me a guilt-free night with Asa, but surely even he wasn't dastardly enough to arrange for an empty house *and* make it possible to skip out on the shop's problems for another day.

Who was I kidding? He was definitely that dastardly. "That's very kind of you to offer, but—"

"Thanks," he cut me off with a wave. "I'll let Shorty know and book a car."

He ducked out before I could haul him back by his wig for questioning, but he'd made his point.

Gah.

Meddling golem.

Now, instead of relieved to get home, I was debating if I could buy an orcess costume online to avoid the alone thing. And the intimacy thing. But I owed it to Asa to confront this relationship stuff head-on, even if it meant telling him how I felt—*gulp*—using my big-girl words.

15

"Home again, home again," I murmured under my breath. "Jiggety-jig."

I pretended interest in the fridge, but I wasn't hungry, and all the good stuff had expired anyway.

Mostly I stood in the open doorway, letting cool air escape around me, wishing it would douse my libido.

I was going to murder Clay for this.

"I'm going to shower," Asa called from down the hall. "I'll leave you some hot water."

Getting him naked was part of the plan, but how did I volunteer to play loofah without making it weird?

"Okay," I called back, snapping out of my trance. "I'll, um, be...unpacking."

Halfway to my room with my suitcase, I caught a whiff of smoke and picked up my pace.

Spread open on my pillow, soot smudging the comforter, sprawled the Proctor grimoire.

"Why am I not surprised?" I picked it up, checked the cover. "Not a charred page."

The residue must have come from burned wood already in the fire pit when Aedan tossed it in.

Proof of incineration hadn't arrived, but I could nudge Aedan for it tomorrow. I was betting he thought it was a done deal, but no. The tricksy grimoire had fooled him by popping into my bedroom to save itself.

A quick wipe down returned it to pristine condition, and I shoved it in its spot with unnecessary force.

"I don't have the emotional bandwidth to deal with you right now." I closed the safe. "Nighty-night."

I ought to take a page out of Asa's book and jump in the shower, but it felt a million miles from here.

Across the hall, water drummed in the basin as he cleaned up, giving me time to think and—*ugh*—feel.

"I'm pretty sure I love you too."

Not the most impressive declaration. Not what a guy wants to hear after pouring out his heart.

As the product of an improbable romance myself, a somewhat legendary one, I could do better.

Before I could talk myself out of finishing what we started in that geriatric elevator, I shucked my clothes in a heap where I stood then sprinted across the hall into his bathroom like a gold medal was on the line.

"Rue?"

"Yes? I mean, yes. It's me. Rue."

"Is everything..." he drew the curtain back, and his eyes rounded to cartoon proportions, "...okay?"

A flicker of reality revealed his horns, curving back over his head, and his fangs grew longer in his mouth.

"I'm not great with words." I scrunched my toes on the bath mat. "I'm better with show than tell."

"Are you...?" His gaze latched onto my face and stuck. "You're naked."

Boobs out. Soul bared. Buns catching a draft.

I was as exposed as a person could get.

"This was a bad idea." I flushed from head to toe. "I should have respected your privacy."

I was definitely going to murder Clay for putting this idea in my head.

"No." He killed the water as I stepped back. "Wait."

Embarrassed to have put myself out there, I dashed across the hall and slammed my door then locked it.

"Do I face him," I muttered to myself, "or do I climb out the window and run until my legs fall off?"

The inner debate lasted a good thirty seconds before I sized up the window and grabbed for the lock.

I kicked out the screen and had one leg through the opening by the time Asa burst into the room. He winced at the knob he dented, and the way my door hung uneven on its hinges, but it didn't slow him.

"You're paying to have that fixed," I yelled as my feet hit the grass. "I hope you know that."

"Rue." A strangled noise caught between laughter and anger lodged in his throat. "You're naked."

"Yes." I flung my arms out to my sides and spun a circle in my yard. "We've established that."

Asa, whose horns refused to be packed away, was forced to give up the window and use the front door.

"Thank you, goddess," I panted, already on the run, "for not allowing Clay to see this."

I would never live it down. Ever. Never ever. Never times infinity.

Aedan was probably asleep, but I veered to avoid the creek anyway.

Mrs. Gleason was my best bet. She could give me a blanket, and she would cackle with glee to hear the story of how naked shenanigans blew up in my face. The edited version, of course, minus the horns.

"*Rue.*"

"I think I left the fridge open," I called over my shoulder. "Mind going back to shut it for me?"

Impact knocked the breath out of me, and Asa snaked his arms around my middle in an ironclad hold.

"When I pointed out you were naked—" he growled as I wriggled, "—I wasn't complaining."

"You looked horrified." I stomped his instep. "Let me go."

With inhuman strength, he twisted me to face him then threw me over his shoulder.

"No," he said casually. "I don't think I will."

Fists clenching in the damp ropes of his hair, I yanked on his scalp. "I told you to *let me go*."

"You and I are going to have a discussion." He turned toward the house. "After which, you can leave."

"It's my house." I kicked and clawed at him. "Take me back there, and *you* will be the one leaving."

"I can live with that."

"Why can't you let me die of embarrassment in peace?"

"I won't let you die." He nuzzled my hip. "Period."

Heat speared my core, and I forgot to struggle for a heartbeat as his teeth closed over my skin.

"What are you doing?" I sucked in air, but I couldn't gulp enough. "And are you…wearing a towel?"

"You didn't exactly give me a chance to dress before you became an Olympic hurdler."

"Here." I scratched at my wrist. "I'll give you the bracelet back." I groaned in defeat as it stuck. "One day, you'll find a nice daemoness who isn't a total headcase, who will be worthy of you. Someone who knows your customs and how to do things right and talks about their feelings instead of cornering you in the shower like a sex-starved maniac. With no clothes on. A naked sex-starved maniac."

"Rue?"

"Yes?"

"Hush."

"Don't hush me," I grumbled, slumping down his back, which was smooth and smelled nice. Not that I noticed because *grr*. "You're already treating me like a sack of potatoes. Don't treat me like a child too."

Sadly, with his long legs, we reached the house in record time. He rooted around in a drawer then dumped me into a chair. He used brute strength to subdue me long enough to bind my ankles to the chair legs and my arms behind my back. With twine. From Thanksgiving.

Sweet as sugar, I asked him, "Having fun?"

"Yes." His eyes met mine, hot and bright. "I should have thought of this sooner."

"I'm not a turkey dinner."

"You're making me hungry." He trailed a finger down the valley between my breasts. "I could—"

"If you say you could eat me up, I will..." I considered my options. "I'll bite you."

"Promise?" He leaned in closer. "Will you leave a mark?"

"I'll chew off your lips and swallow them."

"Hmm."

His gaze dipped to my breasts, and my breath caught in my throat.

"I don't trust that look." I scraped the chair legs with each hop I took across the floor to escape him. "Especially while I'm tied up, and I can't fight back."

The sexual tension burst like a balloon. Not like I pricked it with a needle, either. More like I stabbed it with a butcher knife.

"Hold still." A shadow crossed his features, drawing his eyes tight and his lips thin. "I'll cut the twine."

"What?" I stopped in my tracks. "Why?"

"You're struggling," he pointed out. "You're obviously not into this."

"That's not—"

"I won't force you. That's not who I am."

A ton of bricks fell on my head and crushed my brain to pulp that oozed from cracks in my thick skull.

Okay, so that didn't happen, but it might as well for the force of the epiphany that struck me.

I can't fight back.

Me and my big mouth.

"You're not your father."

Asa, *very* obviously not into this anymore either, cut the twine and backed away slowly.

The mention of his father had to put him in the mindset to recall how he was conceived: by force.

"No, I'm not, and I have no plans on becoming him either."

"Asa…"

"I'm going to attempt a new blanket for Colby." He stood there, dripping. "I'll be in my room if you need me."

"I need you," I shouted before he could turn his back on me, maybe for good this time.

"Rue, you don't have to do anything that makes you uncomfortable."

"Everything about you makes me uncomfortable." His stricken expression gutted me. "That's not—" The words refused to come. "You push me out of my comfort zone, okay? You're so perfect, and you get me. You don't care about my past, and you're like this husband I ordered out of a catalog or something."

Frozen to the spot, he barely breathed while I rambled at him like a crazy person.

"I want to have sex with you. Or make love. Or whatever you want to call it. I'm not sure. I've never been in love, so I have no idea what qualifies." I covered my face with my hands. "This whole thing is confusing, and you're over there, pure as the driven snow, and I've had orgasms that fueled spells that killed people. I don't know what to do or how to do it. I don't want to taint you."

Virginity wasn't a gift. You don't give it away. You don't lose yourself or your worth when you share your body. But it *is* a moment, and you only get to experience it once. He deserved it to be special.

"Maybe we should stick with yes or no questions to avoid confusion." His warm palms landed on my bare thighs, but when I refused to look at him, he pried my hands away from my face.

"Okay." I studied the knot of his towel then felt like a perv and shut my eyes. "First question?"

"Do you love me?"

A frustrated tear slipped through my lashes. "Yes."

"Do you want me?"

"Yes."

"Now it's your turn." He wiped my cheeks dry. "Ask me."

Part of me wanted to shrivel and die on the spot for being so terrible at relationships I had reduced us to this.

The other part, the one who stripped naked in the first place, wanted to lick beads of water off his chest and straddle his hips while he sat in this chair, maybe with *his* hands tied, so I didn't give her much credit for reading the room.

With terrible effort, I forced the question through the knot in my throat. "Do you love me?"

"Yes."

"Do you want me?"

Fingers threading with mine, he used them to pull me to my feet. "Yes."

Naked before him, muddy feet and all, I found courage. "Is that a *yes* for the future or a *yes* for now?"

"Now." He wet his lips. "And in the future." His horns flickered, glimmered darkly, then vanished again. "Please."

Hands linked behind his neck, I buried my face in his throat. "Since you asked so nicely."

"Where?"

"Your room."

The grimoire might cockblock us just for funsies in mine, and I was about to combust.

"Okay."

He slipped in a puddle left from earlier and banged his shoulder on the frame with a hiss. I kissed the small hurt then continued my slow progression to his neck and up to his jaw. I nibbled a biting line to the corner of his lips then brushed across them gently, determined to get this right.

"Do you want candles?" I traced his carotid with my tongue. "Music?"

"Chocolate-covered strawberries?" A hoarse laugh hitched in his chest. "Oysters on the half shell?"

Smiling into his skin, I chuckled at myself. "I'm a walking, talking cliché factory."

"You're not walking," he pointed out, nearing the bed. "How do you want...?"

"Any way I can get you." I reached low and tapped his knotted towel. "Mind if you lose this?"

"No," he breathed, and then the fabric hit the floor.

Fingertip pressing down on his shoulder, I guided him to the edge of the mattress. "Sit."

The brush of his erection, hot and hard beneath me as my knees hit the comforter, hitched my breath.

I wasn't ashamed to admit I had put a *lot* of thought into this moment. It made me a hypocrite, yes, but I wanted his first time to be special. Perfect. That was why, after much consideration, I chose this position to give me total control, to prove I couldn't be fuller of consent if I were a pinata stuffed with condoms.

Which reminded me... "Condom?"

"I'm not fertile."

There were questions to be asked about that, yes, but I only managed, "Good."

With gentle hands, I pressed him flat onto his back then leaned over him to taste and touch every inch from chin to navel. I bit his hipbone next, and he shuddered, so I bit the other. Harder. I wrapped my hand around his firm length, flicked my tongue over the tip, then blew across the crown.

"Rue," he rasped, his hips jerking. "I…"

A strangled noise escaped him when I took him in my mouth, and his fingers speared my hair, not pulling or pushing, just anchoring himself to me in the moment. I grinned as each bob of my head tensed his muscles until they were strung tight and ready to burst from his skin.

Mouth swollen, his taste on my tongue, I asked, "More?"

"Yes," he growled, his hands sliding down to cup my face, his thumbs hot on my lips.

"More of this?" I licked him base to tip. "Or do you have something else in mind?"

Look at me, being a communicator! Actual words coming out in real sentences that make sense.

Who knew all it took was getting naked and rubbing against him to generate words of affirmation?

"I want it all." His touch gentled. "All of you."

His thighs might be quivering, but his feet were planted firmly on the floor. I leaned back, adjusted my position, and braced my knees on either side of his hips on the mattress. I teased us both with long slides of my sex over his, until my skin was humming and his was slick with sweat and strain.

Locking gazes with him, I gripped his base to hold him steady for me. Then I sank onto him with a gasp as he filled me. He kicked back his head, his canines long in his mouth. They pressed against his full bottom lip until a drop of blood welled that parched the back of my throat with the desire to taste that too.

Taking his hands in mine, I guided them to my breasts and showed him how to make me squirm.

Ba-bump, ba-bump, ba-bump.

The frantic beat of his heart warned me he was close, but I hadn't gotten started yet.

Moaning approval as he explored my body with tentative fingers, I leaned backward, bracing my palms on his upper thighs.

And then I began to move in rolling waves that caused his fingers to spasm on my skin.

"Tell me…" His eyelashes fanned his cheeks. "How…?"

Understanding flooded me, warming me, and I shifted one of his hands to the apex of my thighs before I caved to the desperate urge to rock against his fingers. He let my whispers and sighs teach him, and he held on until the cords in his neck pressed stark against his skin before a snarl ripped from his throat.

Control fled when he sat upright, linking his arms around my waist and clamping his teeth where my neck met my collarbone as instinct drove him to thrust into me, harder and harder, until we slid onto the floor with a thump that didn't cost him his rhythm.

Tighter and tighter, he held me, and tighter and tighter the coil twisted in my lower stomach.

As Asa growled his release, he returned one clever hand to my center, eager to help me catch up to him.

"Yes," I murmured, riding his fingers until the tension in me burst in kaleidoscope colors behind my eyes.

Until now, until *him*, sex had lacked any depth beyond the pleasure of its culmination.

This was…

…I had no words.

Arms weighted with lead, I hefted them onto his shoulders and held him until our ragged breaths eased.

"Thank you." Asa kept me locked against him. "For loving me."

For the millionth time this week, I fought the hot sting of tears that threatened to overflow my cheeks.

This I could do. This I could use to make him understand. This was more than words.

This was us.

Not him.

Or me.

Us.

"Thank you." I licked the salt from his shoulder. "For letting me."

Intimacy was an alien language I heard others speak in, their whispered secrets shared with tender grins, but I didn't understand the words or comprehend their meanings. There was a blockade between my head and my heart, built stone by stone over the long years I spent with the director, withering away from the lack of affection until the shriveled remains of my soul met with his approval, and my tattered memories tasted of imagination and wishes and dreams of a better life than a girl like me deserved.

"Come to bed with me." He toyed with the ends of my hair. "Let me wake up with you like this."

Cheek resting over his heart, I was asleep before he got his legs under us.

16

A thump and rattle dragged my consciousness up from a dead sleep, and my eyes popped open.

I was in Asa's bed.

In Asa's arms.

In my birthday suit.

And someone was stomping around in the kitchen.

Brilliant witch that I am, I left my wand in my clothes in my room.

The night swam before me in vivid details that made me flush to recall the late-night trip to the fridge for snacks that devolved into letting Asa finish what he started with the twine.

Focus.

And not on the warm dae curled around my hips, his hair tangled, and his horns denting the pillows.

Focus, focus, focus.

Swinging my legs over the edge of the bed, I touched the floor with my toes. I shifted my weight, little by little, until I could slide off the mattress without waking Asa, whose arms looked mighty empty without me in them.

Oh my goddess, Rue. There is someone in your house. Do you want to die?

FOCUS.

Only a handful of people could cross the wards, and I hadn't felt foreign magic picking at their anchors.

Okay, okay.

I got this.

Brain switch flipped into the *on* position, I put together that if the person in the house had crossed the wards, and—from the smell of it—they were brewing coffee, then they had permission to be here.

I was in no danger. Neither was Asa.

Mmm.

Asa.

With great effort, I blocked him out, buttoned myself into his discarded shirt, and cracked open his door to find a pink-haired golem helping himself to creamer. He wore black jogging pants and a faded lilac tee that read *There's No Better Karate Instructor Than A Spiderweb In Your Face*. Beneath the words, a chubby unicorn lashed out toward a psychedelic web with a powerful kick.

Pointing toward the front door, I invited him outside for a chat.

We sat on the steps together, and he quivered with what I quickly identified as laughter.

"So," he drawled, "you got laid last night."

Heat rising in my cheeks, I elbowed him hard enough to regret it. "Just because I came—"

"I'm sure you did." He snickered and hooted while I spluttered. "I've got two words for you."

"I don't want to hear them."

"Security." He passed me his phone. "Cameras."

With a flourish, he pressed play, and the video feed from the property spun to life.

"They say what you're doing at midnight on New Year's Eve is what you'll do for the rest of the year."

I watched in horrified fascination as I climbed out my bedroom window, Asa in hot pursuit.

"Colby heard the alarm, but we were in a panel. She asked me to check her phone for her, and…"

A groan ripped out of me, and I leaned forward, burying my face in my lap.

That was when I noticed even Clay's shoes fit the theme, the iridescent laces in complementary pastels.

"I owe you." I passed him his phone, unable to look him in the eye. "Can you delete it?"

"Already done." He rubbed my back. "She won't find a trace of it in the cloud."

Snapping out of my slouch, I narrowed my eyes on him. "Then what did I just watch?"

"Oh, I made a copy. I sent one to you. You can share it with Ace, if you two like that sort of thing."

"And you kept a copy."

"Eh." He deleted it in front of me. "It saved automatically when I formatted the clip. The program always backs up what you're working on in case you lose your connection." He showed me his trash bin then he emptied that too. "See? Gone. You're in the clear."

"Goddess bless, what a mess."

Since we had no idea if the wards kept out the *y'nai*, I had decided to pretend they weren't there. This? I couldn't pretend away a video clip that would warm the cockles of Clay's metaphorical heart for all time.

"You do realize this is actual footage of you running from your feelings?"

Another groan tore out of me as it sank in how badly it could have gone if Colby had seen, which told me I had worse priorities today since I hadn't even asked, "Where is Colby?"

"Down at Camp Aedan." His eyes twinkled. "She's dropping off some Mystic Realms swag."

"I don't trust the way you're smiling."

"Just thinking of your future children. How they'll sit on Uncle Clay's knee, and I'll tell them—"

"Nothing." I swatted him. "You'll tell them nothing. There will be no children. And they'll know nothing."

"Fae fertility will work against you," he said earnestly, "but daemons breed like rabbits."

"Asa told me he wasn't fertile." I caught his shoulders bouncing. "I didn't know that was a thing."

Did dae track it, like ovulation? Pop birth control pills? Condoms were out. We didn't use those.

"You just grabbed the stick and shifted into drive, didn't you?"

"*Clay.*"

Wheezing laughter gasped out of him, and he slapped his thigh as tears wet his lashes.

"Dae control our fertility with contraceptives brewed to match each individual's heritage."

Twisting on the step, I found Asa standing in the doorway, his hair down and tangled from my fingers.

"Many dae aren't willing to chance the genetic lottery," he continued, "and decline to have children."

Clay had recovered enough to pivot toward our conversation, but then did a double take at Asa.

"That's new." He pointed out the gleaming horns that hadn't gone away. "What's up with those?"

Grateful Clay had asked so I didn't have to, I threw my weight behind his question. "What he said."

Asa prowled over to me, crouched to put us at eye level, and wound his hand in my hair. He pulled until I tipped back my head, and he pressed a kiss over last night's bite mark near my collarbone. It was tender, probably would be sore for days, and I didn't mind one bit.

"I woke up like this." His lips trailed my throat. "I've tried, but I can't conceal them."

Hide them was what he meant, to make himself less threatening, less daemon, just...less.

"I like it." I caught his chin and guided his mouth to mine. "A lot."

Hand over his eyes, Clay damn near giggled. "Is anyone else thinking he's horny because he's horny?"

Ha! For once, I had beat him to a punchline. "Been there, done that—"

"Yeah, I know." He broke into peals of evil laughter. "I saw the video."

"Video?" Asa swung his head toward Clay. "What video?"

"We tripped the motion detectors," I told him. "Clay watched our romance unfold in real time."

The blush I expected from Asa burned up my throat, but he was more at home in his skin than I had ever seen him. Even the presence of his horns didn't bother him, when once, he would have locked himself in his room until he discovered a way to mask them. From me. From Clay. From Colby. Even, I suspected, from himself.

"That's not why you came home early, is it, Clay?" I stroked Asa's jaw. "You could have called."

I hadn't expected him and Colby back until dark, but it was noonish, as best I could tell.

"And miss your face when I told you?" He snorted. "Some things are worth waking up for, Dollface."

"You're *such* a good friend."

"I know." He grinned at Asa. "That's why I'm going to tell you a story that might help your situation."

Afraid of the rating on the story, I managed to get out, "Okay?"

"There was a couple, maybe thirty years back. Two agents. He was fae. She was a siren." He laughed, the memory a good one. "His wings popped out the night they mated, and they wouldn't fold back in." He shook his head. "Took him a month to get them to cooperate, and they still *boinged* years later whenever he got...you know."

The anecdote sparked my curiosity. "So, it's a fae thing?"

"Far as my experience goes, yes."

"Hmm." I managed to yank my attention from Asa's horns to his outfit. "What are you wearing?" Asa and Clay were matchy-matchy. "These are real clothes."

"I always wear real clothes."

"You know what I mean. They're casual." I shoved Asa and glared at Clay. "What are y'all up to now?"

"That's my cue to skidoo." Clay got to his feet. "I'll go check on Shorty."

"Chicken," I yelled after him then turned back to Asa. "What has he talked you into this time?"

For him to emerge dressed for chaos, they must have texted about their plans for the day.

"Canvassing the streets of Samford. Clay says it's time to enroll students in the self-defense classes."

Meaning he wanted to get Asa alone to see how he was doing post-sex. Or he wanted to threaten him in private. Clay might not be my biological anything, but he was like a big brother to me. The temptation to warn Asa not to break my heart *or else* might prove irresistible once they were alone for guy-talk time.

After they left, I would call Camber and Arden and tell them to spread the word about the classes to their friends.

"Aedan is at the shop, waiting on the electrician." I stretched out my legs. "Do you need him?"

Now that I was home, I could relieve him, handle the electrician, and do a thorough sweep of the store.

"Clay plans to use him as the BOB." At my blank expression, he explained, "Body opponent bag."

Poor Aedan would be eating a lot of foot-scented mat then. "What about Clay?"

"He'll work one-on-one with the students to correct their forms and boost their confidence."

That sounded like the best allocation of their talents. "And you?"

"I'll be teaching at the front of the room. Aedan will partner with me, as required."

"To prevent any hand-chopper-offering."

"Yes," he said a beat too slow for it to be the only reason.

Before the blood oath, I would have suspected it was an excuse for Asa to beat Aedan senseless.

Now I figured he wanted Aedan trained to protect himself, and the girls, against threats.

Like my cousins.

Or my grandfather.

Or my grandmother.

Pretty much anyone related to either of us qualified.

"There is one thing. Two, actually." I cleared my throat and pointed to his head. "What about those?"

"The one element missing from Clay's story was a clever witch."

"Mmm-hmm." I arched an eyebrow at him. "You're buttering me up to cast a spell on you."

"You already have." His lips twitched in the promise of a smile. "The day I met you."

"That was terrible." I snorted a laugh. "You must be scraping the bottom of your barrel of one-liners."

Enjoying the ribbing, he gestured to his horns. "Would you mind?"

Innate fae talent left manufactured glamours in the dust, but I could spin a concealment that would hold for a few hours with Colby's help. The tricky part was intangibility, making them both unseen *and* unfelt.

"Not at all." I dusted off my pants. "Let me grab my kit from my room."

Past the sagging door, I dug through my clothes from yesterday until I located the necessities.

Asa stood in the hall, testing the hinges and drawing his bottom lip between his teeth.

"I can fix this." He smoothed his thumb over one of the dented screws. "I'll buy supplies while I'm in town."

"Hmm?"

The ease with which he stood there told me last night had been a release in more ways than one. As if our roles had been reversed with that one act. He was looser, more relaxed, while I was ready to volunteer for the full-time job of Asa's lip biter.

One taste of him had me craving *more, more, more* with a familiar urgency reserved for juicy hearts.

More kisses.

More caresses.

More sweet words.

This, I realized, was how Dad had conquered a black witch's hunger for power.

He replaced it with an equally addictive drug that hurt no one and could be gotten only one place.

Mom.

"You're a million miles away." Asa slid his hand into my hair. "Where did you go?"

"To a place we shouldn't visit until we have wards on our rooms for privacy."

His eyes promised me those wards would be set before bedtime, and I couldn't wait to test them.

"Let me know if I can help." He rubbed a lock through his fingers. "Where do you want me?"

Climbing onto the bed, I sat in lotus position. "That's a loaded question if ever I heard one."

Smiling softly, Asa mirrored my pose to make sitting knee to knee more comfortable.

"What Clay said..." I cleared my throat, "...about your horns."

"Yes?"

"I thought I was alone in my suffering, since I had the verbal diarrhea, but fascination is prodding you too." I reached up to run a fingertip the length of one horn while watching his eyes shutter from the pleasure. "You were raised fae, so I'm guessing that means you have some natural resistance to certain urges." I lowered my hand to his cheek. "I suck at feelings, so it's been forcing me to word vomit—"

"I thought it was diarrhea."

After tweaking his nose, I rolled my eyes. "I've had it coming out both ends."

"Fair enough."

"You suck at accepting yourself, and you also suck at believing anyone else will either." He leaned into my palm, but he didn't say a word, so I rambled on. "That's why your inner daemon pops out, and stays to chat, when he never did before." I eyed his horns again but kept my hands to myself. "It also explains why, when it became apparent that I accepted him, you allowed your horns to show."

With curious fingers, he explored the ebony curves as if they were a new feature rather than being born under the weight of them. "Do you think I'll be like this for a month?"

"Would it bother you if you were?"

"No," he said after careful deliberation, "but I would be forced to take leave."

There were exceptions, even for Black Hat agents, that could get you out of fieldwork for a time.

An inability to blend in among humans was right at the tippy top.

"The director won't be thrilled with the excuse."

Your granddaughter literally makes me horny, and I need nakey vacation time with her to fix the problem.

"Does it bother you? That your family might not approve?"

"You're mine." I slid my palms over his knees, down his shins, to his ankles. "Every single inch."

And yes, that sounded pervier out loud than in my head.

But no, I didn't care one whit.

"Hmm." He caught my wrists before I could trace the arch of his foot. "Does that mean you're mine?"

In the past, say, *yesterday*, I would have snarled I wasn't a piece of furniture, that I couldn't be bought or borrowed or sold like one. But this wasn't ownership. He was a part of me in a way no one had ever been. That made him mine, and it made me his too.

"Maybe." I tapped my chin. "I'll have to think about it."

A growl revved up his throat, and it revved me up too, but Clay was waiting.

Okay, fine. I didn't care so much about that as the fact I had no door on my room, and a little moth girl could flit through it at any moment.

"Hold still." I lifted my wand. "This won't hurt, but it might itch."

Palms on my knees, he watched me work, as if I were his personal miracle.

Eyelids drifting shut, I drew a trickle of light from Colby, then tapped Asa's horns. "Ta-da."

"Thank you." He smoothed a hand over his head. "I'm sure Aedan will appreciate it as well."

"You won't win over your students if you impale them on accident."

His sudden growl left me squirming until I realized it wasn't meant for me.

The grimoire sat on the windowsill, sunning, as if it had any right to be out of the safe.

"Son of a biscuit." I jumped up and stalked over to it. "What do you think you're doing?"

With a thump, it hurled itself onto the floor, its pages flung open on cosmetic uses for daemon...

"*Eww.*" I scuttled back from it. "No." I kicked it shut. "Just no."

Granted, I had smeared questionable substances on my face (and other places) for rituals' sake, but I wasn't going to use Asa like a walking, talking bottle of high-grade retinol with a handy built-in pump.

A crinkle in his brow, he joined me over the book. "What's wrong?"

"The grimoire thinks it's a comedian."

As I was scooping it up, Clay bounded into the room with Colby on his head.

"Ready to go?" He clapped his hands. "This is going to be great."

This would be the first time she and I had been alone since The Incident.

Great wasn't the word I would use to describe how I was feeling right about now.

"Ready." Asa flicked a glance at Colby then back to me. "You've got this."

"I hope so," I murmured as they left then faced Colby. "Hey, smarty fuzz butt."

"You will not believe the door prize I won." She whirled. "A code for a saber tooth pterodactyl."

"That's only the coolest thing ever," I crowed with excitement, as if I'd had a clue they existed before today.

Waving her into the living room, I gave her a minute to settle on the perch above her favorite chair.

That was when I noticed she wasn't clutching a towel, but her missing blanket. "Hey, you found it."

"An agent discovered it in the suite Sorie was using. They logged it as evidence, but Clay stole it back."

"Jilo must have suspected it would offer you protection against boo hags if she had Sorie steal it."

"How cool is that?" She flapped her blanket-covered wings. "I'm boo hag proof."

"Very cool."

The strain in my voice leaked out, and she touched back down on the perch.

"You want to talk about Charleston." She huddled deeper into her blanket. "The daughter thing."

"Um." I would rather extract my own teeth first. "Yes."

"I know you didn't mean it like that."

"I don't..." I sank onto the couch. "It's just..."

"You don't want me to think you're trying to replace my mom."

"Yes." I sagged with relief. "That."

"I'm not my mom's little girl anymore." Her antennae slouched a bit. "I love her, and I miss her, but she's not..." Her wings twitched. "She couldn't be my mom now." She drew patterns on the perch with a foot. "She wouldn't understand me, and she couldn't protect me." A sigh moved through her. "I think, if I did go back, it would make her sad."

"Colby..."

"She would see the girl I used to be instead of the girl I am, and it would be too hard. I would be trapped there, and anyone who saw me would think I was a pet. Over time, she might see me that way too. It would be easier. Simpler. To have a pet rather than a moth-girl daughter. I wouldn't blame her for that."

"She might surprise you," I forced myself to say, the words cutting a path out of my throat.

"You see me for who I am, Rue." She drew herself up taller. "You understand me, and you value my opinion. I'm not a thing to you. I'm *me*." Her speech reminded me of Clay, and it made me ache for them both. "You only know me like this, and I only know you like this, and I think we're better off if we keep growing into our new lives together."

"I just want you to be happy."

"I *am* happy." She flitted over to land in my lap. "You gave up everything for me. You *saved* me. You helped me figure out how to be this new person. You never put limitations on me. You always believe I can do anything I put my mind to, and I always believe you." She butted her head against my stomach. "I believe *in* you, Rue. I always have, and I always will. I don't need a mom, but I need you. I don't know what that makes you or me, but maybe we don't need labels."

"You're very wise for a fluff ball." I kissed the top of her head. "How did you get to be so smart?"

"I played an oracle for a few months."

"Ah." I pretended like I understood her gamerese. "That would explain it."

Snort-giggling, because she knew I was full of it, she snuggled closer.

"You can call me your daughter," she murmured against me. "If you want to."

"We'll figure it out," I promised her. "Did Clay tell you where he was going?"

"To round up students for the self-defense classes you promised Camber and Arden."

"What do you say, I change clothes, put on my favorite hair bow, and we have a girls-versus-boys race to see who can sign up the most students?"

Aedan wouldn't hold it against me if I stuck him with the electrician, right? He was already there, and no one knew we were home. Really, he should thank me for sparing him from playing punching bag for Asa.

Plus, it would give Colby and me much needed one-on-one girl time that was in short supply these days.

"I'm in." She kicked off to glide a loop around the room. "Want me to call Clay?"

"Heck no." I made a production of jerking back. "Do you know how charming the ladies find him?"

One flutter of his lashes, and he would have them eating out of the palm of his hand.

"Oh." Her eyes glittered. "A stealth mission." She rubbed her hands together. "I like it."

While she folded her blanket, I changed into leggings, a fitted tee, and a pair of sneakers.

I *might* have also cast a teeny spell to make my outfit matchy-matchy too.

Blending in with the guys was paramount to not giving away the game.

Clay and Asa had a tiny head start, but I wasn't worried they would win.

When my phone rang, I tucked it between my shoulder and ear while I searched for my keys. "Hollis."

"I have Aedan," a low voice informed me. "I won't harm him. I simply wish to speak to you privately."

"You're the black witch who's been sniffing around my shop."

The girls had pegged him right. He did have an odd speech cadence and a formal tone.

A peculiar tingle in the back of my mind spread like an itch I couldn't reach.

He sounded...familiar...but I couldn't match a face to his voice.

"Do I need to tell you what I'll do to you if you hurt that boy?"

"I'm aware of your reputation. I understand the peril I have placed myself in."

"I'll meet with you, I give you my word, but leave him out of it."

"I'm afraid that's not possible at this juncture."

Hands balling at my sides, I demanded, "Let me talk to him."

"Of course."

Rustling filled the background, then muttered words, and wood scraped on metal.

"Rue," Aedan breathed into the receiver. "I'm sorry I—"

"I'm the one who owes you an apology for not coming home sooner."

A few murmurs hinted the kidnapper was ready to reclaim the phone.

"I'm coming for you," I promised Aedan. "You're going to be okay."

The handset passed from him to the black witch, and I grated out, "I can be at the shop in ten minutes."

"I won't harm him," he reiterated. "I simply wish to talk."

Famous last words.

17

Hands trembling, I dialed Camber as I pocketed my wand and strapped on my kit. The black witch might not be working alone, and Aedan might not be the only hostage. The Black Hat rogues—and what else could he be?—traveled in covens. I couldn't plan my next move until I confirmed the girls were okay.

Ring.

Ring.

Ring.

Ring

Ring.

With Colby looking on, I ended the call and told her what I feared most. "No answer."

Less than a minute later, my phone screen lit, and the display showed Camber's number. "Hello?"

The beat of silence prior to an indrawn breath on the other end stretched for an eternity.

"Hey," she panted. "Rocko got out of the pen, so I had to drop everything and chase him."

"Rocko?" I soaked up the sound of her voice as Colby flew a victory lap. "One of the puppies?"

Her grandmother, Dotha, bred Cavalier King Charles Spaniels.

"Puppy? No. That's the wrong word." She snorted. "Ringleader. Instigator. Troublemaker…"

"Have you spoken to Arden today?"

"No."

That single word spread ice through my chest in a crackling sheet of uncertainty.

"Remember how much trouble Mrs. Gleason got into last year on New Year's?"

"She almost burned down my house." I had to file an insurance claim for a new roof. "It rings a bell."

"On the way home from work yesterday, we noticed her unloading boxes of mixed fireworks. She had at least six of them on the porch, and her trunk was still open. We told our parents, in case things got out of hand. Again. But last night, her display was weirdly subdued. Hardly a fire hazard at all.

"Arden's mom is worried Mrs. Gleason is stockpiling, and she knew Arden had a free day, thanks to the outage. So, she dispatched Arden to investigate. Mostly, she wants to know if the police need to be called, which is almost always *yes*. I would have gone with her, but Gran needed help."

For all our sakes, I volunteered, "I'll warn Aedan to keep an eye out."

"Arden was going to ask him to join her after the electrician left, but he didn't answer his phone."

Poor Aedan was too busy being kidnapped by yet another crackpot who tracked me to Samford.

"He's still at the shop," I assured her. "The electrician ran late."

"Oh good. She's always paranoid if he doesn't answer he's ghosting her."

"I have another call," I lied to clear the line. "I just wanted to check in while I had a minute."

"We're all good here." A puppy barked in the background. "Hope I see you soon."

"Me too."

Before the screen went dark, I dialed Arden, but the call ended after one ring.

>>*Can't talk.*

>>*I'm on a secret mission.*

>*So I heard.*

>>*Camber must have missed the memo about it being secret.*

Mrs. Gleason's shenanigans were known far and wide, but it was a Samford conspiracy to ignore them.

Oh, we talked about them. Extensively. We kept an eye out for them. Frequently. We tried keeping her out of trouble. And by trouble, I mean jail. There was even a tip jar in the diner where everyone chipped in for bail money or to cover minor property damage.

Samford's willingness to embrace the quirky, the strange, and the downright weird was what made it home.

>*Camber said Aedan wasn't answering your calls. He's just busy with the electrician.*

>>*Oh good.*

>>*I mean, I knew that.*

>>*I didn't go to your house to check if he was hiding from me or anything. I just thought it might be nice to have company on a stakeout, and he ought to know how crazy folks are around here before he decides to settle down, you know?*

>*It was nice of you to want to include him.*

>>*That's me. Nice. Cute boys friendzone me from a mile away.*

>*Are we still talking about Aedan?*

>>*No?*

>*Are you sure?*

>>*Yes?*

>*Then why all the ??*

>>*I can't surveil and text.*

>>*Later!*

"Thank the goddess." I stared until the screen went dark then smiled at Colby. "They're both safe."

Antennae aquiver, she sailed onto my shoulder. "What do we do now?"

"You're going to play Mystic Realms with your friends and stay as far away from this black witch as I can get you." I scratched her head. "I'm going to text Clay to get his butt home ASAP, even if he has to drive. I'll call Asa and pick him up, and he can go with me to get Aedan." I kissed her cheek. "Please, stay put."

"I will." She nuzzled back. "I promise."

The boo hag incident must have spooked her more than she would ever admit, if she wasn't fighting me.

I dropped her at her rig on my way out then checked and double-checked the wards behind me.

Asa in tow, I rolled into my usual parking spot behind Hollis Apothecary and killed my SUV's engine.

"Give me five," I said, exiting the vehicle, "then get into position."

Head up, shoulders back, I marched to the rear entrance and knocked twice.

Of its own volition, the door swung open onto the dark hall, but a candle burned in my office.

Had there not been a power outage, I would have blamed it on black witches' love of theatrics.

"We're in here," Aedan called. "We're playing Monopoly."

Wracking my brain, I combed over possible meanings if the board game was a code word, but nada.

Aedan smiled, tight and wary, when I arrived in the office. Then he gestured to my desk.

They really were playing Monopoly.

Weird.

I didn't own any boardgames. Colby preferred to play online.

Aedan wasn't restrained that I could tell. He wasn't hurt. He was anxious, but that was understandable.

The man sitting opposite Aedan, his back to me, had perfect ringlet curls a cherub would envy.

A memory tickled the back of my mind when candlelight glinted off the golden locks.

The kidnapper played his turn then raised his hands where I could see them and stood slowly.

As he pivoted toward me, and I got a good look, I fought the cold sweat drenching my shirt.

Thanks to hours spent memorizing the photo Colby gifted me for Christmas, I recognized his face.

Hiram Nádasdy.

My *father*.

"No," I breathed. "It's not possible."

"Hello, Cate."

Cate.

Cate.

Cate.

The echo bouncing between my ears shook loose a certainty that quaked through my marrow.

Catheryn.

Cate.

Only two people had ever called me by my birthname, and they were both dead.

I killed them.

"Who are you?" I locked my knees to keep from bolting. "*What* are you?"

"Let me show you."

Ink dribbled from his pores, masking his features in magic so dark and vile, I lost sight of him in its midst. A foul breeze stirred his hair, and fetid whispers breathed down my neck, hot and rank and putrid. What stood before me resembled a man dipped in tar, plump dollops dripping onto the floor, and the smell…

All those teas the director poured down my throat when I was a kid drowned me in memories, but I couldn't trust them. I couldn't trust *him*. Either of them. I had to remember caution, because I didn't remember anything else. The director saw to that. I learned the history as he taught me, without ever questioning its authenticity.

Damn him for erasing my past, and damn me for letting him, for never suspecting a liar had lied to me.

Hot tears slid down my cheeks, burning my eyes, as tiny fissures crackled over my heart.

A roll of his shoulders cracked the blackness as if it were a dark chocolate shell coating ice cream. Jagged pieces slipped and slid to the floor, evaporating, taking the malodor along as if neither had ever existed.

"I vow to you, on the dark heart of Eire, the cold stone of Tran, the darkness of Mirk, I am your father."

The invocation was as dated as the rest of him, but it bound him to his word in unbreakable chains.

"You really are Hiram Nádasdy."

"I am."

Had he lied, he would have been struck dead, but he remained standing.

"I heard you're in fascination with the prince of Hael." His voice held echoes of a long gone past. "Your mother taught me love is unexpected, a treasure, so I won't pretend I know what you need better than you do, but I had hoped you would settle down with a nice witch for the most ordinary life imaginable."

"You're really him." I was stuck in a loop, and I couldn't break free. "Hiram Nádasdy."

"I am, I am, I am." He smiled. "Thrice spoken, thrice vowed, thrice proven by my vow to the ancients."

Dad.

This was my dad.

How was this my dad?

Warm hands gripped my tense shoulders as the comforting scents of tart green apples and sweet cherry tobacco allowed me to relax. Asa was here. I could get through this, through anything, with him. He linked his strong arms around my waist, and I melted back against him.

"This is…" I swallowed, tilting my head up at him, "…my dad."

"Are you sure?" Asa held me tighter. "I thought he was…"

Hiram sat on the edge of the desk, facing me with an unspeakable agony carved into his features. He stared at me, into me, and he shattered my world to bits.

"Everything your grandfather told you is a lie."

That same little girl in me sobbed with joy and relief and—most damning of all—hope.

I couldn't afford hope. It cost too much. It *hurt* too much.

"I don't remember…" I pinched my lips together, "…most of my childhood…"

"I'm aware." Hiram angled his head away, but the set of his jaw was hard and tight. "Father told me. He wanted me to know I had been replaced. That he was molding my child in his image."

Asa kept me steady, plucking questions from my head I couldn't voice. "What caused your rift?"

"I was already questioning Father's tenets when I met Howl." He cleared his throat. "Vonda, my wife."

A distant memory tickled the back of my mind, a certainty Mom had called him…Saint?

"After we married," he continued, "I broke ties with Father, and his Black Hats. I wanted a peaceful life. I wanted to be with Vonda. I wanted… It hardly matters now." He took a fortifying breath. "He had always hated my lack of ambition, but my contentment was not to be borne."

"If he couldn't have you," Asa summarized, "then no one could."

With a wry twist of his lips, Dad nodded. "Just so."

As if I were a child on my father's knee at story time, I asked him, "What happened next?"

"Father demanded I return to him, to Black Hat, time and time again over the years, but I always refused him. Your mother was meant to be his leverage over me, but she was beloved by the wargs, and they guarded her too well. After you were born, I gave my father another target, and he has excellent aim. He set his sights on you, and we made an innocent mistake that cost us everything.

"That night..." grief, somehow fresh and raw, twisted his features, "...the pack was running under the full moon, and Vonda begged to go. I hated to deny her anything, so we went. Only to watch. Only for a little while. I hoped it would help her to heal after Megara's death, but instead it left us exposed."

Back in her wilder days, Mom had run with Meg's pack, who viewed her as family.

Asa, once again, found his voice before Dad or me. "Your father attacked you out in the open?"

"The wards around our home were too strong for him to breach. He had to find another way."

With thoughts of Meg at the forefront of my mind, I had to ask, "What happened to the pack?"

"He put silver bullets in their skulls."

"Against all odds, you survived the massacre." Asa erased any censure from his voice. "Your wife...?"

"As far as I am aware, she is truly dead." He closed his eyes, collecting himself, then he explained to me, "That night, your grandfather stunned you with a spell too strong for use on a child. We thought it killed you." His aura darkened until a black-gold halo of power ringed him. "When your mother ran to you..." his eyes, trapped in that moment, held the vast darkness between the stars, "...he killed her."

"He killed her. Not you." I broke on the words. Not my voice. *Me*. "He killed Mom, and you *left*."

There were more questions, bigger questions, but that was the one I couldn't trap behind my teeth.

Where have you been?

Why did you leave me?

Did you ever love me?

However much of him I had forgotten, standing before him, I wanted to hurl caution to the wind and fling myself into his arms.

I wanted him to absolve me. Of what I had done. Of who I had become. Of *what* I had become.

But his hands were as red as mine, his heart as black, and neither of us could exonerate the other.

"I lost myself to rage, trying to protect you and your mother's…" He couldn't say body. He tried. More than once. Then he stopped, as if giving permission to quit tormenting himself. "He riddled me with bullets to slow me down, and six of his henchmen pinned me. They took my wand, broke my hands. I killed them, but it required time, and it distracted me from his real target." He set his jaw. "When I got to my feet, he held you in his arms, his wand to your throat." He spoke through his teeth. "I had no choice. I would have done anything to save you. Even become his prisoner."

"You've been incarcerated all this time," Asa confirmed, for my sake. "How did you escape?"

"Four months ago, a woman paid me a visit. Luca. She offered me freedom in exchange for a favor."

Four months.

It fit the timeline for Clay and Asa showing up on my doorstep, assuming the director had waffled before pulling the trigger on contacting me. He'd had one shot at reeling me in, tempting me back, and only the case he brought me would have done it. So had he orchestrated the copycat? Or merely cashed in on it?

"What favor?" Asa held me in check. "What did she want?"

"For me to dismantle Black Hat and destroy my father."

Oh, so no big then.

18

Dismantle Black Hat? I saw Hiram's mouth moving, but my brain was on vacation. *Destroy the director?*

Just two tiny little items on his to-do list, both waiting for a lazy pen to scratch them through.

He was a black witch of immeasurable power. I knew that. I *knew* it. But this was insanity. Even for him.

No stories about Hiram Nádasdy shied from the atrocities he committed, both before and after my mom stole his heart. (Not literally.) She was the delicate chain holding him back, acting as his conscience while he developed his own, but it snapped clean when she died. Now, goddess help us all, he was unleashed.

The faint brush of Asa's lips on my skin yanked me to attention, and I noticed Hiram grimace at the PDA.

"I was kept chained in a cell beneath the manor," Hiram continued. "Father released me a time or two, offering me freedom in exchange for loyalty. I was too far gone to comprehend the first attempt, but I almost killed him. I would have finished the job, if he hadn't kept me weak. The second attempt failed as well. There might have been a third, but I can't remember much of the first few decades, if I'm honest. I was grieving your mother, and you, too hard."

The director's choice to mix magic with water when he designed the Black Hat compound partially under the sea had always baffled me. But it made sense, if your son was half aquatic daemon, and you wanted him to flourish in his element.

"Why cooperate with the woman," Asa asked, "but not your father?"

"She fed me, gave me water. She allowed me to regain my strength before she released me." He raked a hand through his golden hair. "Her reasons didn't matter half as much to me as her ability to unlock my cell, my chains."

Much as I hated to admit it, in his shoes, I would have felt the same and damn the consequences.

"How did Luca gain access to you?" Asa studied Hiram. "Does she work for Black Hat?"

"She was in the compound, so she has ties to the Bureau. The way she dressed, and the times when she chose to visit, made me think she was posing as a guard, but I can't swear to it." He exhaled through his teeth. "I can't verify how long she worked to gain my trust, but it must have been years."

Anyone who risked working against the director right under his nose had a serious death wish.

Or good reason to believe they could handle the fallout if they got caught.

Like, say, a contingent of rogue black witches, ready to sacrifice themselves to the cause.

"Time held no meaning for me down in the dark." Hiram's expression shuttered. "I wanted to believe Luca could deliver on her promises, but I was convinced it would be too late. I felt certain when I got out, *if* I got out, you would be as much a slave to my father's teachings as I had been at your age. That it would have all been for nothing." He forced his gaze around the shop. "You weren't what I expected, and if I believed in any god, I would have fallen to my knees and thanked them for your deliverance."

"How long have you known where to find me?" I dredged up my voice. "How long have you been watching?"

"Your location was part of our bargain." A faint smile lifted the corners of his mouth. "You left on a case the day before I arrived, so I toured your shop and got a feeling for your town."

"I knew this day was coming, but I hate it arrived so soon." I glanced over my shoulder at Asa. "The director unearthed me, and now every Tom, Dick, and Harry can find my address."

"The director," Hiram echoed. "That's what you call him?"

"He didn't want to acknowledge our familial tie, and neither did I."

His first real smile broke across his face, subdued, yes, but there, and a knot formed in my chest.

"Your mother would be so proud." He rubbed the spot over his heart. "You're a remarkable woman."

"Yes," Asa agreed. "She is."

"This Luca you mentioned," I cut in, "she's behind the rogue black witches we've been tracking?"

"Yes."

"Then she was responsible for the Silver Stag copycat."

"She placed demands on my release, and I agreed to her terms. That's all I know."

"The original Silver Stag case altered the course of Rue's life. She left Black Hat, embraced white craft." Smart man, Asa kept Colby out of it, not confirming or denying her existence. "The director used a copycat case to lure her back as a consultant."

"The girls who work at my shop were taken by that black witch." I curled my nails into my palms. "They were spelled and caged in a swimming hole not far from here."

A popular trend among black witches, it seemed.

Got a problem?

Dunk it.

Maybe that's where the phrase *drown your sorrows* originated.

"I've been softening those memories for months." For their sakes, and mine. "So far, so good."

"The girls are healing." Aedan spoke for the first time in forever. "You've done well by them."

"This is your…?"

"Cousin."

"How unexpected that you bonded with that side of the family. Though you chose a daemon mate as well."

"We're not mated," Asa told him before I got tongue-tied explaining. "Yet."

"Yet," I mumbled weakly. "We're, uh, working on it."

For several hours, just last night. Not that I needed to tell Hiram that.

"She's reluctant," Asa teased, "but I'm persistent."

Amusement curved my father's lips as he drank me in. "In that uncertainty, you take after me."

The topic of genetics brought me around to a sticky topic. "I found your mother."

Not so much as a pucker of his brow indicated concern about my discovery. Or about her.

Apparently, no one was worried Granny might break free. That dismissal had to burn her biscuits.

Good thing she had all that swamp water to cool her temper.

"That's why I broke my silence." He rubbed his whiskered jaw. "I had meant to remain a ghost."

That hurt, but I didn't want to fight, so I made a peace offering. "The ward containing her is brilliant."

"It was your mother's design." His eyes crinkled at the corners. "And some of my finest work."

The idea that a light and dark practitioner blended their know-how into a cohesive whole stunned me.

Gray magic existed? Who practiced it? What were its limits? Its costs? Its benefits?

There was so much I wanted to ask him, so much I wanted to know, but I couldn't help feeling there was a ticking clock floating above our heads. As if this were a timed interview with a final buzzer at the end.

"You left me a warning, at The Devlin Wildlife Center."

"Which you ignored." He scoffed lightly. "Your mother predicted as much."

The chastisement oddly warmed me. "You also keyed the lock to me."

"The spell was stronger with a blood tie, so that was the choice I made. You and I are the only ones who can set her free, but I would advise against it. She's had a long time to decide how to take her revenge, and her throne. You're better off forgetting you know where she is or that you ever saw her."

"What about you?" I forced out the question. "Am I supposed to forget this too?"

"It would be for the best." He stood and approached me, giving me enough time to withdraw. "I can't stay. I have a vow to fulfil."

"To Luca."

"To your mother."

"You vowed to kill your father for taking her life," Asa, who was no stranger to dreams of patricide, stated with absolute certainty. "You might die in the attempt. Is it worth it to avenge a woman you will never see again, when you could stay here and fight beside one who has borne the guilt of your deaths most of her life?"

"Father told you—" the air behind him pulsed with its own heartbeat, "—that *you* killed us?"

Everything the director told me was a lie, he said, and he'd had no idea of the truth of his words.

"He said I came into my power early," I rasped, recalling the details. "That there was an accident."

"Dark gods damn his black soul." He rushed me then, bundling my tense form in his arms. "My sweet girl, you did no such thing. Nothing that happened to your mother or me was your fault. You're innocent, Cate. You have done no wrong." He held on tight, until I couldn't breathe, or maybe that was the sobs hitching my chest that kept me mute. "I failed you and your mother, but I won't fail in this."

With his voice fierce in my ear, and his love for me a light within his darkness, I couldn't deny it. Deny him. This was my dad. He was alive, and he was here, and I didn't want him to go.

"Stay." I tried not to, I tried so hard, but I melted against him. "Please."

"I made a vow." His awkward embrace grew more certain. "I am bound by my own magic to fulfil the bargain, or the spell I used will rebound on me."

"All that power..." I shivered at the thought. "It would kill you."

There was no point in confirming it. He knew. That was why he had to go. Part of the reason, anyway.

"Modern technology confuses me, but we can exchange letters. You can write me. We'll stay in touch."

"Let me help you." I clung to him. "We can work together—"

"No." He kissed my forehead then withdrew. "You will continue on. You must. Or Father will suspect."

"You don't have to do this." I fisted his old-fashioned coat. "You can stay. I can protect you. I—"

"You struck an animus vow," Asa said slowly, as understanding darkened his expression. "That's the only reason I can fathom you wouldn't fight to stay with your daughter."

"What does that mean?" I glanced between them. "What's an animus vow?"

"Your mother and I were soul bound, in the daemon way." Dad did not appreciate Asa's epiphany. "We would have died together, we should have, but I swore revenge on her killer."

"Okay, so you said earlier." I rolled my hand to get them around to the point. "What am I missing?"

With a flourish of his hand, Dad gave Asa the floor to finish smashing any remaining illusions.

"The moment he satisfies his vow," Asa said, unhappy with the spotlight, "he will die."

Old grief soured my mouth and left me tasting ashes as I told Dad, "You should have stayed dead."

Now I would have to mourn him all over again. This time without the burden of his death, or Mom's, on my conscience. No. Now I would live with the guilt of gobbling down every word the director had spoon-fed me. I had lived in that miserable manor, floors above my father, and I never suspected he was there. I should have searched for him, for my own answers. I could have saved him, but I left him there to rot.

This visit had ripped open old scar tissue, and I was bleeding out on the inside.

"I apologize." He withdrew after pressing a tender kiss to my forehead. "I shouldn't have come."

Without another word, he strode toward the rear exit.

Warmth trickling down my cheeks, I ran after him into the parking lot as if sprinting through a dream.

I wanted to yell at him, hug him, hit him, scream until I tasted blood then spit in his face until his leaving, his choice to go, didn't skewer my heart. Until I convinced him to forget revenge. Move on. Stay. For me.

Stay.

Please.

Just stay.

Do this one thing for me, Daddy, please.

Please, please, please.

For what might be the last time, he turned his back on me and flung out his arms to his sides.

Black wings that reeked of carrion and decay burst from his back, glittering and pulsing with dark magic.

With a great downward thrust, he leapt into the sky, stirring a rancid breeze.

Right there in downtown Samford for anyone to see.

"Dad," I hissed, darting frantic glances left to right. "What are you doing?"

"Do you truly believe I would risk your safety with such a display if I couldn't cloak myself?"

Right.

Dumb question.

A black witch with that much control over their powers could ensure no one saw them coming.

Until it was too late.

Drawn forward with childish wonder, I wished I could remember if he had ever flown with me. "How?"

"Perhaps I will share the secret." His eyes burned with love, so much love. "*If* you answer my letters."

Before I could snatch him out of the sky by his pantleg, leaping after him like an eager puppy begging for a car ride, he disappeared into the clouds as if he had never been.

It was one thing to be told your father was exceptional, his powers miraculous, but it was another to witness them with adult eyes and an education in craft behind me that said this shouldn't be possible. It was almost as improbable as a black witch falling in epic love with a white witch in the first place.

"Your dad is frightening." Aedan joined me. "He didn't hurt me or anything, but he's got a lot of daemon in him. He didn't have to use magic on me. I sensed his dominant nature and obeyed him." He shook his head. "That's never happened to me. I'm not an alpha personality by a mile, but it was eerie."

"I felt it too." Asa tipped back his head. "I fought it down easily enough, but the compulsion was there."

Until they agreed on it, I hadn't realized how much daemon nature had in common with warg culture.

Maybe that was why Mom fell in with Dad so easily. Her friendship with Meg was the learning curve.

As he said, she had been beloved by Meg's pack. Her nickname—Howl—came from her wild heart.

Well, and the one time she ran naked with the pack under the full moon.

Meg still laughed about that, still found joy in their friendship, and I had no idea how to tell her.

About Mom.

About Dad.

About me.

"Tomorrow I will wake up," I decided, "and this will all have been a dream."

"We'll find out in the morning." Asa, kindly, didn't press the matter. "Do you want a ride, Aedan?"

"I'll walk." He stretched his arms over his head. "My butt fell asleep waiting on you."

"It's a long walk home." I hated to let him out of my sight. "Are you sure?"

"I need to shake off his hold on me." He rolled his shoulders to loosen them. "I'm going to hunt."

"Keep your phone on." I touched his shoulder. "Call if you so much as stub your toe."

As much as I hated to suspect Dad, I couldn't afford to accept his miraculous reappearance at face value. Now that he was gone, and I had room to breathe, I felt my brain kicking into gear, sussing out his story.

"Do me a favor?" I waited for his nod. "Call Clay and Colby. Let them know you're okay."

And if they happened to keep him on the phone, say, the whole time, I would be fine with that.

"I'm okay." Reading my unease, he swooped in for a hug. "Nothing happened."

"I wouldn't call rising from the dead nothing." I squeezed him tight then reared back. "That reminds me." I cocked an eyebrow. "How did the electrician escape?"

"Um." He flushed to the tips of his ears. "About that." He scuffed his shoe. "There was no electrician."

No electrician meant he had flipped a breaker to set the scene then lied to the girls about the problem.

Given how flustered Arden had been about Aedan not answering her call, I could guarantee the girls had no part in this. Since he wasn't the scheming kind, I had a good idea who put him up to the whole thing.

"You were just hanging out in the store for the heck of it?"

"For authenticity's sake," he corrected, chin tucked. "Clay said to give it a few hours then I could—"

"Go on. Hunt." I flicked my wrist. "I don't need the details." I smiled. "See you at home."

Already bouncing on the balls of his feet, Aedan set off at a brisk jog and left me alone with Asa.

"Clay enlisted Aedan's help in the blackout, I take it."

If Asa was as embarrassed as I was that Clay had orchestrated his deflowering, he didn't show it.

"Looks that way." I turned to Asa. "We should flip the breakers before we leave."

That dedication of Aedan's to authenticity meant the store was still powerless.

"How are you holding up?" He studied me in the sunlight. "You've had a big shock."

"It's only going to get worse. The drop-ins. The surprise guests. Can you imagine how bad it will get if we do mate? How long before you're the one who gets kidnapped?"

"I won't get kidnapped." He gripped my upper arms to halt my retreat. "And if I do? I'm happy to wait for you to rescue me. I'll even braid my hair and toss it out the window for you to climb."

"That's not as comforting as you may think."

The mental picture of Asa as Rapunzel would have tickled me any other time, but not today.

"I can't imagine how it must feel to know your father is alive and out there in the world."

"And playing for the wrong team." I rested my forehead against his chest. "The Bureau gives purpose to those who would otherwise be executed by their factions for their crimes. Dad wants to dismantle it. I'm not sure I agree with him."

The last place any sane person wanted to stand was in Hiram Nádasdy's way.

Daughter I might be, but he had made a vow designed to drive him to its completion.

Before I stepped in front of his speeding bullet, I had to be certain the Black Hat Bureau was a target worth saving.

Including agents like Marty.

"You'll do the right thing." He rubbed his thumb along my jaw. "You always do."

"You have way too much faith in me." I nipped his finger. "I might turn supervillain and join him."

"You won't." His eyes flashed, hot and hungry. "That's not who you are."

"Anymore," I corrected him. "I could relapse."

"And take Colby with you?" He caressed my neck. "Never."

The reminder of the familiar bond forced me to ask him a hard question. "Will you and I soul bond?"

Already I carried Colby's life in my hands. I wasn't sure I could hold his too without dropping one.

"I would have said no." He traced my carotid. "But your father is half daemon, and he bonded to your mother." His lips thinned. "With you carrying daemon blood, I would say our chances are higher than theirs."

"That's a lot of responsibility to put on another person."

"The fae part of me will want that," he confessed. "You bring my daemon traits to the surface, but I was raised by a fae mother with fae ideals and fae instincts."

"You would be tied to Colby and me."

And we would be tied to a dae who routinely fought other daemons for his survival.

"It's a big decision we don't have to make yet." He captured my hands. "We can reject it."

"Does biology work like that?"

"I won't pressure you into a bond you don't want." He lowered his gaze. "Or without Colby's consent."

That last bit hurt the most, because he meant it. She and I were a package deal, and I had no right to make decisions that impacted her on a life-or-death scale. She deserved as much say in it as either of us.

Awkward?

Yes.

No adult wanted their future happiness dictated by the whims of a ten-year-old girl, but there you go.

"I'm a lot of work." I winced, attempting to pull away. "I'm sorry things with me aren't simpler."

"Simple is overrated." He reeled me in against him. "I prefer to put in the work."

"Admit it." I linked my arms around his waist. "You stay up at night reading books on perfect one-liners."

"You're right." A chuckle jostled him. "I read eBooks on my laptop but pretend I'm writing reports."

"That explains it." I slid my hands to his hips. "I always thought you took reports too seriously."

"Let me turn on the power." He kissed me softly. "Then we'll go home."

"Home sounds good." I kissed him back. "No, home sounds *great*."

Big Trouble and Little Trouble waited for us on the porch when we pulled into the driveway.

"We're going to blow stuff up," Colby squealed from Clay's shoulder. "It's going to be *amazing*."

"I picked up a few boxes from the fireworks stand while I was in town." Clay shrugged at my scowl. "You, who knows me better than anyone else, left me unsupervised near an explosives display. On *clearance*."

Mayor Tate allowed fireworks vendors to set up stands in one parking lot in town. That was it. Just one. I suspected it was meant to nudge the town toward attending her extravaganza rather than enjoying solo celebrations, but that might just be me.

Either way, I *never* would have left Clay alone there had I not been so panicked about Aedan.

"Some…" he waited a beat then bounced his shoulder, "…might say that makes it as much your fault as it is mine."

"Shoot." She fluttered until he settled then landed. "I missed my cue."

"Ixnay on the ue-cay," he murmured out of the side of his mouth, rustling her antennae.

"Save it," I told them, afraid what her lines might be. "If you want to do fireworks, we'll do fireworks."

And pray that Mrs. Gleason didn't see them and join in with whatever shenanigans she had on tap.

"We'll start a new holiday tradition." Clay punched the air. "Let's ring in the Not-New Year."

"Your talent for originality is breathtaking," I told him dryly. "The eons have been generous."

"Just for that, I'm scrapping the part of the program where we write your name in the sky."

"Please do." I groaned. "I don't want the police to see it and view it as a confession."

"Let's start setting up." Colby rubbed her hands together. "Rue, can you bring the scissors?"

"You're in charge of the kids until I get back." I pointed at poor Asa. "Don't let them have any matches."

"Hurry up with those scissors, Mommy." Clay took the stairs down at a clip. "I can't run without them."

A snort propelled Colby right off his shoulder and into the air, where she barrel-rolled with laughter.

"Please hurry," Asa agreed when he saw whatever horrors Clay had crammed into the trunk of the SUV.

The fact their pyrotechnics display required this many hours to prep should have scared me more than it did, but I had lived next door to Mrs. Gleason for too long to be frightened so easily.

Hmm.

For the sake of the town, and my new roof, I ought to invite her over and encourage her to detonate her surplus under adult supervision. I could bribe her with hot wings, cold beer, and assorted chips and dips.

A bounce in my step, I took the stairs, let myself into the house, and rummaged through the junk drawer with no luck before recalling that was where Asa had found the twine. Had we used scissors to cut it? Or claws? Teeth? I was hazy on the details, and I wasn't sure where either of them landed in the aftermath.

Eyes on the prize, I set out to toss Asa's bedroom before I moved on to mine.

All I needed was a firm headcount, and then I could hit the grocery store.

I was thinking maybe a Coca-Cola cake for dessert...

Ten minutes later, I had no scissors, but I did have a vague memory of my closet.

About to check there, I tripped over the grimoire and smacked my shoulder into the wall to avoid falling.

"What is your problem?" I stood up and marched over to it. "Why can't you stay where I put you?"

The book would have me believe I knocked it open with my foot, but the page before me said otherwise.

There, written in red ink so dark it might as well have been black, was a list of names.

Authors.

Dozens of them.

The topmost one caught my eye.

Hiram Nádasdy.

"No, no, no," I chanted at it. "You're pulling my leg."

The grimoire called my bluff, allowing me a brief glimpse of the spell Dad used to conjure his black magic wings. Before I could do more than recognize the striking illustration's purpose, it flipped back to the list.

"Goddess bless."

This wasn't, and never had been, the Proctor grimoire. There were simply too many other signatures.

That night, when I read the Proctor name, the book must have been showing me the portion he wrote.

These names meant there was more, much more, to this book, and it left a hard knot in my stomach.

On autopilot, I placed the grimoire at the foot of the bed, but I couldn't tear my gaze from the cover.

"Might as well leave you out," I told it. "You'll just be creeping around when I get back anyway."

Bad idea, talking to a grimoire of its power, but I blamed it on the shock.

Had the book always been meant to end up with me? Had I been meant to hold it until Dad fetched it?

Few safer places existed for dangerous arcana than in the possession of a witch with my reputation.

Aedan suspected Dad had broken into the store. Had he come here searching for me, or the grimoire?

And if he came for the book, then how much of his imprisonment story was true?

I didn't know.

But my Not-New Year's resolution was to find out.

ABOUT THE AUTHOR

USA Today best-selling author Hailey Edwards writes about questionable applications of otherwise perfectly good magic, the transformative power of love, the family you choose for yourself, and blowing stuff up. Not necessarily all at once. That could get messy.

www.HaileyEdwards.net

ALSO BY HAILEY EDWARDS

Black Hat Bureau

Black Hat, White Witch #1

Black Arts, White Craft #2

Black Truth, White Lies #3

Black Soul, White Heart #3.5

Black Wings, Gray Skies #4

The Foundling

Bayou Born #1

Bone Driven #2

Death Knell #3

Rise Against #4

End Game #5

The Beginner's Guide to Necromancy

How to Save an Undead Life #1

How to Claim an Undead Soul #2

How to Break an Undead Heart #3

How to Dance an Undead Waltz #4

How to Live an Undead Lie #5

How to Wake an Undead City #6

How to Kiss an Undead Bride #7

How to Survive an Undead Honeymoon #8

How to Rattle an Undead Couple #9

The Potentate of Atlanta

Shadow of Doubt #1

Pack of Lies #2

Change of Heart #3

Proof of Life #4

Moment of Truth #5

Badge of Honor #6

Black Dog Series

Dog with a Bone #1

Dog Days of Summer #1.5

Heir of the Dog #2

Lie Down with Dogs #3

Old Dog, New Tricks #4

Black Dog Series Novellas

Stone-Cold Fox

Gemini Series

Dead in the Water #1

Head Above Water #2

Hell or High Water #3

Gemini Series Novellas

Fish Out of Water

Lorimar Pack Series

Promise the Moon #1

Wolf at the Door #2

Over the Moon #3

Araneae Nation

A Heart of Ice #.5

A Hint of Frost #1

A Feast of Souls #2

A Cast of Shadows #2.5

A Time of Dying #3

A Kiss of Venom #3.5

A Breath of Winter #4

A Veil of Secrets #5

Daughters of Askara

Everlong #1

Evermine #2

Eversworn #3

Wicked Kin

Soul Weaver #1

Printed in Great Britain
by Amazon